"YOU ARE HUNTED!"

Thyri sat up. "I am hunted?" she asked. "By what?"

"A man—a dark, powerful man. He took our *felnina*. He killed my wife."

Thyri spat. If he was strong enough to take a *felnina*, dark powers were at work. "Can you describe him?"

Ai'reth nodded. "Blond hair, low-born, has dwarven sword—"

"Wait!" Thyri interrupted. She unsheathed her sword before Ai'reth's eyes.

The *felnin* gasped. "Same sword! He wants to kill you. You must flee!"

"No," Thyri said. "He is my brother ..."

Avon Books by
Michael D. Weaver

THE BLOODFANG TRILOGY
WOLF-DREAMS
NIGHTREAVER
BLOODFANG

Bloodfang

MICHAEL D. WEAVER

AVON BOOKS ◆ NEW YORK

AVON BOOKS
A division of
The Hearst Corporation
105 Madison Avenue
New York, New York 10016

Copyright © 1989 by Michael D. Weaver
Front cover illustration by Gary Ruddel
Published by arrangement with the author
Library of Congress Catalog Card Number: 88-91364
ISBN: 0-380-75584-X

First Avon Books Printing: May 1989

AVON TRADEMARK REG. U.S. PAT. OFF. AND IN OTHER COUNTRIES, MARCA REGISTRADA, HECHO EN U.S.A.

Printed in the U.S.A.

K-R 10 9 8 7 6 5 4 3 2 1

for Tana

Book VII:
QUEEN OF THIEVES

Sometimes I wish I could start over. Not with my life—that is too much to ask—but with this, with Thyri's story, my story. I've only had this one chance, and time is running out. Still, I fear I've failed in every way. I read what's already written and weep at my words; they haven't captured the *life* of it all. Immobile they are, dead on their pages of parchment, and so what use are they? Who will read them and understand? Whoever does will know Thyri only through me, through this work, as poor and lifeless as it is. I want them to see her smile, smell her hair, feel her presence, taste her agonies and passions. But I've been vain; I've stained her story by betraying myself in the words. Can you understand that? If so, you're beyond me, because I'm not sure I do. I only know that, so far, I've written selfishly; I've written, I realize, so that I, not you, might regain Thyri's world. Lifeless ramblings I've written, so I would start over and make Thyri more alive for you, but I can't. And if I could, my heart tries to tell me that I would fail, again. Words can mean only so much.

Have my years made me wise? I don't think so; I still proceed on this reckless course, racing for my destiny. I think, though, that I've learned love, if love is a wisdom. My wife—it is she who has lifted me above this thing I do—she lets me see it clearly, lets me see my selfishness and injustices, and helps me understand why I do what I do, even though it pains her terribly.

"And, Gerald," she says, "for good or ill, you must continue."

For good or ill.

I continue:

1

Warriors

Thyri stooped to the ground and touched the grass thoughtfully. She was closer and gaining, only minutes behind. She tested the air for magic; it was everywhere, the air a latticework of subtle, shifting sensations. Given time, she might separate the peculiar qualities she sought, but she didn't have time, not if she wanted to keep gaining. Still, she took a moment to stand and savor the thrill of the chase, begun hours before in the early morning. It felt so good to be out of the city! And so close to her prize as well.

She wiped the sweat from her forehead, lifted her hair a moment to let cool air onto her neck, and started off again.

From the wood she was watched, her watcher full of fear and awe and reverence. Moments before, he had observed the chased; by rights—and orders—he should have followed then. But to be caught by the chaser, from behind and unawares? No, Ai'reth was a warrior and not that stupid.

This one—the chaser, the hunter—short by low-blood standards, but his first sight of her made him tremble. She was high-trained, Tuathan-trained by her stance, and she carried a dwarven sword, very *fei* and alarming, for why did she have it? How had she come by it, and what brought her here? The hunt, surely, but how could a low-born know how to follow? He would have expected a dragon of Svartalfheim, or Nidhogg himself—considering the darkness of the days—before this.

Still, this usurping of order could not explain his trembling, the way his hands had shook and his heart had

2

thumped in his chest. That had come from a glimpse at the battle inside her, the clash of dark and light that afflicted all low-borns of Midgard— the Midgard curse the Sylvan jokingly called it—the playground of the High Gods, the mortal pawns the Creators had given the high-born to test their powers—the *yangyi* as Ai'reth had once heard it called by an initiate of the Ishtan mysteries.

The *yangyi* of the low-born, always before a joke whenever Ai'reth had seen it: so weak it was, so pathetic and dim, scarcely bright enough to power a beating heart, and so easy to twist and shape. Even when the light was strong, it could flicker out in the most simple magical breeze, or, on its own, with no help, continue its battle with the defeated dark, nurturing it, keeping it alive in a phantom battle that only the Creators could possibly understand. Ai'reth certainly didn't. His spirit was a bright flame, the last traces of darkness banished aeons before, in his childhood. He was a bright warrior, and no trick within himself could turn him. He knew this well because his sense for spirits—light, dark, or *yangyi*—was the finest he knew. Dark masquerading as light had never deceived *him,* and whenever S'kiri desired a second judgment, it was Ai'reth she summoned.

As the woman-warrior with the dwarven sword started away, Ai'reth still trembled at the memory of what had happened when he'd opened his sense to her *yangyi*. It had struck him like the fist of a giant; its light had burned his eyes, and its darkness had enveloped him so suddenly and completely that he'd almost lost control and cried out. He'd had to *fight* just to shut off his talent and regain his normal senses, and after that he could only look at her in wonder. This low-born of Midgard—for she certainly was that—turned the Sylvan joke of *yangyi* into a joke of itself. Her spirit was as wild and strong as any he'd seen in any realm. Her darkness made him fear for the strength of his own light. Her light urged him to fall on his knees and beg her to take him into her breast, but this he didn't do for she moved away too quickly.

When she was gone, he scrambled from behind his leaf-shield and into the clearing where she'd stopped. He, like her, touched the grass, then he bent close to it and sniffed, finding her strong, low-born scent. Before, it might have choked him, the way a forest-dweller might crinkle his nose in the midst of pigs, but now, after he'd *seen* her, he wanted her smell to be stronger, to surround him as if it might solve her mystery, as if he might find in it some clue to her presence here and what that could mean to himself and his people.

Some months before, he had heard it said that low-borns had brought down the great Tuathan sorceress Morgana, not merely capturing her, not merely defeating her, but actually *slaying* her, banishing her power and influence from all worlds. He'd laughed at the tale then; now he could almost believe it. This was his thought as, carefully, as silently as a cat, he became the hunter of the hunter and followed in the chase.

Thyri's heart beat faster as the trail twisted, doubled back, and twisted again, back onto the shadow-path. When the world suddenly shifted she barely broke her stride, and then only to make sure she didn't rush headlong off a cliff or into a pool of fire. Instead, the shift dropped her at the *bottom* of a fifty-foot cliff, and her senses urged her upward. Thyri grinned and cursed; if she didn't push her body to its limits she'd lose all the time she'd gained. Still cursing, she attacked the wall of rock, ignoring the screams of her muscles, racing haphazardly ever upward.

At the top, she found a field of barley. The ripe crop filled her nostrils, as did the tang of magic, but she didn't lose the fresh scent of her quarry, and she kept on its trail, her muscles fatigued for the first time all day.

Ten steps into the barley, the earth erupted in a shower of black and silver that fell on her, wrapped around her, and lifted her into the air. She struggled against the sorcerous grip as it tightened, and through gaps in the sorcery's claws, she saw her prey floating level with her, another ten paces ahead.

Megan of Kaerglen Isle smiled at her as the sorcery continued to flow from the ring finger of her raised hand.

Thyri fought fiercely, trying to swim through the air toward the sorceress, but the magic blocked her, and then suddenly, unexpectedly, the bones of her right shoulder wrenched and a dark hunger began to grow in her stomach. "Stop!" Thyri screamed. "Megan, please!"

The sorcerous grip loosened, and Thyri felt herself falling slowly. Still, her vision went red and her hunger grew as the beast within her struggled to break free. She glanced at Megan and felt saliva fill her mouth, and she screamed, spitting out, fighting to beat down the wolf's sudden rush of bloodlust as the magic laid her gently down among the barley and quickly retreated.

For a few moments, Megan hung still in the air, watching her friend on the ground as she shook and wimpered and finally let out a strangled howl before going still. Even then Megan waited a little longer, until Thyri looked up at her wearily, before descending.

"Goddess," Megan whispered as she smoothed Thyri's brow. "Can that happen so easily?"

Thyri felt tears rising to her eyes as she nodded. "Not *so* easily though; only when I'm beaten." Hadn't she told Megan about the other times? About the time on the *Black Rabbit* when the wolf had emerged in broad daylight and slain the entire crew before leaving her? *Oh, Megan—it would have killed you!*

"Never," the sorceress said softly. "Our love is too strong."

"I'll be all right in a moment."

Quiet! There's no hurry.

Megan stretched out and laid her head on Thyri's breast. The heartbeat within was rapid; she ran her fingers gently over Thyri's bare stomach until the heartbeat slowed.

"Careful," Thyri whispered distantly. "You're starting something."

"Thyri?"

"Yes?"

"Did I do well?"

"What do you mean?"

"Did I practice well? Did I make any mistakes? If it were a real battle?"

Thyri laughed lightly, remembering herself that morning when she'd told Megan to play for real, to take it seriously even if it was a game, to start *thinking* like a warrior because if she didn't she was going to get herself killed one day. She'd gone on: *"Then next time we get in real trouble, I want you at my side, not near death and on your back and useless! Use your sorcery, but don't ever abuse it. Conserve it, don't throw it around as if it's boundless because it isn't."* Megan had taken the hint. Aside from a couple of very subtle sorcerous attempts to throw Thyri off the trail, Thyri had encountered nothing of Megan's ring magic during the chase until the final confrontation. The sorceress had conjured no beasts to guard her path, laid no elaborate traps, and chosen her own field of battle, in a place where she knew Thyri would be weakened after the exertion of climbing a cliff. Thyri actually found herself wondering if Megan had purposefully slowèd before the cliff, allowing her to gain so that when she faced the wall of rock, the need for swift climbing would be all the more urgent. Thyri knew that her friend hadn't climbed; the sorceress had floated, spelled herself fairly effortlessly to the top.

"Yes," Thyri said finally. "You did well." She unclasped her weapon's belt, grabbed Megan's shoulders, and pushed off with her legs so they rolled and tumbled through the barley. "You ambushed me!" Thyri said, landing on top.

Megan nodded, smiling. "I did, didn't I?"

Thyri touched her cheek, traced her lips with her fingers. "You did," she said. "And you caught me."

Megan growled playfully. "I'm glad."

Ai'reth

He peeked through the tall stalks, watching the two women, glad the hunt had been but a game. He kept very still; he didn't fear discovery in particular—no, his charms would hide him from all scrutiny but the sorceress's ring. He kept still, rather, out of reverence, for fear of shattering the beauty of what he saw. He watched power mingle with power, power caressing power, and, wonder of wonders, the powers were both low-born! At first, when he'd seen the sorceress race by him, he'd thought her Tuathan, but she had low-blood in her; he could definitely smell it now, and her *yangyi*—it was nearly as strong as the other's, though much lighter.

What had he found this day? What had he witnessed? Two powers at play while such darkness hung over all the worlds?

He watched awhile longer, dared to murmur a quick charm of following, backed away, and scrambled down the cliff's face while the two women lingered on their bed of barley.

Back in his familiar wood, Ai'reth wondered more deeply. The powers he'd witnessed—they were not low-born powers. And the white-haired one—so obviously Tuathan in style, in grace. Likewise the taller one of dark hair. Perhaps they were hybrid, like he and his people; women of high blood were wont at times to lay with anything it seemed. He'd once heard of elven owl-people . . . But more was amiss than that. He had to know more before returning to S'kiri with any news of this. Perhaps there were prophecies . . . So he wondered and wandered. The birds in the trees chattered of the dark armies; he shut them out and only thought of them again when the chattering stopped.

Instinctively, in the sudden silence, he froze, beaming out his talent in all directions. The cloud of darkness hung on a limb directly over his head. He shaped it; *vulture,* he thought. *Or dark raven? Scout or warrior?* He remained still, waiting for the flyer to move. It had to be a scout; a warrior would have fallen on him by now. But it was so high; if he attacked, he would surely miss, and it would fly back to its masters with news of him, or worse, stay high above and watch his every move. That thought burned in him; he would not be rendered powerless by a stupid bird!

Slowly, he began to look around, but never upward. He stretched his arms out, then plopped down on the grass under the tree and decided to eat, opening a pouch full of dried rabbit meat. He ate slowly, hoping the flyer would grow bored and fly away with nothing more than news of a hungry felnin. But the stubborn scout stayed high above, out of reach and unmoving.

Time for tricks! Ai'reth thought angrily. *Stupid tricks for a stupid bird!* He muttered a minor charm of making, and a white spell-mage leaped from the bushes across from him.

"Evil felnin!" he had the spell-mage shout at him. *"You face the great Zesthistedamir! I have slain dragons and giant armies, and now I slay you with but a click of my fingers!"*

The spell-mage clicked its fingers, and Ai'reth toppled, wide-eyed and motionless, onto his side. In a colorful explosion of smoke and fire, the spell-mage disappeared.

Now Ai'reth stared directly up at the giant raven. That's good! he chuckled silently. *Stupid bird now does two things. It flies away with news of the great Zesthistedamir, or it comes down for a closer look. Either way, Ai'reth wins!*

Ai'reth stared blankly; slowly, the ravan flapped away. Ai'reth chuckled again; probably the raven knew him, his name and his greatness, for why would a scout of the dark powers shadow an unknown felnin? Now to all the dark powers Ai'reth was dead. He would teach them in the end.

He leaped to his feet, but before he could start away, a

silver wall sprang up before him. He stamped on the ground. "What now?" he cried out. Behind him, he heard light laughter and clapping.

He spun. "Dryad!" he growled angrily. "Take down wall!"

She was pretty with light brown hair and almond eyes and olive skin. "You save me," she giggled. "You're so handsome! What is your name?"

She stepped toward him; he quickly pulled out a knife and waved it in the air between them. "No time for dryads! Don't you know? Is war on all worlds!"

"But you ate in my shade! That means you love me!"

"Love nobody! Take down wall, or I slice your tree!"

The dryad burst out crying. "Am I not beautiful?" she sobbed.

"Beautiful, ugly, who cares? Take down wall!"

He lunged at her, and she stepped back, merging into her tree's trunk. As the silver barrier began to dissipate, Ai'reth leaped through it and back out onto the path. "Ravens and dryads," he mumbled, brushing traces of silver from his vest. "What did Ai'reth do to deserve such things?"

Now, he thought, calming down. Now what? Prophecies, yes; no more time to waste! He would seek the oracle.

She dwelt in a lake a short distance from Ai'reth's home. He reached her shores and summoned her: "Klorista! Ai'reth the felnin calls!"

Only silence answered.

"She sleeps," he sighed wearily. "Must wake all the powers of Light? Is Ai'reth alone the ready one?"

He sat on the lake's mossy shore and took out his pipe, packing it carefully with his herbs of calming. Lighting the herbs, he began to will his angers and frustrations away. He exhaled the smoke out over the water, watched it swirl there and mix with the lake's light mist. He concentrated on the water's light lapping on the shore, then reached out gently with his magic and set the lillies below spinning, making a slow, dancing circle.

From his belt, Ai'reth took his finger drum and brushed it lightly a few times before starting into a rhythmic tap-

ping. He straightened his spine and closed his eyes, keeping the image of the spinning lillies before him, making
them into a tunnel, and opening the tunnel into a world of
light on the far side. *Klorista!* he beckoned. *Come forth!*

His drumming grew louder and more resonant. Light
swirled at the end of tunnel. *Who calls?* she whispered.

It is Ai'reth, dear Goddess.

Ai'reth? What brings you, felnin?

*I have seen low-borns of great power, and I do not
understand such strong* yangyi. *The great wars come,
Goddess.*

Low-borns? Show them to me.

Ai'reth conjured up likenesses of the two women and
sent them into the tunnel of lillies in his mind.

Ah, said Klorista. *I understand. What troubles you?*

Who are they? Why are they?

They are low-borns. One of Light, the other of Chaos.

But so strong!

The High Ones made them so.

Will they fight in the wars?

They do so already.

On whose side?

I cannot say.

Ai'reth sighed. *What now for me, then?*

Look to your people.

*But the worlds are ending! All will perish! So spake the
Sybil.* Fimbulwinter *descends on Asgard!*

Ah, Klorista countered. *But not Midgard. What does
that mean, little felnin?*

I do not know.

*The One God grows strong there on Midgard, Ai'reth.
He keeps the fimbulwinter away. He may yet keep the
great war away as well. What if Surt burns all the nine
worlds save one? Save Midgard? Will the One God then
stay there and let the old mysteries be reborn from the
ashes as the Sybil foretold? Will he allow his enemies to
grow strong anew and threaten his hold on Midgard? I
think if all prophecies come to pass, we will destroy
ourselves and nothing more.*

But Midgard is battleground! One God can't rule all!

All battles may be won, dear felnin. And the One God

has his opponent, as Odin has Loki. And there are other gods against which we do not war, but the One God does.

What gods?

Do not think of them. Think of us. Think of the questions I have asked, for they are very good questions.

Tell Loki to think of your questions! Is his fault!

Loki is blind to prophecy. He feels he will cheat it.

Can he?

Perhaps. He is not all dark; he is part Chaos. Go now, Ai'reth. Look to your people and think. Act if you like; thoughts cannot save much.

But what of the low-borns!

He had no answer. The circle of lillies fell apart in his mind, and he was left on the lakeshore, staring out over the water.

The birds in the trees chattered again of dark armies, and Ai'reth cursed softly, wishing they'd be still.

Magic

"Aha," Megan said, stopping suddenly near the trunk of a large oak. "I think I've found one!"

"One what?"

"A *felnina*. The reason I brought you all the way out here."

Thyri's eyes followed Megan's into the high, dense thicket beyond the oak. She raised a puzzled eyebrow and laughed. "A *what?*"

"A *felnina*—a quest-house. Very witchy," Megan whispered playfully.

Thyri nodded gravely, then they both burst out in a fit of uncontrolled laughter. The light sound filled the air as Megan pushed against the huge trunk and the bark gave way.

"Loki's tits!" Thyri laughed, then, "Wait!" as Megan disappeared inside the trunk.

Inside, the old wood twisted into a stairwell that led up, then opened into a large natural chamber on the far side of the tree. The walls and ceiling were of interwoven polished hardwood branches, the walls stepping upward and outward in ledges like an ampitheater. A gentle creek flowed in from the far side, and it was blocked into a pool by an intricate circle of stones that both dammed it and guided it to drainage holes in the moss-covered floor. Moss, in fact, was everywhere, on the floor, on the ledges, even dangling down through gaps in the ceiling. In places, it was several inches thick.

Megan removed her boots and motioned for Thyri to do the same, then she dove out onto the floor and sprawled on her back, smiling with deep satisfaction. "Yes," she sighed, closing her eyes. "This is what I wanted to feel again!"

Thyri knelt, pulling off her boots, then touching the moss thoughtfully. "There's magic everywhere, more than outside. In the walls, the floor, even in that water," she said, pointing.

"Oh, yes." Megan's words were dreamy, distant. "Very gentle magic. Magic to soothe, to refresh. Look—by the door there is food."

Thyri looked. There were bushels of nuts and berries, and pouches of dried meat, even three small casks of mead. She stepped out onto the moss with her bare feet; its coolness washed upward, unknotting the tired muscles in her calves and thighs. When she fell next to Megan, it was almost as if the moss pulled her down into its embrace. She had never felt such sensations; she recalled the hut where she'd studied under Scacath, where she and Astrid would lounge on layers of furs. She thought of the pool in Castle Kaerglen, and of the other pools and quiet places she had discovered on her travels. Nothing compared to this.

The moss almost grew into her; it massaged her, staying ever cool. Its scent was like honey infiltrating her mind; the trauma of the afternoon—when the wolf had almost taken her over—grew distant, a memory years old, one that could no longer hurt her, or even one that belonged to somebody else, some other existence outside herself, a tragic existence with which she'd shared life for a time, but which she'd now abandoned for a future of simple, happy contentment. Suddenly, she felt she almost glowed. She felt infinitely safe. No danger outside could enter and harm her. She felt that even if the moon were to rise, her curse would not be able to take her here, to twist her body and mind in this peaceful place. The curse, perhaps, was not even hers. . . .

"Where are we, Meg?" Thyri asked at last. The words bubbled out of her, as if rising from great depths. She heard them—the words of somebody else. Reason began to rear up and survey the unnatural peace within her.

"Alfheim," the sorceress whispered. "I led you all the way to the edge of Alfheim."

"I mean this place." There it was again, that alien

voice. Thyri began to grow uncomfortable. All this peace began to hurt. Little voices began telling her she was good, pure, a servant of Light. She should forget her curse, the killings, the bloodlust—they meant nothing, minor failures of a past no longer hers. In the future, all was bright, love and light and soft moonlight. No worries at all . . .

"The *felnina?*" Megan rolled onto her side, placed a cupped hand on Thyri's shoulder, and rested her chin there. "The quest-houses of old . . . they are everywhere, some older even than the Tuatha de Danaan. The felnin make them; I believe they live in them for a time, and then move on. But always they tend their old homes, keeping them fit for travelers who know how to find them."

"Who are the felnin?" The little voices? No, the voices were magic, trying to deceive her, to make her forget. They were gentle voices, warm voices, the voices of spells meant to soothe, but they instead inflicted pain. They wanted her to *forget* the trials of the past, to look to the future; maybe for Megan that was a good thing, but for her now? Too much horror lurked within, too much terrible death, and she couldn't risk forgetting it, not in the complete sense the *felnina* demanded. She could never forget, because forgetting an enemy was the surest way to lose the battle. Maybe this place *could* shield them from the external world, from external enemies, but internal enemies? Thyri couldn't let herself believe it; her worst enemy was ever within herself.

"I don't really know," Megan answered innocently, unaware of Thyri's internal conflict. "An elder race, a light race. They are the unseen of the fair peoples, shadow-warriors. Those who have seen them say nothing, out of respect. They serve the forces of Light in their own way. Lore says the Creators made them, even before they made Buri and placed him in his block of ice."

"Odin's grandfather?"

"I've told you before; common lore is seldom trustworthy."

Later, Thyri gazed into the shallow pool. Little silver fish swam there, feeding off the moss that grew down over the rock. She touched the water with her fingers, and the fish, curious, swam up for a closer look. When she lifted her fingers out, the fish scattered, flashes of silver radiating out from the center like the flying points of a star.

She wanted to smile, but that *felnina*'s magic still taunted her. She felt shaken; she'd almost believed, almost let herself slip into fantasy and think her curse away, as if it were only one long, bad dream. And as she remembered that feeling, another part of her longed for it again, pleaded with her to submit to it, to be carried away into happiness. Hadn't she forgotten her curse at times before? Hadn't she loved and let the worries melt away? Wasn't that what she lived for? Yes, yes, and yes, but not like this, never so fully and disarmingly, never quite so euphorically.

The magic of the *felnina* made her feel helpless, like a child or a baby. It tried to force innocence upon her, an innocence she knew she couldn't keep because it wasn't real. For those who once lived here, perhaps for them, this was the most wonderful magic of all, so wonderful that they kept it alive for others, weary travelers, elven warriors, white sorceresses like Megan. For them, this innocent comfort could be transcendent, but not for Thyri. She couldn't accept the helplessness, but she couldn't help longing for the careless oblivion.

Yet she couldn't succumb. She would want to keep that feeling forever, to take it away with her and carry it wherever she went. Right now, the memory of *almost* having it hurt. She felt how she imagined a blind person would feel if suddenly given the power of sight for a few moments, only to have it stripped away again. Which would be the greater torture? To be blind, experience sight, and lose it? Or to be blind, never see, and long for it?

After a time, she realized she was crying. Megan slept, blissful in the embrace of the *felnina*'s gentle magic. She had brought Thyri here out of love and unknowingly caused pain. She looked to Meg, stared long at the mass of silky black hair splayed out over the green moss, at her breast which rose and fell on the slow tide of her breathing. Thyri looked and felt herself apart from her friend and lover as she never had before. Always, they'd shared everything. Most of the time, just being in Megan's presence elated her, making her feel whole and alive. It wasn't working now. Megan had brought her here, intending this place as a gift, and Thyri couldn't accept it. Neither could she bring herself to wake the sorceress and flee. For once, she couldn't see herself admitting her pain, even to her best friend. Somehow, she felt that that might destroy everything, Megan might finally see the darkness within her and hate her for what it was. . . .

I'm mad. . . . She knows me. She's seen inside me. We speak, half the time, from mind to mind. Why did she do this to me? Why didn't she tell me how much it would hurt!

S'kiri

The sounds weren't right.

As he approached his home, the birds no longer chattered. He cast about with his talent; above was no vulture or dark raven to silence them this time. All the trees shone white, a defensive, frightened white. The frogs near the water pined croakingly for their lovers, but the females didn't answer. No felnin maiden sang out the music of the night. No young felnin chased after rabbits in the bushes. The moon behind the clouds, even, did not moan of the Midgard tides.

"Dryads," Ai'reth whispered. "Dryads, what passes?"

No answer.

Stupid dryads, he thought. *Be silent, then! Ai'reth is friend! He asks; you do not answer, and he will remember.*

Outside the *felnina*, nothing stirred, not even the frogs. The Queenstone's light-magic on the stairs shone weakly, beckoning his entrance.

From his belt, Ai'reth took his sword and held it before him, then, step by cautious step, he ascended through the oak.

Inside, the tribe gathered, lying restlessly on the ledges, all eyes turning toward him. Across from him, beyond the pool, on the ancestral ledge of the queen, a blackness sat, a low-born blackness—another low-born bearing a dwarven sword! At his *feet* sat S'kiri.

Ai'reth smelled blood in the air. As the eyes looked at him, he looked at them, counting. "Where is Ai'dana?" he asked at last. "And Ai'pez?"

No one spoke. S'kiri looked fearfully at Ai'reth, her eyes rolling up, indicating the low-born. Ai'reth's gaze

17

finally settled there, booring into the low-born blackness. The low-born smiled at him. "The great warrior has returned," he said, chuckling.

Ai'reth stared. "Come here, wife," he said softly to S'kiri.

"No!" the low-born commanded. The dwarven sword fell down heavily in front of S'kiri, barring her path. The man's gauntlet, silver mail, shone like the moon in the black of a starless night.

Ai'reth's eyes stopped on the runes near the sword's hilt. "That is sword of Light!" he said angrily. "You are not worthy!"

"But I am," the man said. "It was given to me. Have you seen such a sword lately?"

"No," Ai'reth answered, half falsely, half truthfully. Two dwarven swords in one day . . . He'd never seen the woman-wolf's bared.

"You lie," the man said darkly. "Your tricks are up, Ai'reth. I know you were scout today. I know who you've seen."

"Who's that, stupid low-born?"

"Eiriksdattir."

Ai'reth shook his head. "Low-born stupid. Low-born dreaming or drink too much."

"You lie," the man said calmly. "I want you to bring her to me. Bring her, or I will kill your wife, and you, and everybody."

Ai'reth glared around at the felnin on the ledges. "Do you let him take your queen? Do you let him take your home and kill young felnin? Are you not warriors? Think Ragnarok is bad dream! Curses on you!"

"Silence, Ai'reth," S'kiri shouted at him. "He holds the Queenstone!"

The man behind her grinned and raised a fist. He opened it slightly, and the blue light of the tribe's ancestral talisman shone out from between his fingers. Passed down from queen to queen, only S'kiri's hands had touched it for the past millennium—until now. Its power had shaped their home, and all their homes before this one.

Ai'reth laughed. "Stupid rock!" he exclaimed angrily. "Just stupid rock now, felnin. The worlds will end, and you mourn theft of stupid rock!"

S'kiri's eyes pleaded with him. How had the low-born taken it from her? Ai'reth wondered. Had she given it up willingly after he slew Ai'dana and Ai'pez? The Queenstone meant much, he knew; it was the source of all S'kiri's magic, and much of the tribe's itself. For all he knew, it could guard their very immortality. . . . But Ai'reth felt the vast, impossible weight of Yggdrasil and all the worlds on his shoulders. The balance of Ragnarok—Klorista's words bespoke prophecy for the woman-wolf, and Ai'reth knew without asking that she was whom this man desired. Even would she let him, he could not deliver her to him and make himself the first traitor to Light in the end of all things. Next to the balance of Ragnarok, the Queenstone meant nothing.

Ai'reth took a knife from his belt, and returned S'kiri's pleading gaze, hoping she would follow his thinking. Then he flipped the knife in his hand and sent it spinning through the air toward the low-born. Ai'reth took a terrible chance. He hoped—he prayed—the man knew his sword. The runes—Ai'reth knew at first glance that one would deflect missiles. S'kiri had to know as well. At the same time, the man would have to *use* the sword, lift it, giving S'kiri one brief moment in which to escape.

Ai'reth breathed easily as the man watched the knife and grinned. He did know his sword; it came up to block the knife, and S'kiri leaped—but not away! She leaped for the Queenstone! Ai'reth watched in horror as the sword came around and bit into S'kiri's side and she screamed, her claws falling away from the hand that held the Queenstone.

"Flee, felnin!" Ai'reth shouted as he leaped forward. "Flee for your lives!" Furiously, he grasped at spells. S'kiri was dying, and he had to have the stone now to save her. He glanced only briefly to make sure the tribe had obeyed him; then he whispered the power of Thor into his sword and struck at the low-born's dwarven sword with all his might.

The blow knocked the man back, and, as Ai'reth hoped, the Queenstone dropped into S'kiri's ledge as the man came forward, his blade now in two hands.

Ai'reth closed his eyes against the sight, held up his sword, and frantically whispered another spell. As the dwarven blade came down, Ai'reth, the Queenstone, and S'kiri all disappeared, leaving the man alone in the *felnina*.

Outside, Ai'reth caught his breath. His muscles ached and his mind was dizzy with fatigue from the powerful sorceries. Still, he pushed himself, taking up S'kiri and the Queenstone and running without pause until he reached Klorista's shores. There, he whispered a ward of guarding before laying S'kiri gently on the grass. "Wife," he said, his voice choking with sorrow. "Hear me!"

He examined her wound; blood already soaked the grass, dark in the moonlight, red in his tears. He pressed the Queenstone into the wound, drawing on its magic, trying to heal her.

"Ai'reth," he heard her whisper, "you saved the stone!"

"Yes," he said, excitedly, looking into her face. "I heal you!"

"Too late, my love," she coughed, blood flowing out of the corner of her mouth.

She lifted her head slightly to look at him, then it fell, lifeless, back to the ground.

Ghosts

The points of the stars contracted, nibbling at her hands as she scooped water out of the pool and splashed it on her face. She drank. She looked back at Megan who still slept.

She thought of Rollo; on the seas of Jotunheim, when she'd faced a full moon at dusk with Megan near death on the bed in their cabin, he'd given her strength, strength she'd needed then, strength she needed now. She hurt all the more as she realized that it wasn't Rollo she really wanted, *just his strength*. She felt weak, helpless, besieged by this magic that pulled at her, taunted her, forcing her to see herself again and again as the wolf, as unclean and unworthy.

Megan sighed in her sleep, then moaned with pleasure. Did she dream of Thyri? Who embraced the sorceress in her dreams? Did she ever dream of Thyri and dream of the wolf? Was Thyri ever her nightmare?

Rollo was leagues away, worlds away in the city of the Franks. With Rollo were Gerald and Rui Taichimi, and under them some two dozen rogues, all ready—Thyri knew—to face death at her side. They'd built quite an empire since their battle with Morgana and their return to Midgard. They'd pillaged for a while, then taken *Nightreaver* up the Frankish river into the heart of Charlemagne's old empire, if empire it still was over forty years after the death of the great ruler's son. Chaos it was in truth, but amid chaos, Thyri prospered, thieving and drinking—that was her world. By herself, she was invincible; with Megan at her side, doubly so. It was a game, but one that kept Thyri's mind busy, one that kept her battle skills honed and deadly. In the city of the Franks, there was no end to the stream of swordsmen who sought immortality in her defeat, only to find their own. Assuming they could find her, but that was all part of her game.

Maybe she just needed to get back. This was only one night, really. One night that Megan had meant as a gift; she could endure it. In the morning they would return and find Rollo, Rui, and Gerald waiting.

Why had Megan brought her here? How had she known of this place?

Just a game it had been in the morning. . . . Practice—a chance to get out of the city and test, at the same time, their skills, both in combat and in navigating the pathways between the worlds that Thyri had more or less avoided since the ordeal with Morgana. Who had suggested it? Megan? No, Thyri had, but the sorceress had quickly grown excited at the thought. Had she unwittingly played into Megan's hands, into the sorceress's desire that they be here, in a world she knew, rather than there, in the world Thyri knew?

Thyri touched the pool's surface again, attracting the fish, trying to turn her mind outward. Megan didn't deserve such doubts, even if she knew this place and had kept it secret from Thyri. Since returning from Jotunheim, the sorceress had not expressed any desire to be anywhere but by Thyri's side. Could Megan help it if she had a past? If she had been places of which Thyri had not even dreamed? Thyri never asked her friend much of the days before they met; she was too afraid to hear talk of lovers past, lovers lost. She'd suspected long before that Coryn, King of Kaerglen Isle, had once had Megan as mistress. If the sorceress didn't wish to speak of it, Thyri didn't wish to ask. But it left a void between them; Megan knew all of Thyri's pains, while Thyri knew virtually nothing of hers. Megan knew Thyri's sword-training under the goddess Scacath, while Thyri, again, knew nothing of how Megan had come to wield the power she did. Thyri didn't even know Megan's age—the sorceress looked scarcely more than twenty, but the ways of sorcery could hide century upon century of experience behind the face of youth. Only Megan's mistakes, her obvious inexperience in battle, hinted

at the possibility that her appearance might at all approxi-
mate her age. And yet nothing guaranteed that a century of
years need be a century of strife and battle.

So did Thyri's thoughts circle themselves, and so it was
what she did not witness Megan's waking until the sorceress placed a concerned hand on her shoulder.

"Is all well, little one?"

Little one . . . What Scacath had named her, what
Astrid had called her.

"How come you by your sorceries, Megan?"

Megan laughed lightly. "By training, Thyri. There is no
other way."

"How? Why? By whom?"

"By the spirits of the air, as I called them. I puzzled for
many years. The will of the gods, I think. Their will that I
meet you, Thyri. That I aid you."

Thyri turned, her eyes blazing with sudden anger. "Then
you are here for them! Not for love? You endure me by
their command?"

No one commands—

"Use your tongue, your lips! I want it out loud!"

Megan lowered her eyes. "No one commands me, Thyri.
I love you for you, for the kindness that I know is in your
heart. Because you love me, and you *do* need me, but I
also need you. I was an outcast when we met, powerful
perhaps, but very alone. You made me whole."

"Then why all this talk of gods!"

"Because you asked. I was not *told* by Odin or Loki or
Lugh or Brigid to find you. I know only that I was trained,
and when I asked why, I received only laughter or riddles.
*'Because the white needs the black, and the black the
white'*—does that sound to you like the command of the
gods? What I've guessed of their will, I've guessed only
since I met you, and not before."

Megan looked up, and the tears in her eyes and the
words that hung fresh in the air dispelled Thyri's anger,
and Thyri fell forward, into the sorceress's lap. *Oh,
Megan, I'm sorry! I did not mean to hurt you!*

Pain for pain . . . I was unaware of the hurt inside you.

*It's this place! I cannot endure its magics. They pain
me; they want a deep forgetting that I cannot give!*

I understand. I'm sorry—I should have known.

May we leave now? Sleep out under the moonlight?
Whatever you wish, my love.

Thyri looked up then, and it was then that she noticed
Ai'reth standing in the portal where the steps came up into
the *felnina* through the great oak. The felnin was scarcely
more than three feet tall. His face was animate, almost
human, but his body that of an erect cat with thick,
powerful rear legs and manlike hands. In one, he held a
sword, in the other a large blue gemstone. A jerkin covered his torso; it, and one of his legs, was slick with
blood.

The little creature looked at Thyri, then fell to his knees
and laid his bared sword down on the moss.

Blood

"You must flee!" Ai'reth said excitedly. "You are hunted!"

Thyri sat back up. "I am hunted?" she asked. "By what?"

"A man—a dark, powerful man. He took our *felnina*. He killed my wife!"

Megan crawled toward him. "Goddess!" she whispered. "Are you hurt?"

"Not Ai'reth. Came close; blood is wife's," he said sadly, holding back tears.

"Come here," Megan said. "Wash at the pool and tell us."

"Flee!" he said stubbornly, but he didn't fight the sorceress as she grabbed his arm and led him across the moss to the pool.

By the time he was clean, they had most of the story out. A man, searching for Thyri, had taken Ai'reth's people hostage to get to her. That made little sense, especially when the felnin insisted the man was from Midgard and had named her Eiriksdattir. Dark powers obviously were at work—dark powers that knew Thyri was here, in Alfheim.

"It stinks of gods," Thyri spat.

"But why didn't this man come to us?" Megan asked. "If he's strong enough to take a *felnina*—why didn't he just confront us?"

"Maybe because he'd first have to find us, and that might warn us, prepare us for danger. So he's strong," Thyri continued thoughtfully. "But not that strong. It still stinks of gods. Can you describe him, Ai'reth?"

Ai'reth nodded. "Blond hair, low-born, very dark inside. He wants to kill you, but you cannot be killed! Ragnarok comes! He is big and dark. Has dwarven sword."

"Loki in disguise?" Megan wondered aloud.

"No," Ai'reth said. "Trickster fettered until the end. Was *man!* Low-born!"

"But possession and manipulations won't be beyond him—"

"Megan—wait!" Thyri interrupted gravely. She took up her sword and unsheathed it before Ai'reth's eyes.

The felnin gasped. "That's it! Same runes, dwarven sword! Twins!"

"Oh, goddess!" Megan said. "He is full of darkness, you say? Powerful?"

"Yes."

Megan looked at Thyri, placing a hand on her arm. Thyri stared blankly ahead at the pool, tinged red by S'kiri's blood. "That's my sword," Thyri said distantly. "I kept Astrid's and gave him mine, and now I've destroyed his life, too."

"Flee," Ai'reth repeated. "You must flee!"

"No," Thyri said, standing. "He is my brother."

As they traveled swiftly through the night toward Ai'reth's home, Thyri's thoughts spiraled backward, back to the days of Astrid's death, the terrible pain and misery when the wolf first took her and she tore out her mother's throat and wished for nothing but her own death. She'd left behind her a trail of blood, her family's blood, and now, Erik, the last relative she cared anything for, sought her death. And he'd murdered, murdered along the way, just to get to her.

How had he come here? What enemy of hers had adopted him and played him like a pawn against her, to torture her? The last she'd heard, he was fierce, a Viking—he'd come to hate her and called out her name in battle, but that hardly bought him passage out of his world, Midgard, into this one.

As Thyri ran, she screamed up at the sky, shuddering as the scream transformed into a high, terrible howl. Now, she thought darkly as they neared their destination, he knows I come.

*   *.   *

Alone, she stalked silently up the stairs. Another *felnina* . . . Earlier, she'd wished never to enter one again. She stopped at the portal, her sword before her. Ahead, all was darkness but where the moonlight shone down through gaps in the ceiling. "Erik!" she commanded softly. "Show yourself!"

"Kinslayer," came a lilting voice from deep in the shadows. "Her mother is dead, her father is dead, their blood on her lips and her fangs and her claws! She is evil, like the dragon in the sea, like the hound at the gates, like the teeth in the giant's mouth."

"Forget the rhymes," she seethed. "Show yourself!"

He stepped forward, a tall, lanky, shadowy figure in the moonlight. His eyes burned red.

"Why do you seek me?"

"I do not seek, sister! I have found!" His exclamations were obscene, orgasmic.

"I will not fight you, Erik!"

He laughed. "She is here, but not to fight, that is good! Let us go then, to my master! I have a spell for you!" Strands of red light coiled out from his fingers and wrapped around her. Thyri fought against them, but they bound her, holding her still. How had he come by such sorcery! Erik stalked slowly forward.

"Erik, stop!" she cried. "I don't want to kill you!" Already, she could feel the bones twisting in the back of her neck and shoulders, just as they had the day before, so easily did the beast emerge when all seemed lost.

"Kill me?" he laughed. "I'm going to kill you!"

"Who commands you? Who did this to you? Who gave you this power?"

"Command?" he spat. "Gave? No one! I traded!"

"What did you trade?"

He stood right in front of her now. She could see his face, see the young, innocent features of her little brother twisted now into something impossibly evil. As he raised his sword, she looked into his eyes, his burning, red eyes, and she saw herself there, all the murder and blood of her past racing up through time to consume her. In that instant, she again wanted to die, prayed for his sword to descend down upon her, even as the agony of transformation twisted her spine and the hunger grew inside her, devouring her thoughts, pushing her human awareness down to where it was helpless to do anything but look on in horror.

As Erik's sword came down, he whispered an answer: "My soul," he said. Before his strike could sink into flesh, the beast took Thyri and twisted violently out of the magic. Erik's sword only grazed her flank, and that wound began to heal even as she jumped away.

Now, the wolf stood before him. The red madness burned in his eyes, and he attacked again. The wolf leaped to meet him, heedless of the point of his sword. She fell on him, pushing him back to the moss, the sword piercing her stomach. Snarling, she writhed, pushing the sword through her body until her fangs reached Erik's throat.

Thankfully, the pain of the wound consumed the little awareness Thyri had left. She didn't see his eyes right before he died; she didn't see the red madness flee, and pure, human terror take its place before the wolf's jaws snapped shut.

Magic

In her dreams, she floated. Everything was white, and she wondered if she were dead. The sky was white, the ground white, nothing even moved,˙ and then a terrible, freezing wind blew through her. The white in the sky grew solid, huge snowflakes falling around her, through her, like spears of ice through her body. In the distance, dark clouds lurked, and above, colors began to shine through the light—the colors of the rainbow.

The Rainbow Bridge. She fell next to Heimdall's foot. Dark armies moved across the distant snows. It was *fimbulwinter*, the coming of the end. She looked at herself, and she was the wolf.

She bit into Heimdall's big toe. . . .

Megan sat, stroking Thyri's forehead as she slept. The sorceress's eyes were red, strained by fatigue. She'd traveled hard through the night with Thyri to reach this place before morning, and once here, she'd been unable to sleep. She still saw, in her mind, the terrible carnage she'd confronted when she'd entered the *felnina*: blood everywhere, the head of Thyri's brother torn from his body, Thyri herself, naked, half wolf, half woman, a sword piercing her stomach and emerging a full foot on the other side.

Ai'reth had helped her remove the sword, then she'd cleaned it and wrapped it carefully with Thyri's other things. She'd then set off immediately for home, using her sorceries to push her burdens before her. By the time they'd made it back to the city of the Franks, Thyri's body had healed, and she'd turned fully back into a woman.

29

Then Megan had cast her spells, tried to sleep, failed, and now waited for Thyri to wake.

Slowly, sunlight invaded the snowscape, and Thyri felt Megan's hands brushing over her skin. She opened her eyes and saw the walls of the large room they shared on the north side of the city. She creased her forehead. How had they come here? The last she remembered, she and Megan had loved, in a field of barley after a hot day's chase on the pathways between the worlds.

"What—"

"Hush," Megan said. "Everything's all right now."

"But what happened?"

Megan smiled sadly. "I've cast a spell, Thyri. I can't lie to you—it's my doing that you can't remember."

"Odin!" Thyri said, bringing her hands up to her face. "What did I do? Did I change? Did I attack you?"

"No, my love. You didn't attack me."

"Then what?"

"I can lift the spell if you like."

"Megan, I have to know!"

"I have done other castings," Megan said quietly. "He was not himself. He was made to hate you, twisted by a power he couldn't resist. I'm not sure what power, perhaps Morgana before she died, perhaps another. I just want you to know that."

"Who's he?"

"Thyri, please. You don't know what you ask."

"I can't spend the rest of my life wondering about it!"

Megan sighed, tears rising to her eyes. "I thought you would feel thus. Do you want the memories back, or do you want me to tell you? Either way, if you ask quickly, I can renew the spell."

"The memories, Meg, else I can't be certain of the truth."

"You can trust me."

"But without proof I might always doubt it!"

"Very well."

The sorceress closed her eyes, took Thyri's head between her hands, and began to sing softly. Thyri felt something sharp, like a knife stabbing inside her mind, then it all came down upon her, not only the memory of slaying her brother, but the anguished hours before then, in the *felnina*, the pain she'd felt there, and her resentment toward the sorceress for putting it upon her. All of it hit her at once in a huge, crushing, agonizing wave. "No!" she screamed, struggling in Megan's grip. "No!"

Megan's song abruptly grew louder, and suddenly Thyri was screaming and wondering why. As her scream faded, Thyri knew only that *something* had caused it, something Megan had again hidden from her. Anguished, she coughed, her body wracked by sobs.

Without, she heard a loud crack—the door to the room bursting open. Rollo Anskarson filled the space, his sword ready. He glanced, concerned, at the two women, his eyes meeting Megan's for a moment, then he nodded slowly and backed out, shutting the door.

"I still have to know, Meg."

Thyri sat on the edge of the bed, her head in her hands. Megan sat across from her, cross-legged on the floor.

"Tell me, Meg," Thyri pleaded. "I'll trust you."

Slowly, the sorceress rose, lifting up a bundle near the door. She took it to Thyri and unrolled it onto her lap. Two swords fell there; Megan unsheathed them, laying them side by side.

Thyri's hand moved to touch the two blades. "Erik!" she whispered. She looked up, teary-eyed, at Megan. *Did I have a choice?*

The sorceress knelt, took Thyri's hands from the blades, and held her gaze. "No, my love," she said. "You did all you could do."

Gerald

In the city of the Franks, on the Street of Merchants, the high end, near the palace, an establishment called The Emporium peddled its wares to rich and poor alike. On its shelves one could find ancient scrolls and parchments in nearly all scripts known to men. Stone and wood carvings from the north sat in cabinets near the door. Bolts of fine silks colored the right side of the entrance hall, while statuary stolen from the old southern empires beckoned the visitor from the left. At the counter, one could request gemstones of all sorts, or fine scents from the far east, pendants and jewelry from around the world, or, in a back room, some of the finest swords and arms in all of the Frankish Empire. It should be noted that the average customer, more often than not, exited with a forgery of one of the above, rather than the genuine article.

Two other chambers, aside from the armory, led off from the main: two taverns, one of the wealthy, replete with silk-draped dancers and fine intoxicants of all sorts, the other for the common man and the servants of the wealthy, where one could purchase only mead or, if he knew who to ask, the services of one or more of the assorted rogues that lurked, by day and night, in the corners of this second public house.

In general, The Emporium enjoyed marked success, catering faithfully to the whims of all who entered. To some in the city, its success provided some small frustration as well as mystery. Thieves, it seemed, came away from attempts at penetration bruised and battered, or they came away not at all. No one, to anyone's knowledge, had successfully exited with anything for which he had not first paid, and two attempts at outright sabotage—midnight efforts to set the building aflame—had ended in equal frustration, the agents involved suffering similar fates to those of the thieves.

In some circles, whispered voices proclaimed The Emporium guarded by witchcraft; in that respect, they were correct. Sorceries permeated the walls and the wares, and much more went on within the building's walls than anyone uninitiated into its mysteries might guess at. No conversation held within, in fact, was safe from sorcerous eavesdropping. No freelance rogue hired from the second tavern left without primary allegiance to one or more of the establishment's generally unseen proprietors who lived in practice in the lavishly furnished rooms above.

One of those proprietors, the exception in that he was ever the most visible and often worked personally behind the establishment's central counter, was Gerald of Jorvik, the offspring of a Saxon and a Pict who had followed Thyri Eiriksdattir from his native soil to the seas of Jotunheim and back to here, the center of all European wealth, the heart of the empire conquered by the great Charlemagne, now ruled by a descendant lovingly known as Charles the Fat, King and Emperor of the Franks. With Thyri, Megan of Kaerglen, Rollo Anskarson, and Rui Taichimi, Gerald had thieved his way into part ownership of The Emporium, and now, with the others, he thieved from it.

Without a doubt, the proprietorship of The Emporium was a high point in Gerald's long, illustrious life. Though the establishment served many purposes of all involved, its day-to-day operations were managed by Gerald exclusively and his success as a trader provided him great personal satisfaction. He chose the wares to sell and marketed them to his customers, and he knew that they all could now live by his efforts alone. *His* efforts kept Megan and Thyri in silks, and himself, Rollo, and Rui in women and the finest meads and wines. He'd even commissioned a secret tunnel in recent months, overseeing the workers led blindfolded to and from their toils, in order to give Thyri safe passage from the city during the nights of the full moon. The week before, he'd presented this tunnel to her as a present, and he'd known by her smiles and tears that the gift was well received. In this, he felt great pride, for he knew that he'd accomplished a feat on the level of the sorceress, and moreover, he'd kept it secret until the gift was ready, and earned in the end the thanks of she against whom all other women paled.

Not that Gerald didn't have lovers. His business brought him the attention of many of the best women the city had to offer. He generally had his choice when he wished; he'd even spent a few glorious days with a pampered, *educated* great-granddaughter of Charlemagne himself. But he'd left even her, though he'd gifted her with a large sapphire fit for the crown of any queen in the world; no method of existence appealed to him more than the management of The Emporium, for only there could he remain close to Thyri and Megan, their beauty, and the greatness he perceived in them both. Even though he knew by now that he might never get close to Thyri, in the way that a normal man possesses a normal woman, he didn't care. Just serving her was enough, and he knew that Rollo and Rui felt much the same way. She had the loyalty of each of them, and it was a loyalty that knew no bounds. Only she could ask him to forfeit the luxuries he'd gained, but if she asked, he would do so willingly, without regret, and follow where she would lead, no matter if it were the seas of Jotunheim again, or the very gates of Niflheim itself.

On that morning Megan comforted Thyri, trying to help her friend face the pains of the night before amid the sumptuous furnishings of their bedchamber (if these were not described it was only because Thyri did not *see* them or perceive herself among them in the depths of her despair). Gerald worked below, entertaining a pair of wealthy travelers from Barcelona in their own tongue, just as he normally entertained Franks eloquently in the Frankish tongue. He'd grown fluent in all the tongues required for his dealings, Megan having cast for him and Rollo and Rui the same spell by which she'd once made Thyri fluent in Irish in the space of a few days. Once, Gerald had had a quiet chuckle when overhearing a gossip state that the king would do well to hire the advice of The Emporium's proprietor because he'd had the finest education of any in all the land.

But to return: Gerald entertained the Barcelonans, showing them silks and fine scents when suddenly Thyri's
screaming above echoed faintly in the rafters. Such were
the magics in the building that Gerald alone heard the
sound, and then only distantly, while his customers went
on bantering cheerfully over the price of silk and the
dangers of the far eastern trade routes. Gerald, meanwhile,
lost the thread of their talk and grew fretful, his imagination racing wildly in attempts to explain the sound he'd
heard. No one upstairs would ever scream so with no good
reason—that he knew well. So, were they under attack?
Had Megan or Thyri been injured or killed by some unknown assailant?

Gerald resisted the impulse to turn and bolt upstairs,
heedless of his business. Rollo and Rui would handle
it—whatever the problem was—and he wasn't certain what
impression his sudden departure would make, or even that
he was definitely the only one in the room to have heard
the scream. So he stood, detached, before the Barcelonans
until Rollo Anskarson came out of the door from the back
stairwell and stood silently, nodding and smiling at the
customers looking his way like an affable, friendly guard.
Gerald glanced at him and felt relief that no emergency
had transpired; at least Rollo didn't signal his undivided
attention, but in another way, the scream grew more puzzling. Had Thyri's nightmares returned? What *had* happened?

One of the Barcelonans clicked his fingers in front of
Gerald's eyes. Gerald looked at him, smiled and apolo-
gized effusively, then the Barcelonan shook his head, held
up a handful of glass vials, and said, flatly, "Two hundred."

A real barterer, Gerald realized dismally. His response
should have been abusive, followed by a firm declaration
of "One thousand, no less!" but instead he smiled weakly
and waved his hand toward the door, "Take it," he said
abruptly.

Now the man stood before him, insulted by Gerald's
refusal to carry out the game. To many, the act of barter-
ing was as sacred as showing piety before an altar. Merchants, in fact, owed their existence to the tactical skills,
the offers and counteroffers, involved in a sale. By not
demanding four or five times the Barcelonan's initial offer,
the traveler could only assume insult, that he'd drastically

overvalued the merchandise he desired, or that he held in his hands something of a quality somewhat less than advertised.

Gerald saw the insult and hurriedly attempted to dispel it. "No, just take it," he said, smiling warmly. "For nothing! Free! I've just remembered today's my birthday, and I must make amends to myself for forgetting." He raised his hands, declaring loudly, "All my customers! Today is my birthday, and I wish to celebrate! This place should be closed this morning, but you are lucky to have gotten in. Please, take what you have in your hands, as gifts from me, but leave now!"

Hearing the declaration, Rollo stepped forward to guide The Emporium's few morning customers toward the door. Gerald looked again to the Barcelonans and placed a hand on the one's shoulder. "Please, my friend," he said. "Take my gifts. Come back another day and I will gladly relieve you of your money."

Shaking his head in slight disbelief, the Barcelonan stepped back. As Rollo showed them to the door, Gerald heard them laughing, and at the portal, the one turned back and promised Gerald that he would, indeed, return.

After Rollo had gone to declare the same holiday in the taverns, he returned to Gerald, smiling. "Don't forget this date, friend," he said. "You'll have to remember it in the years to come and treat it accordingly."

"Just won't open at all," Gerald said, searching the larger man's gaze for some clue to the events upstairs. "It was Thyri, wasn't it?" he asked finally.

Rollo nodded, his dark hair falling down in front of his eyes, his hand brushing it quickly away. In Gerald's memory, the Viking was ever his natural blond, though Rollo had consented to Megan's cosmetic change after learning how unwelcome Norsemen remained in the lands of the Franks. Before Gerald could say more, Rui came down the stairs to join them. The archer appeared as always, his alien, exotic features, his flat nose and catty eyes, setting him apart from other men. Rui resisted any sorcerous disguising of his everyday appearance, conceding this principle only in the most necessary of circumstances. Instead, on the streets, he traveled cloaked like a monk, though he seldom went without his bow and quiver. At Rollo's side, he was usually left alone. Now, Rui came cloaked, though his hood was back, the concern on his face mirroring Gerald's.

"I don't know much," Rollo told them. "Thyri screamed, but she didn't look hurt. The witch was with her; I didn't ask any questions."

For a while, they stood around restlessly, silently. Gerald knew they all thought the same thoughts: They all desired to ascend the stairs and learn first hand of Thyri's troubles. In that she was with Megan, they all felt powerless. They would learn what they would learn, in time and not before. Finally, Rui suggested they get out and wander.

"Take our frustrations out on some poor rogues near the docks, you mean," Rollo chuckled darkly.

Rui looked at him calmly and shrugged.

On the streets, Gerald felt the weight of the sword at his side lift another weight off his shoulders. He'd almost forgotten what it was like to move free, anonymously, among other men. On his cloak he wore a pendant fashioned by Megan; to others he would not appear as himself, as the groomed proprietor of The Emporium, but as an unkempt ruffian on the right flank of Rollo, a giant of a man among the small Frankish people.

They did go to the docks, but they didn't find a fight. They found instead something else: A messenger for the king, fresh off his ship, sat at a table and drank, one mead turning to two, then more, and the mead loosened an otherwise confidential tongue. The messenger's news for the king was good.

A few weeks before, the city had learned of an invasion on the river. Hundreds upon hundreds of Norse reavers had started upstream in search of land. Much talk had centered on the outcome of the bold frontal assault; and the last anyone had heard the Norse only wanted to settle, and though the nobility was up in arms, King Charles in his detached and fatalistically cowardly way, was going to let them. Thyri and Rollo had had something of a special interest in the news, both feeling the bonds of kinship with the invaders, but the king's apparent lack of belligerence had pleased them and they'd been happy merely to watch.

Now, through the king's increasingly drunk messenger, Rollo, Rui, and Gerald heard a different story. Under pressure from the nobility, the king had secretly blockaded the river and, with his ships and armies, now held the seven hundred-odd Norse ships trapped and more or less helpless. At the king's command, the messenger told all the tavern, the Norsemen would be summarily slaughtered.

Hearing this, Rollo, Rui, and Gerald quietly left.

Thieves

Rollo watched Thyri closely as she and Megan came into their council chamber, a second-story room furnished with cabinets and a large oak able where they occasionally took their meals, but more often than not simply gathered to drink and discuss present and future plans. Few outsiders ever saw inside the room; when they met with others, such meetings were held in one of the taverns, or in some location well away from The Emporium. Here, Megan had covered the walls with wards and other arcane drawings, protections she claimed would shield their councils from even the most powerful sorceries. As Thyri entered, she looked at these wards and drawings; they were chalk, and Rollo couldn't know that they recalled for Thyri a room in Castle Kaerglen, to which the Princess Tana had once led Thyri, and wherein Thyri had found many such drawings, as well as a ring, a plain gold band streaked with silver, Megan's ring in Megan's old room. Chalk drawings on the walls, just like here. . . .

Externally, Thyri showed no sign whatever of the wound she'd endured. She seemed her ever confident, calm self—except that her eyes took overly long to meet those of the others. She looked long at Megan's drawings; something about them bothered her. She felt as if she'd thought of them lately, or dreamed of them lately, but couldn't remember when. Was this memory, along with Erik's death, hidden from her behind the shield of Megan's spell? Two swords now stood in her room, where yesterday there had been only one. Chalk on the walls—Megan's past and present. She yearned briefly to know again, to have the sorceress lift the spell again, but they'd tried that once. *Let*

it be forgotten, Thyri heard in her mind. She glanced at
Megan. *Let it rest.* In the sorceress's eyes, there was
pleading and love. Thyri nodded imperceptibly, and saw
Megan smile. "What news have you?" she asked, turning
to Rollo.

"Sit first," he said, taking two flagons and filling them
from a cask of mead.

Thyri and Megan sat, taking their flagons. "What news?"
Thyri repeated.

"Charles has attacked, and the seven hundred are trapped,
awaiting death."

Thyri drank, then set her flagon down. "Then it's war,"
she said.

Rollo eyed her closely, looking again for signs of her
wound. Did she suggest, seriously, a frontal assault on the
Frankish armies? A possible suicide, that idea, but he
wouldn't refuse should she command it. "Shall we prepare
Nightreaver?" he asked carefully. "Recruit the rabble?"

Thyri laughed, and in her laughter, and the sudden
intense concentration in her eyes, Rollo saw that he'd never
learn what had pained her that morning. The news he'd
brought would now command her attention; in effect, it
had already healed her, diverting her thoughts, making her
look fully to present and future battles, not to past ones.
And then he realized that she laughed at him, his sugges-
tions. He failed to understand, though he realized that he
had thought very little about the news before bringing it to
her. Even after learning of the king's treachery, he'd
worried most about Thyri. Now, in the light of Thyri's
laughter, that worry felt burdensome, ill-placed.

"And what then?" she asked him, still laughing. "Do
we attack the castle? Burn the city? Have you been a thief
this past year, my friend?" She grew serious. "No, we
must have a more subtle way. Those Norsemen seek only
land, not war with this empire, or even control of it. If we
make it war, we will be too few to win."

Now it was Rollo's turn to laugh. "With her sorcery?"
he asked, nodding his head toward Megan. "She could lift
the king's palace and drop it on his armies' heads!"

Megan smiled at him, but she spoke calmly, "No,
Rollo. The One God is very strong in this land, but he
slumbers and his followers do not know I am here. I have

been very careful to conceal myself from them, for if they turn certain of his sorceries against me, in this land where his power is so great, I may well die.''

"Subtlety, Rollo," Thyri said. "Our people want land, and they should have it. All lands resist us now, ever more effectively. Once, I thought we might rule the world, but that seems fated not to pass. We must, however, survive, and this empire has no right to slaughter seven hundred ships full of men when it has land to spare them. If we fight incorrectly though, the Franks will not rest until all of Norse blood are cast out.''

Rui tapped his fingernails on the table. "What," he said slowly, glancing at the others, "does the king value most? It is his decision, is it not? Whether or not to attack? Whether or not to wage war?''

"His throne?" Rollo asked, unsure.

"No," Gerald answered, leaning forward, cracking his flagon down onto the wood. "Not his throne, but his gold.''

Thyri smiled at the Saxon. "Perfect. Now, how do we do it? With our wits alone? With sorcery? With the rabble? After this, I doubt we'll be able to stay here, but we should think first of a way to do it alone. I will entrust none of this to any Frank or cutthroat in this city. I will not have what we do undone, whether we stay or leave.''

Rollo stared at her, at the sparkle in her eyes, and his thoughts turned back again to the morning, when he'd heard her scream and seen her, deep in despair, with the sorceress. The questions still burned in him awhile, then the sparkle in her eyes affected him as, slowly, he thought and wondered on what she proposed. Eventually, he sighed and gave his mind over to the future, as she obviously had. Whatever secrets the morning harbored, it could keep them. Adventure beckoned, and the lives of Norsemen, his people, were at stake. And after that, she'd said they might leave, hadn't she? To be back out on the sea? That thought comforted him. Thievery and this city had their good sides, but sometimes, and fairly often of late, Rollo had ached for the feel of a sword in his hand, for the anarchy of battle. He might not get that now, but with the sparkle in Thyri's eyes, and the promise of leaving, battle felt ever closer, as if she moved, and he with her, in a slow flirtatious dance to the sound of clashing swords.

Magic

The plan, in the end, rested mostly on Megan, and such a plan it was that Rollo found himself wondering on the sorceress's earlier words on the power of the One God. Surely this idea concocted by Thyri would tempt the One God's wrath, but Megan consented willingly, even laughing with delight from time to time and adding ideas of her own. It didn't amount to dropping castles on top of armies; in ways, however, it sounded worse.

Most of the time, the men simply listened, each of them thinking, as they all had in the past, on the incredible talents of the women they followed. They sat, smiling in amazement, as each new twist of the plan fell from Thyri's lips.

In the end, it sounded remarkably simple, assuming the One God would fail to rise up and strike them all dead.

Getting inside the palace was the first problem. Megan's sorceries would be sorely tested during the operation, and she didn't desire to use them except when absolutely necessary. So instead of a sorcerous approach, they decided on a covered one.

Gerald, Rollo, and Rui loaded a wagon full of The Emporium's finest wares, then all but Gerald and Rollo concealed themselves within. Once loaded, and its horses hitched, the wagon carried them quickly to the palace gates.

"I must see the king!" Gerald called out to the guard.

"Who hails the palace?" a man returned, opening the gatekeeper's hatch.

"It is Gerald of The Emporium. I wish to see the king."

43

"Come back tomorrow. It is late."

"I cannot," Gerald said impatiently, "for tomorrow is not my birthday—only today, and I have presents for the king on my birthday. I have presents for you, as well, if you will only let me in."

"What sorts of presents?"

"Jewels and scents for your ladies," Gerald said, holding up a handful of necklaces and vials. "Surely you have ladies?"

"Aye," the gatekeeper laughed. "You must wait." The man disappeared. A moment later, the gate came down.

Gerald drove the wagon across and stopped it where they were flanked by two dozen guards. Rollo smiled at them, hopped down, and threw back the canvas covering their load so all might see they carried no dangers for the king. As the canvas came up, it seemed to all that a light breeze descended from the sky, filling them with feelings of great warmth. A few of them looked up and saw, high above the castle, a new star that shone as brightly as the moon itself.

That star was Megan's star blazing in the heavens; she had stolen it from the lore of the One God, from the tale of his son's birth. Rollo glanced at it and shuddered; they tempted great powers, and would do more before the night was through. And such powers he couldn't challenge with his sword. Seeing the star, and knowing that the earth had not yet opened up to swallow him, his confidence in Megan's judgment began to improve. "The One God is not like our gods," she'd told them. "His mysteries are open, free to all, while ours are closed and sorcerous. Any man can become one of his priests, but in our world one must be born into the mysteries and then taught their secrets. We of power are closer to our gods, but those opposing us are far more numerous. Most important, though, he *depends* on his followers to carry his cross, the banner of his mysteries, into battle. They are but men and can be tricked, and they can't fight with his power unless they know there is a battle. We're going to trick them. We're not going to let them know."

Rollo thought on it as he looked up at the star. Odin would never stand for such sacrilege. He hoped the sorceress was right.

* * *

Thyri, Megan, and Rui hurried across the courtyard, concealed by Megan's sorceries but nevertheless fearful of lingering. If the plan succeeded fully, they would have to beat Gerald to the king. Overhead, Megan's star beamed brightly, lighting their way. While running, the sorceress cast other spells, locating both the king and his gold. The treasury was underground, though it had a heavily guarded entrance on the palace's outer wall. To there they went.

The guards, four of them armed with sword and mace, saw nothing until a shimmering silver key materialized in the air, and the door behind them suddenly opened. Before they could shout out, Thyri and Rui appeared before them, but they did not see a short, fierce Norse swordsmistress and a strange archer from far off lands. Instead, they saw two tall figures clothed in white and bathed in white light. Behind the figures, sprouting from their shoulders, huge wings twitched in the air, and one by one the four guards all fell to their knees.

Improvising, Thyri smiled at them, then carried a finger to her lips and pointed up with her other hand, to the bright star over the castle. One of the guards actually began to weep with joy as streams of gold came through the air from behind him and seemed to pass through his chest before soaring up into a window high on the castle's walls.

Megan stayed only long enough to be sure the guards would not see through the sorcerous disguises of her friends, then she spelled herself to where she'd sent the streams of gold. She had, by the way, stolen nothing. All the king's gold remained where she'd found it; she'd wanted mostly to see it, to be sure of the reality of her illusions.

In the room where she went, she found a ready audience, a perfect audience, for he was alone. He sat on the edge of his bed, his mouth agape, his eyes fixed on the stacks of gold bars that had poured in through his window. He was a fat man, and, in a way, a very simple one. But he was also good of heart, and he'd first declined to oppose the small Norse invasion out of dislike of bloodshed, rather than fear of it. It seemed to him that his God, with his son The Christ, had meant to teach men something. Peace was one of those teachings.

As it was, Megan almost felt sorry for the king. She appeared before him, a small dark-haired woman draped in brown cloth. She looked at him sadly, but said nothing until he spoke.

"Who—who are you?" he finally stammered. His body quivered, his rolls of fat shaking with his voice.

She turned to the side and became a man, a bearded man with a crown of thorns on his head. "I am your god," said the man's voice.

"Wha—"

She turned and became the woman again. "I am taking this from you," she said, indicating the pile of gold. "Seven hundred bars, one for each ship you offer Death."

He stared at her, wide-eyed and speechless.

"You have nothing to say?"

"But, Virgin," he said. "You can't mean those godless pagans!"

"I can, and I do."

"So you take my gold?"

"As a start, and a warning, yes."

"A warning?"

She nodded. With a flick of her wrist, she started small, dark, magical fires in the corners of the room.

The king fell to his knees before her. "No, please! I'll do anything!"

"Leave the ships alone, then. Let them ashore. They will fight bravely for you when the real wars come."

"What real wars?"

"You will learn in time."

"Oh, Virgin," he cried. "I'll do anything! I'll give this gold to those ships, if only you will let me! I will let them land, but please leave my life and my soul so that I may worship you forever!"

"You will give the gold to the reavers?" she asked, choking off amazed laughter at the unexpected twist of irony.

"Yes!"

"Then I return it to your treasury," she said, flicking her wrist again, sending the gold streams back out the window. With another flick, she extinguished the fires, and then she stood over the king, looking at him with warm, motherly eyes.

"Thank you!" he said, crying, gazing at her.

"Your life is blessed," she said, and she disappeared.

Downstairs, in the castle's entrance hall, Gerald began to worry, straining his ears for any hint of danger. From outside, the sound of great commotion sporadically reached him; Gerald couldn't be sure whether it was the continuing effects of the star above, or whether something more alarming was happening. He wished for his sword, but he had come unarmed as part of his character. If it came to battle, he could always take a weapon off of one of Rollo's first victims, not that they'd then have a much greater chance of getting out alive. He could see in Rollo's eyes that the Viking felt much the same.

He'd already handed out a fair portion of his wares just getting the castle's main doors opened. Once in, the powers inside the castle had directed him to leave the gifts and then depart. He would not have his audience. The point of his actions began to seem meaningless as he oversaw Rollo and several guards carrying statues and rolls of silk through the castle's entrance hall into the king's council chamber. He yearned to get outside, to find Thyri and see how the plan fared.

But then, as the men worked, King Charles, looking dazed and almost bouyant despite his great bulk, stumbled in. Gerald's heart began to pound in his chest; he watched the king from the corner of his eye. Charles called several men to him, gave them whispered orders, and they hurried off. After an agonizing wait, the king came toward Gerald.

"What's this?" Charles asked, watching Rollo and the guards come in with another huge roll of silk.

"Presents for the king," Gerald said, forcing a pleasant smile. "It is my birthday, and I have presents for the king!"

"Did she send you?"

"She—" Gerald feigned surprise. "Oh no, my king. I am not married."

"No, I mean—" the king stammered, looking confused. "You mean you're bringing all this to me? Gifts? Not taxes?"

"Not taxes at all," Gerald said happily. "It is the night of my birthday, and a wondrous night it is! Have you not seen the bright star in the heavens?"

"Star?" the king asked in amazement.

Gerald watched, finally relieved and chuckling to himself, as the king bobbed merrily toward the door for a look outside.

Warriors

That night, the proprietors of The Emporium laughed and drank until they collapsed under the weight of their merriment. Gerald talked at length of the king, of the rapturous look on his face as he'd started outside to see the star; as an afterthought, Megan had made it explode in a shower of silver before the king's eyes. In the midst of the spiritual euphoria that ensued, they'd have no trouble leaving. Charles, in fact, had commanded the gates be thrown wide so he might invite in his subjects and tell all of his divine visitation.

The story—and its absurd hilarity for Thyri and her friends—had grown quickly. Throughout the castle, it seemed every man or woman had been blessed or visited by all manner of angels and visions. As Gerald and Rollo had mounted their empty wagon, they'd heard three women proclaiming joyously that the Archangel Gabriel had come to them and blessed them all, simultaneously, with child. Departing, Gerald had heard the king's gardener describing in detail his vision of heaven's gate and how The Christ stood before it, kissing those who entered and showing the horrible wounds on his hands to those who were turned away.

Even in The Emporium's taverns and throughout the city the tales of angels and visions flourished. Thyri and the others finally retreated to the solitude of their council room for fear that their laughter and their own words might undo what they'd accomplished. It seemed the entire Frankish nation had been blessed along with its king.

Once alone together, they laughed until their sides hurt,

all save perhaps Megan. She smiled and chuckled at the others' stories, but weariness hid behind her eyes, and occasionally, Thyri thought she saw sadness there.

Rollo, though, relaxed fully. At the height of the celebration, he went to the sorceress, lifted her up, and gave her a hug that threatened to crack her spine. "You are fantastic!" he shouted out, then he kissed her sloppily above her breasts.

Gerald, at the sight, fell silent. It stunned him—the Viking's lips and beard touching Megan's flesh in such a way. When Rollo put the sorceress down, he almost expected her to back away and inflict upon the Viking some terrible, excruciating death. But this she did not do. "Thank you, Rollo," she said, then she sat back down.

Rollo's happy eyes darted about the room, settling finally on Gerald. Gerald stared; Rollo stamped his foot on the floor. "What's wrong, Saxon?" he bellowed. "Seen a ghost?"

Gerald blinked, glanced from Rollo to Megan, and smiled weakly. "No, my friend," he said. "Just a vision."

Later, near dawn, Thyri curled up to Megan and found her tense. She touched her cheek and realized the sorceress cried. "You are troubled?" Thyri whispered softly.

"Yes."

"Shadows on our victory?"

Our end I saw, Thyri. The end of our ways, the passing of our gods. Even you laughed at the idiocy, at the way the visions I started spread like wildfire from the castle out over the city. Yes, it was absurd, hilarious, and laughable. But behind that absurdity lurks the death of our way of life, the death of the natural spirits before the coming of the detached spirit of meaningless, nonexistent visions. See how they spread with all the people of this city so eager not to be left out? Instead of disbelieving the stories, ridiculing them, the hearer simply creates a grander one, or a more mysterious one, and they go on believing each other, interpreting these invented visions until they actually come to believe they had them. Tonight, my love, I have made the One God stronger and quickened the passing of those we know. I have been his miracle, and from this miracle, he spreads and gains even more strength.

Rollo feared his wrath, but why should he be wrathful? I have helped him, in a way he rarely helps himself. And I did it very well; I did it perfectly.

"But you saved the Norse," Thyri protested gently, caressing Megan's breast.

Yes, but for what? So they might hear of the One God's miracles, forsake Odin, and follow the cross blindly with the rest?

"We will tell them the truth."

Will we? How many will believe us, and how long before our truth fades?

Thyri sighed. "We've long known of our gods' passing, Meg. Why such sorrow now?"

To know is one thing, to feel is another. Tonight I felt it.

Thyri lay silently, thinking. She pictured Odin on his throne, with the Thunderer at his side. How could they fall before any power less than that of Fenrir, Jormungard, and Surt? Nothing in all the worlds could withstand the crush of Thor's hammer, not anything real, anything that could be touched. Why didn't Odin and Thor take the battle out, confront the One God and destroy this disease of faith?

Megan interrupted her thoughts: *I fear, Thyri. I fear especially for you. I learned many things yesterday, from one who loves you, but one you will not remember. Fimbulwinter has come to Asgard. Do you feel it here?*

No.

"It is the One God," Megan whispered, her voice cracking and stark in its sudden emergence. "It is the One God who keeps it away."

Thyri stayed silent. The talk of gods, the exhaustion of the day, and Megan's mention of the day before sent her thoughts tumbling into murky, disconnected images: She was the Wolf, the Reaver. Odin's head grew small; Thor's hammer floated among clouds, writhing like a snake. Memories pulsed and burned, straining to break free from their cages of darkness. So were her thoughts as she drifted into equally disturbing dreams.

The next day, far upriver, the Frankish armies pulled away from the banks. Hesitantly, seven hundred ships weighed anchor and started for land.

Though they had no leader, the first Viking to step ashore was named Hrothgar Olafson. He debarked armed, but he did not attack the few Franks that remained near a sole, canvas-covered cart. Instead, he approached them cautiously.

"Hail, friend!" called one in the Norse tongue.

Hrothgar stopped. The Frank reached under the cart's canvas and Hrothgar saw something glint in the sunlight as the Frank stepped forward. At Hrothgar's feet, he dropped a bar of gold. Hrothgar stared down, unsure whether or not he dreamed.

With ceremony, the Frank pulled a scroll of parchment from his vest and read aloud. By now, several other ships had landed, and the Viking marauders had begun to gather behind Hrothgar. "By decree of Charles, Emperor," the Frank read, translating into Norse, "I offer you land and welcome you among my people. For each ship, the King and Emperor offers peace and one bar of his gold. You may divide the land here among yourselves, except that land that is claimed and worked by another. In this, may the Lord God make you prosperous."

The Frank lowered the parchment and looked up at Hrothgar, clearing his throat. "You will, of course, pay taxes," he added.

Hrothgar bent to the ground and lifted the gold, testing its weight. Behind him, cheers broke out among the Vikings as the Frank's words sank in and spread. As Hrothgar walked away, followed by his men, he felt a sudden weight on his shoulder and stopped. Turning his head carefully, his eyes met those of a bird, a small blackbird. He stared at it, and it spoke to him. *"Eiriksdattir greets her fellow travelers,"* the bird said, then it flapped away to a tree and sat there, watching until the next Viking came away from the rest with his gift from the king.

Book VIII:
KAERGLEN

So it all now truly begins, and I only wonder why true beginnings stand so close in time to their endings. Events rush together, gaining momentum, shaking all the worlds in their calamitous joining. That calamity—its thunder— roars like death and life together. I suppose little Ai'reth knew it well, for this vision I have in my mind, of life and death at war, recalls the *yangyi* I have seen through his eyes.

Yes, my power grows; my vicarious sorceries nearly drove through Megan's shields last night. Nearly—but not quite. Ai'reth was easy, though very difficult at first. Once, Tana, daughter of Coryn, king of Kaerglen Isle, was closed to me, but attempting her of late, I've succeeded as well— a timely success as only now have I need again to write of the princess and her family.

Still, I do not understand why I gain strength, unless it be that I am a part of those events rushing to a common, fateful conclusion, gaining speed and power along the way. That is a thought, but I fear I am but an echo. I dream of darkness now in the night, dreams of nothingness so vacant I wake and turn restlessly until dawn, or I steal away from my bed and come to this work, toiling by candlelight. I've come to cherish the silence of sleepless nights, inasmuch as I can escape those dreams. To be aware, aching for light, for movement, but to dream only of this yawning void of darkness. Nothing moves in my dreams; nothing changes, but the dreams themselves feel eternal.

At first—or I should write *Long ago*—I wished to write of those days of chaos when we thieved and pillaged and built the small fortune that grew into The Emporium. It did not take long, not for Thyri, and especially not for Megan: goddesses crushing ants, both of them. I guess now that that is why I have not written of those times. They were times of diversion, akin to all the adventures of Thyri and Astrid before Astrid's death. I must stay focused on the Twilight. Why write of the hero's idle afternoons while the battles remain untold? And, as always, I do not know what time I have left. Satan's Chalice threatens, even now, to run dry before long.

So follow as the tale leads us onward and elsewhere. As events unfolded, we abandoned The Emporium anyway.

Ghosts

Her name was Tana, and she was just fifteen, the age when childhood still bubbles up unexpectedly through memory, as it now did for her. She was fifteen, with long nut-brown hair and green eyes, long, strong legs built like a doe's for grace and speed, and her breasts had already grown larger than her mother's. But she didn't feel fifteen. She felt about ten—no younger than that because until that age she'd never truly felt herself weak, a child. Until then, she'd felt only the magic; she'd felt almost ancient, a child of Brigid, a spirit as old and wise as the sea, as quick and strong as the wind, as bright as the sky. Until ten, her mother could not make her tremble with fear, and the night's mysteries never menaced or haunted or whispered of past evil. Until ten, she'd been more spirit than girl, with all the world her witching ground. *"Touch me,"* the rocks would say, and she would touch them and hear their sighs. *"Feel me,"* the wind would whisper, and she would, feeling more than the wind, feeling the spirits that rode on it, feeling the wind's age, seeing where it had come from and where it had been. Until ten, when the wind touched her, she could close her eyes and race with it over mountains and follow it from one world to the next— over the seas of Midgard to the glittering shores and golden forests of Alfheim; the majestic plains and halls of Asgard to the granite crags of Nidavellir. In dark Svartalfheim, she'd see her own light illuminating the twisted wood, and when dark spirits would join her in the wind, she'd feel a chill and then, simply, open her eyes. . . .

To stand on the hill below the castle or on the rocky shore down from the secret grotto where the wind-dreams would come to her even when she kept her eyes open—oh, the ageless peace of it all! Sometimes Seth would be with her, standing silently, his hand hesitantly reaching out to touch hers. She'd look at him and search his face—his own ten-year-old face, for they were twins—and then she'd ask what he'd seen. "Glimpses," he would say. Glimpses of forest and lake, dragons at the edge of the sky that would transform into cloud as soon as he tried to focus on them. Tuathán gatherings—great bonfires that spit sparks like fiery, hellish eyes into the night. But always only glimpses; he could follow her, chase after her, strain to catch her only to lose her again, but he could never lead. The wind-dreams were Tana's, but she shared all she could, as she and Seth had shared all ever since they'd been born. Whenever her brother finished telling his visions, she would talk, completing them, placing the dragons in context, the lakes among mountains, the Tuathans in their woods, and the bonfires before the temples of the worlds. She would speak until Seth understood, until he assured her that he felt her wind-dream as his own, as if he had never left her side.

Which, in fact, he hadn't, at least not on Midgard. In her heart and mind she would fly, while he would watch over her body. It had happened first when they were six, exploring some forgotten corner of the castle. They'd found a door, and beyond it a passageway, which they'd followed, winding ever downward until it had opened into the grotto. He'd held her hand while the wind-dream had come and carried her away.

Now, Tana was fifteen and wanted that day back. She tried to find the six-year-old inside herself, her old sense of wonder, her elation when she finally *knew* herself and her strength. For years, she hadn't known what gave her those waking dreams. They would come when she wished, wherever she found herself, but always with effort away from the grotto. With tremendous effort these days . . . She'd lost the feeling; she'd been broken. When she'd first spoken with Brigid—when the sad goddess had finally revealed herself to Tana in the grotto late one formless, shapeless day—it had already been too late.

She still felt ten, the age her world ended, when the

wonder within her bled from her wound as she'd found herself suddenly naked before all the world. Even five years later she couldn't fight it. To think brought it all back. To try not to think made it worse.

Autumn had come to Kaerglen, and now, near dusk, the full moon shone brightly down into the garden at the castle's heart where Tana slouched, limp in the wooden chair Finaan had insisted on bringing her. (Finaan—of all men it had to be *him* fawning over her, touching her face and hair, trying to comfort her with his vacant, treacherous smile! Finaan whose heart was black like coal, whose men raped her island, whose insidious sorcery hastened the end of all the beauty that remained in the world. Who—but, no, she mustn't think it. . . . Too late already, though: Here she sat, her own father near death. And who did she think of? Her father? No, she thought of Finaan. And Patrick.)

There was a time—once, so long ago—when Tana's and Seth's world had nearly seduced their elder brother, nearly made him one of them. How ridiculous that time seemed now; Patrick was eight years their senior, and only their half-brother actually; King Coryn's blood did not run in his veins. And yet he was heir, and long ago—six years? Yes, they'd been nine and he'd been seventeen—they'd almost had him. It was after Rahne's death; something then had made Patrick morose, listless. Tana wondered what yearning within him had sapped his strength. It could not have been mourning, for the prince shared no blood with the ancient woman, she being the sister of the king's mother. Perhaps it had been simply the shock of death in the air, with Patrick finally mature enough to sense his own mortality hidden implicitly in the ugly, bone-white wrinkles of the corpse, in the blood-bruised skin of its impossibly thin arms. He had, after all, found her first, collapsed in the hall in a lump outside his door.

When Queen Moira had come at his call, they'd found a long, thin dagger hidden in Rahne's skirts. Was that it? Tana wondered (as she had countless times over). Was that dagger the key to Patrick's near-conversion? She and Seth had known Rahne fairly well; in fact, the old woman had informed them many times of her impending death.

She and Seth had gained much of their knowledge of the castle from Rahne, and Tana had often seen that dagger—it was very slender and all of stone with a bird's head carved into the hilt. Rahne had used it in eating, in sewing, and Tana had known that she'd kept it with her always, hidden in her skirts. But had Patrick known this? If not, he might have imagined the dying woman seeking him out with the last of her strength, intent on taking him with her into death. She'd fallen before *his* door. That was slightly strange; Tana reasoned that she'd actually been trying to reach her and Seth. Only a few more steps, and she might have made it. What last secrets might she have told them then in the last moments before death?

Patrick with his deep voice and cruel muscles—even then she'd thought his physique obscene, as if he'd been shaped of muscle and bone, his maker regarding soft, simple flesh as unnecessary, carving only powerful but *cruel* lines, veins that bulged, sharp muscles that moved like snakes under skin, a belly crisscrossed with lines like the back of a tortoise. And whenever she'd seen him, his flesh had been wet, drenched like the coat of a work horse. "Christ's champion," their mother called him. But when he came to Tana—that day after Rahne's burial—he was crying.

She and Seth took his hands and led him deep into Castle Kaerglen, to where he'd never been, back past the rooms of the old ones and deeper still, down stairs and into a maze of halls covered in dust and debris. The castle had known better days; Tana now knew something of its history and its age, its roots in the many ancient invasions of Erin and how it once was home to Manannan—the very god of the sea—and his wife, Fand. Where she and Seth took Patrick—even Brenden the Priest had never been this deep on his periodic missions of exorcism. So the magic remained ever strong, and they passed through it, to the tunnel, the winding stairs, and the most magical place of all: the *faerie* place, the grotto. Tana had her wind-dream while holding Patrick's hand, and through her he could feel the peace and wonder of it all, the power and strength of the winds that blew through all the worlds.

He cried then with tears of joy, and a week later, Tana and Seth led him again to the grotto and repeated the ritual, and afterward they showed him the exit to the rocky shore below, where one could look away overhead and see a corner of the castle at the top of the cliff. They ate there on the rocks and laughed together, Seth singing for Patrick old songs he'd learned years before from Rath, and the sea crashing lightly below them as if Manannan in his depths knew the tune.

A few days later, their cousin from the mainland, Finaan, arrived, and everything changed. When they went to Patrick, he and Finaan laughed at them, so that was that; the near-conversion ended, and Patrick remained unchanged, his cruel muscles yet moving like snakes beneath his skin.

In the grotto she'd had her defeat; Rahne's death had opened the treacherous door for her own compassion to shape it. It hadn't taken long—maybe a month at most. The days grew darker, Patrick's muscles more cruel, and she and Seth were too young to perceive the subtle shifts in the castle's atmosphere, so when Patrick and Finaan arrived suddenly, exploding in like nightmares to devour the grotto's serene magic, the twins had been paralyzed, unable to act as their world crumbled around them. . . .

Tana shifted in her chair as she sensed Finaan's approach. Above, the full moon grew brighter and she gazed at it with helpless longing, as ever she did when it went full. This attraction was real in a way, for perhaps—if she could reach out and touch it—she might regain the hope that had fueled her one, failed quest. Forgetting the present, she closed her eyes and reached up, but her hand touched something rough—Finaan's face—and she quickly drew it back.

He stood in silence for a while, eclipsing her salvation, the moon's light casting him a dark shadow with the wild black hair around his head paled to dull, glittering gray. His eyes were like dark craters, unreadable in the shadows, the same shadows that turned his nose up, into a snout like a pig's.

As she watched, he moved his hand to his face, touching his cheek where she'd involuntarily caressed him. His other hand held a goblet toward her. "I brought you wine," he said.

The silver vessel flashed in the moonlight, a red liquid lapping over its sides. It made her think of blood, and she shook her head. "Leave me," she said simply.

Instead, he raised the goblet to his lips and drained it himself, then he squatted before her. She could see him more clearly like that. He wore a light mail shirt under his black silks, and the sword at his side made a scraping sound against the ground as he shifted his weight slowly from side to side. She almost laughed; the man went everywhere prepared for battle. As she thought about it, she couldn't recall a single time when she'd seen Finaan separated from his weaponry. He even wore his sword at the dinner table. With him squatted like this, she could see something of his eyes, and his nose looked normal, no longer like a snout. She idly wished he'd stand again and resume his demonic form with the moon behind him; the pig's snout would keep her aware of his true nature. But even as she saw him more clearly, she couldn't think him handsome, not with all the imagination she could muster. The servant girls (and she had heard their gossip enough to know this was true)—let them adore him and vie nightly for his bed. Let them save her the anguish.

"Can I get you anything?" he asked.

"Just leave me," she said. There was no force in her words. There never was anymore; what difference did her words make anyway? He wasn't going to leave, not on her command. Finaan did what Finaan wished, and only that. Her very *lack of force* was her defense. Her defeat was her defense; it kept his passions subdued, at a distance.

And he did ignore her. He scarcely moved, save his slow shifting from side to side. "Anything," he said after a moment. "I'll do anything for you, Tana. If you would touch me again like that—if you wouldn't draw away, if you would sigh when I touch you—I would do anything."

She grunted.

"You can't hate me forever," he said. "I will fight the darkness inside you until you love me, until you beg me to hold you. I will be a king one day myself, you know. My own father is old. When Patrick and I are kings, we shall conquer all of Erin. And I would do anything if you would be my queen."

The darkness inside is all within you, my prince, she thought. But she found herself repeating his word, the word he offered her again and again. "Anything?" she asked listlessly.

"Yes!" he said softly, inching closer to her. She imagined she breathed his breath—an acrid stench, the breath of his One God's hell.

"Then kill my brother," she whispered.

He reached out and touched her knee; she jerked it quickly away, and he cleared his throat. "I will when we find him. I will redouble our efforts, I promise!"

Inside, Tana erupted in a torrent of anguished emotion and unspoken words. She wanted to scream, to leap forward and take him by the neck and say, *"Not Seth, you fool! Not my twin, you idiot! Do you think I believe him the enemy of the throne as you do? Do you think that time has sucked me into your fantasy of Kaerglen, and that I have so forgotten the past that I believe in the one you've invented inside your head, instead of the one I know to be true? Do you not realize that Seth is the one person in all this world that I am sure I love? That Seth is the only one who has never betrayed me, that he is more a part of me than you or any other man will ever be?*

"No, Finaan, you are slave to idiocy. You are blind and ignorant. Were you to kill Seth, I think might finally have the strength myself to kill you!"

These words nearly gushed forth, nearly signed her own death. If she'd said them, she would have lost her last defense. As it was, only the whites of her knuckles as she clutched the arms of her chair betrayed her true thoughts. At last, when she spoke, her voice was vacant of this fury, though the words it spoke made it cold and flat, shocking even herself with their dispassionate ultimatum. "Not Seth, Finaan," she said. "Kill Patrick."

The weight of her treason hung heavy in the air, dispelled only when Finaan rose and laughed, softly at first, then loudly, as if bristling with sudden, revealed irony. "You would be queen!" he declared softly when he finally paused, then he laughed again. When his mirth subsided, he looked down at her and spoke softly again, his voice level and starkly sincere in the wake of his raucous laughter. "If I could believe that would make you love me, my princess, it would be done."

With that he left her, the echoes of his laughter still sounding in her ears. She gazed up at the moon, forcing back tears, cursing the weakness that had broken her resolve and allowed her to ask anything at all. And after all was said, Finaan still hadn't understood her request; he'd translated it into a lust for power on her behalf. Tana had no desire at all for the monarchy. She wished, merely, to be free of her ghosts, and she cursed herself again for uttering treason in the presence of Finaan, for she knew—inasmuch as he was the darkest of all who haunted her—that she could never survive the sort of alliance she might have intimated.

If he carried it through, she would have to kill him, or kill herself. She doubted she had the strength for either act.

She closed her eyes to the moon and went back again in time.

She was ten.

The grotto was the most magnificent place in all the worlds; even her wind-dreams had shown her nothing to equal its wonder. And this wonder began with its light, a light that had once illuminated the halls of the castle itself, a light which had spread from here in the happy days when Manannan sat on his throne high above and ruled over the waves and all creatures beneath them, when the mists around the island set it fully in Alfheim, and when the Tuatha de Danaan would gather here on Kaerglen for their feasts and songs and games and romances. And Fand had built the grotto for lovers.

It had kept its glory, untouched by the violence of the island's history. When she and Seth had discovered it . . . one entered from the spiral staircase that wound down from the castle. The stairs themselves had their own light, and along the way were niches and tunnels that led off to other chambers, mostly empty but some containing ornate chests—some empty, some still locked—and a quick eye might discover the dull flash of gemstones here and there buried under the dust, hinting at the treasures these chambers might once have contained. But the grotto—its treasures had remained intact. At the entrance, tinkling water sounded its greeting from the right where a cold, fresh-water stream issued from a flat gash in the wall. In this first chamber was statuary, birds and beasts carved of shining rock or shaped in crystal. Three quartz salmon leaped from the stream while a hungry fox watched, its amethyst eyes positioned so that no matter where one stood, they held the reflection of one or more of the fish. At the end of this chamber, a tree of brown stone leafed with green shells spread over the far wall, and beneath it a pearly white dryad posed, forever drawing one's attention to the next chamber, a shell-filled wonderland of dazzling reflective beauty. Beyond this was a mossy place (not unlike the *felnina*s of Alfheim) where the stream gathered into a round pool and strange white flowers dotted the green carpet in patches and clumps. Further on was the passage-way that led down to the shore.

The moss chamber was where Tana mostly had her wind-dreams. The grotto's peace was most meditative there, and even when the air outside was still, a gentle, sea-laden breeze always came up through the passageway. To there, she and Seth would escape—until the day when the living nightmares came.

How they made it up the passageway fully armed with-out alerting the twins was their secret. But they made it, bursting in with drawn swords, laughing, a hellish cruelty in their eyes. Finaan grabbed Seth by the arm, carried him through the chamber of shells, and tied him to the dryad. Seth's screams, coming a moment later, chilled Tana's blood and echoed and echoed until she slowly grew aware that some of the screams were her own.

Patrick was on top of her—her own brother. The cold-ness of his mail shirt pressed into her flesh. Her shift lay across from her, half fallen into the pool where Patrick had tossed it after tearing it off her in one violent sweep of his arm. She was only ten; her breasts scarcely larger than Seth's, the hair between her legs more tender than the first shoots of spring. But Patrick took her anyway, filling her with pain beyond her imagination, and all the while he whispered and panted in her ear: *"This is an evil place, sister, a pagan place, but I will save you from it. Even now I am saving you. . . . Feel the power of God inside me. Feel . . . the power . . ."*

When he was done, Finaan—this demon in a prince's disguise!—came and did the same. Through the raging fury inside her head, she could hear Seth's sobbing from where he remained tied to the dryad. And Finaan's pounding against her was worse than Patrick's, for he had already sated himself on Seth and now had to heave and strain to have his full pleasure on her. Through her screams, she heard his voice, but unlike Patrick, he didn't even talk to her. He talked to Patrick who looked on, a broad, cruel grin spread across his face. As he heaved on top of Tana, Finaan looked at Patrick and said, "I do feel it here, Patrick.That evil you mentioned—it must be cleansed." And he went on talking and pounding against her. He never finished though, because, suddenly, another was on top of him and there was a flash of metal and Tana felt a gush of blood splatter against her cheek. Finaan quickly rolled away from her and gained his feet, one hand clutching the opposite shoulder where blood poured freely through his fingers. Seth had only just missed the veins of his neck.

Yet filled with pain, Tana turned to see her twin crouched beyond them, near the tunnel, his eyes alight with a fire she'd never before seen there. In his hand, he held a knife with a blade no longer than three inches. He'd carried it strapped to his forearm (as old Rath had once told him a knife should be worn), and he'd used it to free himself after Finaan had abandoned him and left him alone.

Now, Finaan howled in fury. "I'll gut you, you little imp!" he howled, letting go of his wound and taking up his sword. At that, Seth looked desperately to Tana, then he fled, down through the passageway, to the shore. Still howling, Finaan ran after him.

Tana tried to move, but found she could barely stand. When she did gain her feet, Patrick slapped her down, so she lay back on the moss and watched him, dark brooding on his face, as he waited for Finaan's return.

When their cousin came back, he had not caught Seth. He did, however, set to the grotto with his sword, prying out all the shells inlaid in its walls, gouging out huge chunks of moss and tossing them in the pool, hacking and screaming at the statuary until he'd shattered most of it before his sword finally broke. That was how Tana always remembered Finaan—full of animal fury, his eyes malicious pits, his muscles churning and his sword flashing and chips of stone and shell careening off surfaces that sparked and pleaded for mercy. And the louder their agonies, the more violent the punisher, his body wild, one arm painted crimson by his own pumping blood.

When Finaan finally rested, he and Patrick left, abandoning her to find her own way home.

The pain went on forever, though she healed—physically—within three months. But even with her body as evidence, Moira—the queen and her mother—refused to believe her tale. At least she wouldn't admit it; she wouldn't listen long to Tana's weeping. Ever since Tana and Seth had refused Priest Brenden's tutelage to the point of the man's exasperation, they'd grown wild in their mother's eyes. Though they'd lived their days as they'd wished, the queen had completely abandoned them to their whims and focused all her maternal devotion on Patrick alone. *Christ's champion* . . . When Tana spoke, Moira heard not the truth, but Satan, and she told Tana so.

King Coryn, Tana thought, believed her. But he would do nothing. He told her, in fact, that Patrick was prince and would be king, and if his God wished him to possess his sister, then as prince and future king, he had that right. The assertion brought tears to Tana's eyes, and she tried to flee her father, but Coryn grabbed her and held her close, speaking softly to her until she grew still. It was then that he told her of the fading of Brigid and Lugh and the rest of the Tuatha de Danaan; it was then that he tried to explain everything to her, even though she could hardly grasp it all. Coryn had foreseen the fading of his gods and the sure futility of resisting it. He had been defeated, and even the violation of his own laughter could not bring him to fury, so certain was his own defeat.

Tana couldn't understand it. She tried to tell him of her wind-dreams, but he wouldn't listen.

As for Seth, he had disappeared, and it seemed to Tana that she alone mourned his absence.

*   *   *

In the garden, the sky had grown dark but for the moon, and the night's chorus of insects enveloped her, drawing her back briefly to the present. She listened to the sounds; once she had felt only wonder here, the insects the very minstrels of life. Once she would have spent hours separating their songs, naming them all. Now they seemed alien, an obtrusive cacophony with no power left to awe or inspire. They went on, slaves in this castle to the powers that ruled it, caring nothing for the deaths of those who writhed and faded before the power of the One God's cross.

She had the sorcery—*she, Tana Kaerglen*—had the power of the ancients in her blood, as had Megan before her. So said Brigid, and so she knew it to be true. But all her sorceries failed before the cross. . . .

She returned to the grotto a week after her violation. She found it *cleansed*, all the shells and sculptures broken out and removed. Only the tree remained, leafless and barren. And the moss, it persisted; though fires had blackened it in places, Patrick and Finaan had eventually decided it would grow back anyway. Then—finally and too late—Brigid had spoken to her.

The voice came on the wind. *"Do not despair, my child, for your power remains, if mine does not. I would have saved you if I could."*

Tana fell to her knees and wept.

"Sleep and dream," said the goddess. And after a while, Tana did sleep.

In her dreams, she saw Brigid in all her sad glory: a tall, pale woman with brown hair full of leaves and twigs. *"This is my world you dream, princess, and it is far from your own. I would now that we had spoken in brighter times, but I thought the wind-dreams would teach you all you needed to know. They teach power that comes from the heart, but your heart is now shattered, so you must learn normal spells. Would you have me teach you in your dreams?"*

Tana nodded, and so it went. From time to time, whenever she was sure of Patrick's and Finaan's absence, she would overcome her terror of a repetition of the past, and descend to the grotto, there to sleep and dream and learn spells, all of which worked, but none of which could harm her hated enemies, so surrounded did they remain by their faith and their talismans.

And even in these sorcerous dreams, the fading of the old powers haunted every moment. Brigid's voice came to her from far away, and of it, Tana could never ask questions; she could only listen and learn. When she asked, she would waken unexpectedly, as if a simple question strained the limits of the sorcery. She wanted to cry out to Brigid, to ask her how to overcome her brother and cousin, to ask what *would* work and where was Seth, but none of these answers could be hers.

In Tana's thirteenth spring, Brigid taught her the sorceries of the gate, and Tana set herself on a quest, imagining she had real hope for the very first time. Years before, there had come to the castle a wild swordsmistress named Thyri who had slain the druid Pye. From Thyri, Tana had learned that Megan yet remained on the island, and Tana imagined now that only Megan might aid her in breaking Patrick's hold on the throne. She began casting her sorceries, growing excited as if her heart soared again freely among the clouds of all worlds. Through her spells, she found Megan's home and gated there, only to find it disused and abanonded, a lonely hut in a field of mud, battered by the cold northern winds.

In the hut, she found a single clue to the events of the past. A small white tablet sat at an angle on a shelf, and it read, simply, *I, Megan Kaerglen, do forsake this island of sorrow, to seek my heart, and follow the moon.*

And that was why Tana, at fifteen, sat in the garden at the castle's heart and gazed in yearning at the full moon, while Finaan of Connaught—who had spoiled her life and that of her brother—came to court her heart.

Within the castle, Coryn—long since truly king—lay dying in his chamber. Patrick, his adopted heir, awaited the coming of death in anticipation of his own coronation and his destiny to be king of Kaerglen Isle.

Changes

That night was the third of the three nights of the full moon. Thyri spent it in a forest, far from the city of the Franks. In the wood, the changes came painlessly, and she almost enjoyed her days for the solitude they granted her.

The past weeks had not been kind. She felt wounded inside, and in a sense beyond healing. She had killed her brother, and knew that she hadn't the strength to face the memory. In the solitude of the wood, with the day paced by her own heart and labors rather than the bustle of the city, she was forced to face herself and tend to this wound. At least the wood gave her the peace to handle the task.

Erik was dead; she'd killed him—she knew that much. On Megan's word, she'd had no choice. She couldn't hate herself for it; maybe what bled inside her was that lack of choice. Why couldn't there have been another way? Why had the Norns twisted her life so that she had no choice in the direction of the thread? For instance, all might have been avoided had she not followed Megan into Alfheim, and yet the decision had been hers—she'd felt she'd needed an escape from it all, from the city, from the sweat and the smell, just as she'd come here alone, to get away where the beast within her could run free in the night and feed and not fight her for its right to human flesh. If she hadn't followed Megan, then she wouldn't have killed Erik. But she'd followed blindly, and what was done was done. What law of the gods made it thus? What law allowed her pains, and her curse, and what law forbade her breaking the first?

It all seemed meaningless and cruel. She almost felt as if she'd lost all she'd learned from Scacath, all that had made her a warrior. In her mind, the will to fight had grown arbitrary, as if she could no longer choose her battles as all warriors should. She knew this, and yet she was propelled blindly nevertheless—to battle Erik, to battle the emperor of the Franks. What had spoiled that last battle? Megan's tears in the night. Defeat lurking like a viper in the heart of victory. No matter what happened, she couldn't seem to hold it together anymore, even with Megan. The love they shared was losing its power to comfort and heal. No longer was it good enough to seek out each other and forget the rest of the world, because the world kept intruding on a whim, haunting them, stealing their passion.

She had no desire to return to the city and try to go on with things as they were. At night in the forest she hunted and killed and feasted, at one with the beast. There was a harmony to it, a basic purpose in that cycle of hunger and death. It needed no explanation, no decisions, no consideration of any fact, whether it be the lives of the Norse, the battles of the gods, *fimbulwinter* on Asgard, the fading of the old ways. . . . The cycle stood apart from all this, somehow above it; it simply was.

The cycle went on because it had to go on: hunger required food, and food sated hunger. In the past, Thyri might have reasoned that peace required warfare, and victory in warfare brought peace. But much time had passed since she'd had to fight to guarantee her next day. And now, when the peace after victory did not guarantee her happiness—if it spawned only new vipers meant to torment her—then where was the meaning of her victory?

Over those days, Thyri decided she would find another battle, one in which she could believe. Instinct drove her ever farther from the city, and ever nearer to the land on the riverbanks that she and Megan had secured for the Norsemen of seven hundred ships who would have died but for her intervention.

When she arrived among them, the whispered rumors began and she wished them quick speed with a twisted inner smile. Before the morning passed, she paid a man with a horse to take word to Megan, so that her lover might join her.

As for her welcome among her people, her name was well-known and it did not sit well with many. Though a powerful ally, she was berserk, and cursed. All wondered why she had come to them, and all suspected the worst. Fantastic things had happened; they'd been given land when they'd expected death, and they'd been hailed by a bird that had spoken, greeting them in the name of a berserk legend. Now, so soon after that, she was among them, and they could imagine nothing of her purpose but that she might demand payment for the honor.

Eiriksdattir greets her fellow travelers.

For the most part, they were tired men, weary of battle. They had in truth come south seeking land. Now that they had it, most had little desire for the sagas to continue. What legends they desired, they would keep for nights when, armed only with ale, they could tell them in safety and comfort in front of warm, crackling fires.

Magic

Ai'reth stopped short of the portal where the messenger went in. The wards laced the building in a mystical wall—the work of the low-born Tuathan? He would not assume such a thing, not in these dark days, not with him hiding a cat's breath from Midgard and unsure whether Loki remained chained.

But surely this would be her home; the wards shone white, and had he not followed the man ever since he'd left the white-haired one? The messenger had not strayed, had come straight here, and he wasn't a dark man, just a normal, pathetically weak one. The longer Ai'reth paused, the more sure he became that this was the home of the dark-haired power, Megan, his friend. If he wished to see, he would have to enter and trigger the wards. But what harm in that? It would only tell her of his coming.

Unseen by human eyes—but a cat's breath still from Midgard—Ai'reth plunged through the wall and the wards. Their magic twisted him fully into the world, and he would have laughed at the sorcerous subtlety had he not found himself plunged unexpectedly into a room of men. *She knows her tricks*, he thought wryly as he scampered silently across the floor, taking cover in a pile of cloth before daring to look around, to learn whether he'd been seen.

The place was a treasure trove of human wealth. Why would the powers be here? Were there not battles to be fought?

The messenger spoke with a man behind the counter. Another man—a large one, much stronger and brighter than most—came up as they spoke. The large man took the message and turned, starting up a stairwell. Ai'reth took a breath and ran low along the floor, around the counter, and up the stairs behind the man.

Chaos had drawn him to Midgard, Chaos and his own thoughts, his memories of the night his wife had died, his memories of power where power did not belong, in these two women who had brought death to his wife by their presence—but that wasn't their fault. S'kiri had gambled for the Queenstone. She had died brave but foolish. And during war, all blame fell on the darkness.

With S'kiri's death—after that night when he had followed Megan nearly to Midgard—he had wandered, the Queenstone his burden and his sole reminder of love. He had watched battles, and seen gods die. He had seen giants like mountains fall on Aesir, Tuathans, Vanir, Elohim, and all the forces of light. The end came—grew closer moment by moment—and all the while, Klorista's words tumbled again and again though his mind: *What if Surt burns all the nine worlds save Midgard? We will destroy ourselves and nothing more. . . . They are low-borns, one of Light, one of Chaos. . . .* What would come of it?

And then he'd realized what mattered. It was Chaos—the wildfire—the drums that changed heartbeats and the directions of the winds. So he'd wandered closer to Midgard, and at dusk, with the moon newly full, Chaos had burst like an eruption into the night. Through his talent, it had reached for him, and he'd followed and found her, the white wolf bitch of the elder legends, chaotic power in harmony, the power that the dark Erik had tried to steal, the power that had overcome. Yes, the elder legends—to them he turned. Common skalds declared a wolf-age before *fimbulwinter:* "*An axe-age and sword-age starts the flow of blood, with a wind-age to staunch it, and a wolf-age to howl down the ice.*" What if the common lore was wrong? With Chaos so strong in the wolf-age, it could howl down the end of the ice. Or might it best the fires of Surt, and save the worlds' burning?

He couldn't know, but it had given him hope, and since that hope could be followed, then follow he did.

*   *   *

Megan opened the door before Rollo could knock. He eyed her oddly; something had her on edge, he was sure of it. She took the letter from him without a word, only smiling distractedly when he said it had come from Thyri.

In the doorway, she unfolded the paper and read it, frowning at first, then smiling again. "I will be leaving today," she told him.

"And Thyri?" he asked unsurely.

"She is with the invaders."

"Will she be coming back?"

"I don't think so, Rollo."

He grinned broadly and patted his sword. "Then it is good news!" he said, turning away. "We will follow tonight."

She smiled as he left, then shut her door and let the letter fall to the floor. Some sorcerous presence had accompanied the message from Thyri; her ears burned with awareness of this. She closed her eyes and summoned the power of her ring, seeking out the intruder. She found him under her bed.

Ai'reth revealed himself just as she prepared an attack. He stood before her, trembling and smiling, his sharp teeth white in the curtained darkness of her room.

She relaxed and asked him how he fared. He answered her with hurried riddles and tales of the wars. Lugh had died, and it was said that Jormungard had swallowed Manannan whole. The legions of Jotunheim rampaged, awaiting Loki to lead them to Vigrid. It was all only a matter of time.

As to why Ai'reth had come to her, he couldn't say. Chaos had drawn him, and only in it did he see hope. He was glad now that he'd found her; he'd been afraid to show himself to Thyri, not knowing how she would think of him after her battle with her brother in his home. As he spoke, he pleaded with her, for her aid, for Thyri's aid—for them to join in the fight.

"How?" the sorceress asked. Her eyes were like small, dark fires, burning into him, almost hurting him. "We are not gods! My powers pale before those of Scacath and Odin, never mind Loki and the dark kings of Svartalfheim." Her light grew stronger, even as he heard her say these things. "You have been dreaming, felnin," she continued.

"In desperation, you look for miracles, and, finding flimsy wishes and groundless hopes, you take the fate of Ragnarok upon your shoulders and try to bend it to your will! Don't you think that if Odin wanted us, he would invite us himself? No—the battle is his and he must manage it. Look to him, not us. We are of Midgard—among my mother's people I am nothing, a trifling invalid!"

"You are wrong," he insisted, flinching before the strength of her light. "You do not know yourself."

"You are wrong, Ai'reth," she countered. "I am just like you—a gnat that might bite a giant's toe or two before dying in vain. And do not go to Thyri with your wild stories—you should not show yourself to her at all. She does not have memory of you."

He lowered his eyes to the floor. At his feet, the hilt of the rune-blade borne by the dark Erik jutted out from under the bed. He picked it up and unsheathed it, his eyes running slowly over its length, the iron once stained by S'kiri's blood.

"In this world," Megan continued, "you are in grave danger if you are seen by anyone. If you are caught, they will kill you."

"Ai'reth knows that," he said, looking up from the sword. "But he must do *something!* Light succumbs! All is at stake!"

"Yes," Megan said sadly. "I agree you must follow your heart, however foolish it might be. If you are drawn to Thyri, then stay near her, but that is all. Watch over her. Protect her. If all is as dire as you say, then I fear in any case that we shall not avoid the battle."

"Avoid it! You *cannot* avoid it! She is the hope, the wind-breaker, the wildfire and the Chaos!"

Megan eyed him darkly. "How can you insist on knowing such things?"

He didn't answer; how could he explain to her his thoughts and Klorista's riddles? If she was a power, and couldn't see his mind, then his words would have no power to show her if they hadn't done so already. He *knew*—now more than ever—and that was that.

Megan sighed. "I wish I could believe you." She went to the window and opened the curtain, absently looking out. "Do what you will," she said.

When she turned back to look at him, he was gone, and with him went the sword Scacath had given to Thyri, the blade Thyri had left behind with Erik after taking Astrid's sword as her own.

Ai'reth passed out of Midgard, hurrying along the pathways to a half-world where he could sit quietly and think. He was troubled; he had expected Megan to summon Thyri and for them all to depart Midgard together, to build new armies to stand against the darkness. He had come away with but a weapon, and one he had stolen at that.

In a half-world of trees and waterfalls, he tested the blade. He could never wield it effectively; it was far too long. He sheathed it and brooded. If the armies were not to be, the hope yet remained. Perhaps Megan was right about now, while he was right about the future. Time alone would tell; Light—though wounded—had not perished yet.

So he would look over Thyri, he decided. He would stand as her guard until such time as she came to the aid of Light. He would not reveal himself to her unless he had to, and if the time truly came when all would perish without her aid, he might even be able to trick her into the fray. At any rate, he could not abandon his hope, not when it had grown so strong and not when he saw no hope elsewhere, no matter how desperately he looked.

Slowly, his dark mood lifted. If this was now his path, he had to be prepared. Beneath the waterfall, Ai'reth took up his finger drum and began tapping, conjuring up hazy and uncertain images of possible futures, seeking clues and omens of where it all might lead, and where he might need to be.

Reavers

". . . And so we fled south, meeting army after army, even here," Olaf Ulfson concluded, smiling at Thyri.

She eyed him thoughtfully, then looked beyond him, out of the canvas shelter and out to the fields where Vikings toiled, raising wooden houses from the Frankish soil.

"So Harald is truly strong now?" Thyri reflected aloud.

"Aye, swordsmistress. He rules all of Norway, even the coldest Jarldoms. And those Norse he does not rule, he slays."

Thyri didn't respond. Her thoughts turned back to her days with Astrid and in particular, to a letter Astrid had once written her:

. . . I have fought the Danes at sea as well, though it makes no sense that they would come north into our waters while there is such plunder to be had in the south. . . . It would seem that we Norse have not a direction, but only a lust for battle. I have seen men reach berserk fury and die with laughter on their lips, welcoming the call of Valhalla. Thus it is, though I think, perhaps out of ignorance and inexperience, that it need not be thus. We are of strong blood; you cannot imagine it but must see it in the faces of our foes to the south. And we are many too. I have seen the sea covered with our sails, while each ship is bound for a place different from the next. Were all to sail together, we could crush the legions of Surt! But this, for reasons beyond me, we do not do. Instead, we fight each other as well as the rest of the world.

Perhaps Harald of Vestfold is a leader who might

unite the Vikings. But he is yet young, and his unity may come too late. The strength we have is now, and misuse now may make it impotent twenty years hence. At any rate, I should soon find myself on the battlefield with him, my sword against his, and not by his side. In the end, it doesn't matter. The ways of the warrior, all the ways of the warrior, lead to Valhalla—to serve Odin until Ragnarok.

Time had passed, a decade for Thyri, even more including the years we lost while on the seas of Jotunheim. It was now the year 886 by the calendar of the One God. Viking strength had waxed and waned, and all that time, Norse had killed Norse while Harald of Vestfold had sought to rule all. They might have ruled all the southern lands, all the old empires, had Astrid's wish for unity come to pass. Now it was too late. The south knew them, feared them yet, but ever more often turned them away. The Norse remained as they had been, leaderless, without direction or vision while Harald hacked at their roots. He was a leader. He could have compromised, united, and conquered the south. Instead, he still conquered the north. Thyri blamed it all on a princess of Hordaland, her own kingdom. Gyda, she was. Years past, Harald had asked her to wed. She'd laughed and called him a petty kingling. He'd then set out to prove her wrong.

Hordaland had fallen to Harald. He'd made great enemies throughout the north. He'd won Gyda, but he battled still.

Thyri brooded, the ghost of Astrid—the Valkyrie—shadowing her every thought, making her ache anew for the past, for the days before her curse. Since she'd been a child, she'd borne a hatred for Gyda. Since she'd been a child, she'd known of Astrid's dream of the Norselands united. Since she'd been a child . . .

Astrid stood tall in her thoughts, laughing, her eyes full of joy as she spoke to Thyri of Scacath and the wonders of her teaching. Astrid, her cousin, her first love. Her purest love, before the curse, before Megan, Akan, Pohati. Her dream had not come to pass. The *fimbulwinter* had come to Asgard. All threatened to end. Astrid deserved her dream fulfilled. And Gyda, in Thyri's mind, deserved death.

Slowly, Thyri rose from her seat; Olaf watched her strangely, his hand falling nervously to the hilt of his sword. He didn't understand the distance in her gaze. She had drifted away from him, and while her thoughts had carried her back in time, so had his. He had recalled all the legends and whispered warnings of she they called Eiriksdattir, Bloodfang. He began to sweat, fearing she might attack him. Instead, she looked down at him, her gaze suddenly present and stern. "Erect a tent, and summon all warriors. Tomorrow night, I will address them."

"But swordsmistress," Olaf protested, "they toil on their houses!"

"Houses for which I toiled to allow them," she added flatly.

"Eiriksdattir," he said carefully, "may do not believe that. We have heard tales of miracles—the entire land is alive with them—and the tales say the One God gave us this land."

"Odin's beard!" she seethed, turning on him. "Whether they believe or not, you take them my word! I desire a gathering place, a shelter for those who wish to attend. They may come or stay away, but have it built! I only wish to speak to them; I will command nothing!" With that, she turned and left.

Hope

Tana bent low to Coryn's ear and whispered. "I am of your blood, father, and I despair. Tell me we may win! Tell me that all is not lost, even if it is a lie!" She backed away from him and looked into his eyes: dull, yellow, vacant mirrors. He coughed. "Do not fight her, Megan," was all he said, then his eyes closed, this shortly followed by a pained, croaking snore.

She stood to leave, looking down at his whithered body. She had begged him, and he hadn't even known who she was. Whatever pathways he traveled in his mind, she couldn't find him. Thinking this, she fought back her tears. In a way, they were so alike, he haunted by his visions of his gods' passing, and she a victim of the same haunting. In days past, he would have loved her, cherished her every word, for in a twisted sort of way he'd been a noble king. He'd sacrificed his power to his judgment and his compassion for his people. Over the years, she'd come to understand him better, perhaps because her plight so resembled his: He'd abandoned the battle after foreseeing his inevitable defeat; in essence, that was an act of noble virtue, for why should he cause blood to flow and wars to be fought if it was true that the One God's followers would win in the end? What right had he to oppose it? Hadn't he married Moira and brought her and Patrick here specifically to hasten the end, to shorten the battle just where the old powers rooted in Kaerglen might have prolonged it for centuries? And wasn't Tana the product of this union of faith and power? She and Seth both—born of Coryn, King of Pagans, and Moira, Queen of Christ.

She looked at the old man and loved him and hated him

in the same moment. Perhaps he was right and noble, but in another way he'd betrayed them all, betrayed them simply by being a man, by allowing seduction by his wife, by fathering children at all. By rights, Seth should gain the crown upon his death. Patrick wasn't even of his blood! Yet since Seth had disappeared, Coryn had scarcely uttered his name.

Coryn was already dead, Tana realized. He'd been dead before they'd suffered their first breaths in this world. He'd been dead from the moment he'd given up, and he'd been dead even when Thyri had slain Pye to save his life. Moira had ruled Kaerglen since she'd come there, so Coryn's death would mean . . . absolutely nothing, a senseless formality that would legitimize his entire philosophy, a philosophy he'd ensured by his own inaction, his own death nearly two score years before.

Such thoughts left Tana morose as she left her father's bedchamber. When he died, all hope would fall finally on her shoulders. And Seth's—if he were truly still alive.

Patrick would have her wholly in his power then, or he would kill her. She would be a fool to think differently.

Her thoughts propelled her from the castle, there to stand on the hill that looked down over Port Kaerglen. The sea breeze brushed against her skin, and the pale autumn sun only darkened her mood. She stood—forgetting time—until the sun grew red and the breeze cold, then suddenly it filled her with a chill and then a tingling and a rush through her mind like fire and ice, wind and rain, and she was torn away and . . .

Flying!

As easily as before, with no effort, no exhaustive hours of preparation, no strain on her heart like the talons of death! She flew . . . over the castle; from above it looked so small, a dark mountaintop with its deep green heart, the garden of the insects and Finaan and her brooding and weakness. . . . She was free! The wind blew and the world shifted; a lush, deep forest spread below her, a leafy quilt over the hills split only by a mighty river that roared down from distant mountains, over falls and cascades, wending like a snake, dipping and meandering below her.

The winds blew her down, among swallows and hawks.

Aerial harmony—the hawks picked fish from the river while the swallows sang and bats chittered beneath the waves of leaves. She soared over the water, racing for the peaks, up the waterfalls and on. And then she saw the fires and the smoke looming on the horizon. Huge tracts of gutted forest cropped up in the green sea like great wounds, their trees charred and scattered like twigs over blackened earth. And as the wind blew her, the leafy sea itself turned black as life gave way to death and she grew ever more near the fires that licked the edge of the black sea like great, monstrous tongues. And even farther away, she could see giant figures among the flames, figures to whom the trees were like grass and the river but a trickling stream—this was not their world!

Closer still, she saw the elven armies, crackling with sorcery, fashioning great spears of white magic to hurl into the fray. Here and there, acres of reeds lay crushed under fallen Jotun. The battle raged on; legions of arrows swarmed with deadly accuracy at the faces—the eyes—of the invaders. Clouds of smoke billowed in waves across the battlefield. The winds blew Tana down, and the roar of fires grew deafening. She tried to open her eyes, to return to Kaerglen, but the effort failed. The winds blew her down into the Tuathan host, to its heart where Lugh bellowed desperate commands out to tall, beautiful gods colored black with ash and grime and red with blood.

For a moment, Tana hung motionless, her eyes filling with the carnage. In every direction, she saw Tuathan dead, fallen gods. The wind, like animate breath, nudged her and set her spinning, pirhouetting through the ranks of her gods; everywhere was blood, desperation, and death. Slowly, twirling, she became the wind. The ranks parted, and she spun over Brigid; the goddess lay on the ashy grass, white and yellow petals spread around her in the rough shape of a leaf. Her dress was turned gray by the smoke, her pale face blackened and wan. Tana dropped down to her bosom, and Brigid smiled sadly. *"All ends now, little one,"* she said. *"I can teach you no more."*

As the wind, Tana couldn't speak; she whistled mournfully through the petals, lifting them in small whirlwinds to dance around the goddess.

"You must hurry," Brigid whispered into the wind.

"Go to your grotto, and close your eyes in the room of the dryad. In your mind, you can make it whole again. Spin three times and step into the water.

"You will find Fand's haven, and talismans there you can use. Wishing stones full of blue power whose limits are but those of your dreams. Use them well, but hurry! The last battles have begun, and this is the last gift I might give you."

Tana lingered over the goddess, weeping a light mist. She brushed over Brigid's cheek, kissing her, then rose high above the army, and opened her eyes.

Now it was night, so still that her dress hung motionless above the grass. From the chimneys of the port below, smoke rose in pillars that solidified in the moonlight, like long white arms reaching up for the stars.

Tana stood, looking out as if through new eyes, as if the tears on her cheeks had been cried by another, younger self. All she had just seen. . . . Within, she felt a warm power—a tranquil strength—blossoming around her heart. Her wind-dream had reshaped Patrick and Finaan—so small they seemed now compared to the enemies her gods faced. What if they did spoil her sorceries? What if they had stained her island with the blessing of a god she did not know? The power yet lived, and if it failed, that did not make it weaker. If a spell shriveled and collapsed, it could not lose its *meaning*. Not if she persevered; not if she kept it alive in her heart.

As Tana turned away, she was watched. Far below, against the dark line of the port wall, a solitary figure hid in the shadows, gazing up.

He was young and strong, his muscles shaped by sail and rigging, by fish-laden nets and battles with the wind and waves of the sea. For years, he had fished and forgotten, seeking solitude on the water where the past could become a dream, or a wasteland like the endless blue expanse spreading out in all directions beneath him. On the sea, only what the fisherman brought up in his nets and kept mattered; the fish thrown back was nothing. On the sea of the past, it could be made much the same, the painful memories discarded, pushed back under the surface into the depths of nothingness. And so he'd lived his days discarding the past, naming himself Sean, an orphan. He'd fled to the doorstep of an old fisherman and been taken in, going out daily on the waters where he could forget.

Two years back, the old man had died, and he'd inherited the boat. The old man's wife, Maire, cared for him like a son, so after the old man's death, nothing much had changed—he brought in the catch to Maire, and she cleaned it and took it the next morning to market. Together, they survived.

But now his father was dying and he could no longer escape the memories. Rumors that the king might perish even before dawn had spread through city and port earlier in the day, and those rumors had greeted him on his return from the sea. At his side now, he wore an old rusted sword he'd won from the son of a blacksmith in a wrestling match. He'd taken the day's catch to Maire and left quietly, moving through the shadows, inching up the port wall, and stopping only when he'd spied his sister standing out on the hill. That sight had brought the memories flooding back, the good memories of their youth. She had grown, as had he, but in seeing her he realized how much love remained inside of him. He'd wanted to rush out from the wall and embrace her, to lift her into the air as she had done for him so often with her magic in the grotto.

He'd wanted to run to her, but he couldn't. He'd abandoned her and left her to face the aftermath of that fateful day in the grotto alone. For a few days, he'd gone back, hoping she might come so he could take her away with him. But one day he'd found Finaan's guard there, and he'd fled for the last time, alone. He'd become a fisherman, and fought his battles with the past on the sea; while from the port, he'd watched his homeland invaded as his mother brought architects, builders, and armies from Erin to raise churches and chapels all over the island. These men had come, the old, simple folk of Kaerglen powerless to stop them. The city and port had become very dangerous places, though ironically, the fisherman's village on the port's southside was his haven. He seldom dared to leave it. Over the years, he'd suspected the old man had known his true birthright, but he'd never been betrayed. When the guard had first scoured the port, the old man had told them he was his grandson. Seth had cropped his hair before they'd arrived, and the guard hadn't looked at him twice.

Since then, Finaan's search for him had not abated, but it had focused mainly—in vain—on the forests in the north to where more than a few followers of the old ways had fled. Bandits were there now, Seth knew. Bandits making travel unsafe on an island where all had been peaceful in the year of his birth.

So much had changed. He watched Tana disappear up the hill, and he began to grow afraid. What could he do now? He'd had no sword-training, while Patrick and Finaan were veterans with their weapons. All on the island knew of their mock duels and of a good number of foolish souls who had dared to challenge either or both of them.

What could he do? Tana had halted his progress up the hill, and now he was frozen in place, unable to take another step. His senses began to heighten, both within and without as fear took over him. Nightbirds cooed above him from their niches in the wall. Insects chittered all around, and he heard a roar in his head like the pounding of waves, like the sea of forgetfulness calling him back to its safe, constant bosom. Just then, he heard a dull thud behind him, and he whirled, drawing his blade.

At first, Seth saw nothing, but then his eyes caught on a band of darkness in the moonlit grass, just out of the wall's shadow. He approached it cautiously, until he saw that it was a sheathed sword. "Who is here?" he whispered out into the night.

From the shadows, a voice answered. "If my magics don't fail," it said, "then you be the true prince of this place."

"What?"

"Is sword for you," said the voice. "Sword to befit a prince. Sword of Light."

Seth peered hard into the shadows all around him, but he saw no one. He had frozen again, scarcely able to move. "Who are you?" he asked.

"Just a felnin," answered the voice. "No more questions. Take sword, but beware. Is blade of power, so carry by scabbard. Go to where you are most strong, and only there unsheath it. It will test you. It might even kill you."

In the windless night, Seth heard the faintest breath of movement. "Wait!" he whispered desperately, but the voice had spoken all it would.

After a time, the young prince inched toward the blade resting in the grass. He gazed at it awhile, then picked it up by its scabbard and pressed it to his breast. Then, glancing up one last time toward the castle, he started back down the hill.

Magic

She could feel the ghosts in the halls, the aeons of intrigue, love, and battle that the castle had known. Dead and dying gods had thrived here. How often had the feet of Brigid herself touched these stones? How often had Manannan's laughter sounded out for all to hear? All present now were just transient visitors, fated to die, but the structure itself would live on.

Tana passed her mother who seemed pale, nonexistent— less real than the dead for whose memory she ached. She held them close to her heart, striving to keep them strong, drawing their strength into herself. For had she not seen them—even them—engaged heroically in a battle they seemed doomed to lose? How petty her own struggles seemed in comparison! She fought men, not giants. Simple, greedy mortals.

She walked in long, resolute strides, straight for the depths of the castle, to descend to the grotto. Her mother faded behind her, like a ghost into memory. Voices came and went; nothing phased her or caused her to pause until Finaan materialized in her path. She tried to brush past him, but he grabbed her and she spun away, backing up against the stony wall. The torch she carried clattered to the floor.

"Where are you going?" he asked abruptly.

She didn't answer. Torchlit from below, Finaaan looked taller, a beast with a chin and deep shadows for eyes. She bent quickly and lifted the torch up between them. A sizzling crackle and sharp stench filled the air as the torch brightened, its fire catching on strands of Finaan's long hair.

He didn't back away. "Please answer me, Tana. I didn't mean to frighten you."

She laughed. He *was* small and petty, though she knew he had killed time and again, remorselessly, like a dog trained for violence. Yet in his eyes—she filled them. They softened with her reflection there. Perhaps she had misread him in the garden. . . . With a word—no caress required—she could make him hers, her obedient servant. For the first time in her life, she felt within herself the power of womanhood. Before Brigid had renewed her, she'd been a child, and as a child she could only have submitted, not controlled. Now, all that had changed. This—this confidence that swelled her breast, that held her head high—made her someone she had never been before. She could take him, control him like a dog, pet him, make his strength a part of her own. These were evil thoughts, she knew. But the knowledge that she *could* was all that mattered. She was changed. She was a woman now, with the power to choose.

At first, Finaan shrank from her laughter, then anger flared in his eyes. "Here, bitch!" he seethed. "Be still, or I'll take you here."

"No, you won't," she said softly. He approached her, reached for her arm, but she skipped to one side. "You won't because you wouldn't enjoy it. I would scream and bite you, and claw your pretty face." She scratched quickly at the air with her free hand, smiling as his eyes locked onto the movement. "You'd have to kill me and then settle for a lesser queen. You'd spend the rest of your life in agony, wondering whether I might ever have loved you willingly, hating your queen because she couldn't be me, feeling the worms of my death crawling around inside your head." These abruptly unleashed words amazed her, so easily did they pass from her lips. A day before—even a few hours before—she could never have said them. Just thinking them in Finaan's presence would have paralyzed her—body and soul. But spoken now, they bolstered their own truth. Rage yet burned in Finaan's eyes, but he kept his distance, his mouth twisting into a feral grin.

"You acknowledge me," he said, a maniacal warmth edging his words. "For the first time, you've admitted that I will win."

She shook her head. "I simply spoke the truth—for the first time. You think that I don't know you, that I would love you if only I gave you a chance. But I do know you, Finaan; do you think I could not? How could I not come to know one who abused me and abused my brother and chased him away? I have watched you when you didn't even know I was there, when my soul ached with a desire to tear my eyes away from you, but my eyes refused to stray. And alone in the night, I have thought of you, much more often than I suspect you've thought of me. I've hated you and feared you, but I refuse any longer to chain my every waking moment to that fear." As she spoke, she felt her body trembling, her recurrent waking nightmares pleading for her to stop, but it was too late now. Had she said too much?

Finaan stared blankly ahead, taking in her words. "I was a boy," he said distantly.

"You were a man," she countered. "I suppose you've all but forgotten it. But I haven't. If Seth is alive, neither has he. I hope he kills you." With that, she turned from him and walked, ever deeper into the castle.

Finaan ran after her, grabbing her arm again and spinning her to face him. "I love you, Tana," he said fiercely. "Why do you think me evil? I worship the most powerful god of all, and he is a just god."

She laughed and clutched at the silver cross hung on the chain around his neck. "Just, you say? Just leave me, Finaan. Go pray for your just god's forgiveness."

"No, Tana. You have spoken your heart to me, and my own will have its say."

"Will it?" she spat at him. *You mean I've drawn first blood*, she thought. *I've drawn first blood, and the warrior within you will not let you abandon the battle. . . .* "Come then," she said, turning again, leading him silently ever deeper, down the stairwell to the grotto where all things for her began and ended.

In the chamber of the dryad, scant traces of magic yet lingered; she could feel it when she could not before. With each passing moment, something was growing within her, a new strength, of womanhood. This strength—a pool of serenity swelled at its heart. She had rediscovered something she had lost long ago. She had come to where she had to be, to where the goddess had directed her. In the same act of strength, she had brought her tormentor to this ancient place that he had long ago defiled. What first? she wondered. She felt Finaan behind her; she turned on him, capriciously testing her power. "Take it off," she said.

"What?"

"The crucifix—take it off. This is no place for it. If you want to know my heart, you must take it off and feel what truly belongs here. And if I don't believe you know my heart, then I'll not listen to any words of yours."

For a moment, she thought he might refuse her, but then, slowly, his hand went to his neck, and he lifted the chain over his head. She smiled and looked away from him. "Do you remember this place?" she asked. "How it looked before you spoiled it with your One God's iron?"

"A little," he said uncertainly.

"Your blade is blessed as well, isn't it?"

"Of course."

"Then you must drop it with the cross." She half closed her eyes, gazing at the remains of the dryad's tree, slowly fitting each lost green leaf into its proper place in her mind. She didn't look back at Finaan; only when she heard his sword clatter to the rock did she turn. She smiled to herself; so easy this had been, after all the years of hopeless conjuring, of secret spell after secret spell, she had finally brought down his defenses in the most unmystical, mundane way she could imagine. And in this place, what she planned would require virtually no effort at all. . . . She whispered a preliminary charm and crossed her fingers in the sign of the Sybil. Her eyes still half closed, the dryad began to take shape in the image in back of her mind. As she turned toward Finaan, she moved her hands, completing the spell. He stood before her, confused, misunderstanding the light way her wrists had brushed over her thighs, thinking the sudden hardening of her nipples betrayed desire, not sorcery. "Come," she said gruffly, and he approached her without thinking.

He came within arm's reach of her, and she disappeared. He looked around; the grotto had transformed, regenerated itself, the old glittering statues staring at him from all directions. And he felt smaller; his head was dizzy, his mind unclear. His sword and cross were gone, disappeared along with Tana.

Footsteps sounded behind him, and someone grabbed him roughly by the shoulders and lifted him into the air. He twisted to see the face of his attacker, and it was a face he knew well, his own face, his eyes leering, his mouth slavering like an animal's. One hand held him up, the other fumbled at his trousers, ripping them from his body. He was thrown violently against the dryad and lashed there with rope, then he screamed out in agony as his attacker entered him lustfully from behind. The pain rushed through him, filling his entire body. He could feel his own blood running down his leg.

When the assault ended, the pain came and went yet in waves. He began to breathe more easily, then suddenly the dryad faded into mist and he was on his back, fully naked with a terrible weight on top of him, a weight bearing the same face—his own face. This time, the pain was even worse, and his attacker wouldn't even look at him. He was looking at somebody else—Patrick, his best friend—and talking detachedly about evil. . . .

Tana stared down at Finaan's jerking, weeping body and frowned. She *knew* what he suffered: every moment of her agony, and every moment of Seth's—double the pain even she had felt, but it was all pain that he'd inflicted. He'd claimed he was a boy. Perhaps she'd misjudged him; perhaps he had felt remorse in recent years. No matter—she'd ensured future remorse with this revenge, but it didn't please her the way she thought it would. The warrior looked so pitiful now, writhing and moaning, screaming out like a child, the child her sorcery had made him. Knowing what he relived made her remember again. . . . Yet this was her victory. Now she could kill him; all she had to do was take up his sword and run it through him. Then he could never warn Patrick, never reveal to her brother how powerful she had become. Patrick might even be seduced by the same trick. He'd never hinted at any remembrance of that day, but she'd lately seen lust in his eyes when he'd thought she wasn't looking at him. She'd won a battle, and now had victory of the war within her grasp.

She took one step for the sword, then realized she couldn't do it. She hadn't the strength to kill him—no, she *had* strength, but such an act would abuse and defile it, as surely as she had been defiled in this place five years before. The maliciousness of her sorcery—the pain she inflicted at the moment—already caused her grief. She wasn't an assassin; her power grew out of life, not death. That was why she'd been so weak all these years. The will to murder did not reside in her heart, and she'd interpreted it as weakness rather than strength. She'd made herself weak, without understanding anything.

The revelation settled uneasily, cleansing her spirit of the refuse of her darker thoughts, but leaving at least one doubt unresolved: If she couldn't kill now, with success assured, how could she possibly manage it later, when much more—perhaps even her own life—might be at stake? She looked away from Finaan and his sword and crucifix, trying to shrug off the doubt, forcing herself to remember Brigid and the words that had summoned her here. The gods were dying. Each wasted moment might spell disaster and deny her forever the talismans of Fand's haven.

She stood at the stream's edge and calmed her heart, continuing again to reconstruct the grotto in her mind. Green leaves affixed themselves to the branches of the tree behind her; the dryad smiled and bent slightly, offering her arm to guide all noble guests onward. A fox perched across from her, smacking its lips, then freezing, its amethyst eyes shining with the reflections of three pink salmon that leaped from the water to hang suspended in the air. Birds settled to the rock on all sides; she could almost hear the flutter of their wings as they settled stonily on their perches. Tana held all this in her mind and began to twirl—once . . . twice . . . thrice. She stepped into the water and fell forward.

Far away—nestled in a chamber high up in the rock above the grotto—he bent into the candlelight, his forehead creased, his eyes straining to follow the miniscule scratchy writing in the black volume he'd retrieved from the library. It was a strange book; as many times as he'd scoured the shelves of his father's library, he'd never seen it before today, the day, certainly, of Coryn's death. The day that would make him king.

So he tried to read, growing more angry each moment. He would decipher a word and move onto the next, but by the time he'd handled the second word, the meaning of the first would be lost. Beneath his right hand lay leaves of blank parchment, the topmost covered in illegible scribble, further evidence of his frustration. He'd sought to defeat the book by recording the meaning of each word as he discovered it. He'd thought it a worthy idea, what Arthur might have done confronted with the same puzzle. But when he looked back at his writing, it too had grown mysteriously meaningless. Something was wrong with the night. The day had brooded uneasily from dawn until dusk, but the night—the night had escaped its shackles of reason. What he did, perched here with this damnable book torturing him, made no sense. It was like a dream or a nightmare, except he was awake. He slammed the book shut, turned from it, and froze. Not two feet away from him, a pillar of fire rose up from the stone floor. He could feel no heat, and though the fire was bright, it illuminated nothing, nor did it cast shadows. The air in the room grew suddenly cold. "You are betrayed," said a voice that came from all directions. "Betrayed on the eve of your ascension."

Patrick looked deep into the fire and swallowed. "You know who I am?" The voice asked, awaiting no reply: "You have called to me after your prayers to Him. You've cried out to both of us without an answer, tears wetting your pillow as you've entered sleep with my name on your lips more often than His.

"What do I offer? Read again and you will see."

Patrick fumbled behind himself for the slender black volume, never letting his eyes stray from the fire. He let it fall open on his lap: Connaught has betrayed you for your sister's heart, *read the opened page.*

"Now—what will you do about it?" asked the fire that offered no light.

Above her, the stream remained, flowing through the air like a living, watery bridge, a crystalline airborne snake. Beneath her, the ground felt soft, like velvet. She touched herself hesitantly; having passed through the water, her clothes and skin felt completely dry. She fought the urge to take off her boots and lie down on the velvety rock from where she might watch the stream moving above and let the softness below envelop her. Fand's haven was a chamber, of stone all around and but half as large as the dryad's chamber above, but the rock was soft and blue, dimly lit by some magic in the air itself and bathed in gentle, moving reflections off the overhead stream. If only she'd known of this place long ago! So often she might have escaped here. This was a place for thinking, and so soft! A place for lovers to turn an afternoon into eternity.

She raised a hand and touched the stream, feeling its wetness. A slight trickle—no more—ran down her arm. She lowered her hand and touched the water to her lips, then peered around, in search of the room's other secrets.

There was a place where the rock rose, as if to form a bed, and beyond this she found three chests, lying open, filled with dresses the beauty of which she might never have imagined. Among the dresses were candles and sticks, and a warm tinderbox—everything fresh and new. Fand's haven knew nothing of dust or time. She dug deeper into the chests, finally deciding to remove the dresses, which she piled reverently in neat stacks on the bed (If only these were happier times and she had a worthy lover!). There were rings and necklaces, hats and scarves, boxes of powders and vials of lotions—what games Fand and Manannan must have played here! She could easily spend hours puzzling over each piece, but she had come here for a reason, and though she'd never seen the stones Brigid had bid her to take, she somehow *knew* she would recognize them when she found them.

This she did. They were stored in a plain leather pouch—a handful of large aqua gems. Poured into her palm, she could feel the tingling of their magic.

She left by reaching up into the stream until she touched rock, then pulling herself back up, through the water. In the chamber of the dryad, she found herself alone, her spell on Finaan having run its course and the foreign prince departed, gone to lick his wounds. She smiled sadly. She wondered what changes his eyes might reveal when next they would meet.

Ghosts

Yes, something was wrong with the night—even in the land of the Franks. The waning moon rose orange, and mists fell on the streets, coming in rolling banks off the river. Such was the atmosphere without as the followers of Thyri Eiriksdattir prepared their final departure. They walked the streets awhile after Megan left, Gerald filled with a deep foreboding sadness, Rollo boisterous and rowdy, his yellow mane and beard freed of Megan's disguises, and Rui, as usual, indifferent. By the time they returned to The Emporium, an abundance of wine surged through Gerald's veins, and it was a wine that added mysterious swirls to the mist and a curious waver to the moonlight. He wobbled through the entrance, and his eyes passed over all they had collected within. Rollo and Rui went upstairs for their packs; Gerald went alone into the room of armaments, for a task he'd put off until the latest of hours.

By torchlight, he gazed long at the rows of swords, weaponry, and mail, much of which he'd personally polished to perfection. With the wine dancing in his head, the armor seemed almost alive in the flickering light, a spectral army ready to leap away from the wall at his command. He knew the feel of each piece, its strengths and weaknesses. He walked along slowly, touching every one, recalling its origin, its memories. In reality, he wanted only a sword, and he chose, at last, a fine, Norse-forged sword, which he scabbarded and tied to his belt. As he waited for the others, his own pack ready under the shop's counter, he drew the sword and tested its weight, thinking grimly of the days that might come. He scarcely sensed their entrance.

"It is time," Rollo said, recalling him from far away.

Gerald looked up at him and motioned at the rows of metal. "Take what you like."

Rollo shook his head and patted his belt. He wore his axe and his own sword, both heavier and finer than the one Gerald now held in his hand.

Slowly, Gerald turned away, leaving the spectral army behind. In the main chamber, Rollo had pulled several feet of material away from one bolt of cloth. The material lay there like an uneven carpet; Gerald approached it, lowering his torch. He staggered slightly as the wine in his belly shifted the floor beneath him, and the cloth became a flowing, elusive wave.

Moving quickly, Rui Taichimi caught him. From the archer's arms, Gerald looked up. "I filled two sacks with gold," he said, smiling wildly. "In the tunnel; don't let me forget them." The archer only grunted, correcting Gerald's balance.

Standing, the Saxon again lowered his torch. Errant threads at the edge of the silk shriveled and writhed away from the fire as if fleeing in agony. Tiny infernos sprang up at their ends and flew like sprites to collide with the rich eastern hues. At the cloth's edge, the sprites grew brighter and rose up, twisting, glancing at their brothers on either side before lowering their heads—as if in agreement—and growing longer, laying down on the cloth to merge into one unified wall of flame, a sprite army which then moved in unison over the silk, whose colors shone brightly a moment—a final moment of glory—before succumbing to the enemy's might.

Bathed in the bright light of this battle, the three warriors stepped back and watched as the wall of flame advanced, and the rolls themselves caught fire and burned.

He stayed until the roar of the flames filled his mind and the smoke left him teary and choking. Even then, it took Rollo to pull him away.

Through the tunnel he had dug for Thyri, they left, pausing briefly for him to retrieve his fortune. Laden with the heavy sacks, he thought of Thyri—over him, watching him. A week had passed since he'd seen her, since she'd left shortly after their victory over Charles the Emperor. During her absence, the full moon had come and gone with her away, deep in the Frankish forests, letting the beast within her run free. *What did she plan now?* He asked it aloud as they walked along the tunnel, the pyre of The Emporium fading to a faint, distant crackling.

Next to him, the Viking shrugged. "Battle, I hope."

Rui walked silently behind them until they reached the tunnel's end.

Through the ill-forged night, they skirted the city toward the river, and there sought a raftsman. *Nightreaver,* hidden by Megan's spells, stood at anchor a good journey downstream.

The raftsmen all lived in a small village of huts at the edge of the city. Rollo went in alone, leaving Gerald and Rui to gaze up at the stars and shift restlessly, awaiting Rollo's return. Behind them, an orange glow rose over the skyline of the city where The Emporium burned. Above it hung the orange moon, suspended in the night sky as if it had just ascended from the wreckage, risen from the rolls of silks and the vapors of incinerated perfumes, not a heavenly light but simply a child of their labors.

In the first hut, Rollo found a sleeping man. He nudged the raftsman with his foot; he didn't waken. The hut stank of wine. He moved quickly to the next hut, where he encountered the same thing: a drunk, slumbering raftsman. Exiting the hut, he cursed: "Odin! Are they all drunk!"

"I'm not," said a voice.

Rollo turned for the source. A tall, lanky man emerged from the shadows. On the streets, despite the man's ragged garb, Rollo would never have taken him for a river man. He was clean shaven, with elusive, laughing eyes. Rollo gripped the hilt of his sword. "You're not a raftsman," he growled.

"But I am," chuckled the man. "I am pale, I know, but I am the night raftsman. I only work at night."

"Why?"

"Because I love the moon? No—my friends need sleep. I allow them." The man's eyes glinted in the light of Rollo's torch. "Come, let me take you downriver. Your wish is my command."

Rollo stared long at the man, then grunted. "We are three," he said.

"No matter," the man shrugged. "I make four, and my raft will carry eight. Please come."

"We will meet you at the river," Rollo said, turning away for his friends.

The light of the orange moon burned the river with flames of swirling mist. For a moment, the moon, the river, and the mists seemed all one to Gerald, mirrored reflections of the flames behind his eyes, the dancing, orchestrated sprite army. The raftsman found by Rollo moved slowly, whistling off-key, sending spears of dissonance into Gerald's melodic chorus of flame. Gerald began to wonder whether he dreamed; at any moment, he felt as if the entire vision might melt before his eyes, reduce itself suddenly to some uniform, limitless plain of fire.

Rollo's fingers dug into his arm, forcing him to move. The tall raftsman held out an arm, inviting them onto a large wooden craft. Sleep began to cloud Gerald's mind; he wanted to fall forward, embrace the wood, and let his dream of fire carry him away. As he staggered ahead of Rollo, Rui's arm shot out like a bolt to block his path.

"This is not right," Rui said distantly.

Gerald gasped for breath. Flames leaped high out of the water like fountains of dragon's breath. His eyes turned to the archer; Rui's arms moved like liquid, the thin line of an arrow arching over his head, notching against bowstring, pivoting, eyeing the smiling raftsman, then dropping askance to target the raft. Rui loosed the arrow, and it bit deep into the wood. The flames Gerald saw on the water roared. The raft itself seemed to shudder, then its bindings snapped and it unraveled, the grain of its wood squaring off and turning to scales. Like a serpent, it uncoiled and raised itself, a hissing tower of darkness, Rui's arrow jutting out like a spike from its eye.

To Gerald, all moved slowly, like some play of fiery shadow. Rollo's sword sang out of its scabbard. Rui's bowstring rustled softly as another arrow fitted into place, then it too sang as the archer let the arrow fly. Before it could strike its target, the strange raftsman had disappeared.

Briefly, an odd laughter erupted around them, a laughter

as unsettling as an off-key whistle, then all grew suddenly still. The laughter resounded faintly among Gerald's flames as Rollo's fingers wrapped again around his arm, and they moved quickly away along the riverbank. After a time, Rollo let go, and Gerald stumbled along on his own. Somewhere along the way—much to his later anguish—Gerald abandoned the sacks of gold as he fought to keep one leg moving in front of the other.

Away from the city, Rollo found a small boat tethered to the riverbank. Rui tested it carefully, then they boarded, Gerald's exhausted body falling down to embrace the planks. And then they were out on the water, speeding for their rendezvous with *Nightreaver*. Gerald bundled his cloak under his head and drifted off into dream. In the moments before sleep came, he glanced up; the moon now shone bright and white above them.

Water

It was a windless night—after Tana's flight, all the Midgard winds went still. On the sea, Seth's sail hung slack and limp, fluttering only with the motion that Seth himself created as he rowed out and away from the port, into Kaerglen's wall of mist and beyond, his eyes never straying from the strange weapon with which he'd been gifted, its hilt propped up against the stern gunwale, its length resting on his carefully folded nets.

Destiny had visited him on the hill. He knew not of felnins, but the blade before him was real, its hilt alone intimating its sturdy, fine quality. He had seen its like before, but he couldn't remember where; it was a simple, strong, leatherbound hilt with a Norse cross-guard. He gazed at it and rowed ever outward, under the stars, away from Kaerglen until all was sea around him, the island's mist but a distant band of white on the horizon.

When he shipped his oars, his little boat came to a halt, as if it had never moved. "Go to where you are most strong," the felnin had said. This was it—away and alone out on the water, on the calm seas where he had banished all the demons of his past. He knew every creak of his craft, even knew where to cast his net whenever a large school of fish passed beneath him and tipped the boat ever so slightly to either side. He knew no fears here; the sharks never bothered him, and when the great leviathans came near, he knew only wonder. When they rocked his boat, he called to them; in the past, they had never come too close, but if they had he might have leaped out, onto one's back to join in its journey. He'd dreamed of this—life on the back of a whale, knowledge of all the mysteries of the sea. He knew he could never survive such an act, but the thought so seduced him that death did not seem to matter.

Yes, he was strong here. He drew his strength up through the planks from the water. He smiled in his solitude and reached forward, grasping the felnin's blade of power by its hilt. With his other hand, he grasped the scabbard, then he slowly pulled the weapon free.

At first he felt little, a tingling that crept up his arm, a slight burning in his palm. A moment later, something exploded in his head and agony screamed in his every nerve; his flesh tightened around his skull. An unearthly wail parted his lips. He felt on fire, but he held tightly to the beast that tormented him, holding it over his head, then bringing it down, its edge cutting deep into the gunwale. There, he gripped it; in his mind it became the leviathan of his dreams, the monster of the depths that would reveal to him all its secrets if he could only stay alive, if he could only breathe the water and cling to its back and ride.

In his mind, the winds blew anew and the waves crashed. The beast writhed, trying to shake him. He dug into it with claws and teeth, locking onto its flesh, sapping its stamina, its fight. It burned him, but he kissed it while its fires grew ever more fierce. After an eternity, its struggling lessened, then subsided, and Seth rode the beast and gazed out in wonder. He breathed, his lungs like gills, pulsing in the ether of the sea. He saw the depths, the cavernous homes of great monsters and the palaces of sirens and mermaids. From the leviathan's back, he knew all, as if he were Manannan reborn.

Seth took in the beauty of his journey and cried, his tears flowing down his cheeks, falling to the deck of his boat to mix with the water of his dreams. After a time, he opened his eyes and looked along the edge of the sword, at the pinprick reflections of the stars above that danced along its length. He felt changed, gifted with more than just a sword—gifted with the granting of his dreams, if only for a few wondrous moments.

The sword of power had given him this; it felt strong in his grasp now, a part of his body, like an extension of his arm. For a long time, he looked at it, bathing in its power, then he sheathed it and took up his oars, the mists of Kaerglen beckoning him now from the horizon.

They called him prince.

Reavers

Thyri squatted, moodily scratching the earth between her feet with a dagger as she eyed the moon riding high overhead. Megan stood next to her, dressed in the brown, drab garb of a servant girl. "It is time," the sorceress said. They could hear muffled grumbling coming from the direction of the hastily erected shelter a hundred paces on. Thyri rose, sheathed her dagger, and started forward without a word.

The Norse had assembled as she'd requested—at least a fraction of them had, maybe four hundred but no more. They sat on freshly felled logs and unpolished stumps, the best they'd been able to manage. One group leaned up against the hull of a small warship dragged that afternoon from the river. Kegs of mead were scattered haphazardly through the assembly, and to these Thyri pointed as she walked among them. "Drink!" she shouted heartily. She slapped one man hard on his shoulder. "Why is your cup empty, man? Go fill it—this is not a night for the weak at heart."

Her words drew hesitant laughter, and she smiled at them as she stepped up to the small platform they'd built (as she'd commanded). She looked out over them and shook her head. "They say in the city of the Franks that the Norse are a pathetic lot!" Angry eyes fell on her from all sides, and what grumbling had persisted after her entrance gave way to an abrupt silence. Thyri laughed. "I see I have your attention! Well, I don't believe that. You're warriors—Vikings—all of you. Your teeth were cut on the points of swords, and your hearts carry all the fury of the north. No—pathetic you're not."

"We know this!" shouted an impatient man in the back. "What do you want from us? Why have you called us here?"

"Battle," she said grimly, stamping her foot down on the wood.

"For what?"

"For your blood," she answered. "Is this your birthright—to beg for land of a king who knows not your tongue, your gods, and your ways? Are these the followers of Thor before me, or are they tired old men content to scramble like dogs for scraps fallen off the table above them? I want battle! I want the Norse united, and the deaths of any who stand in my way!

"I have had a vision, of Norwegians, Danes, and Swedes united. Of fleets that cover the seas from horizon to horizon, fleets to make emperors and kings tremble with fear."

Someone laughed. "You have no right to command us, Eiriksdattir!"

"I have no right?" she asked, letting her anger boil quickly to the surface. "I have no right! How do you think you came safely to this riverbank? Why do you think you now possess half the treasury of the king? Was it your looks?"

"There were miracles!" The shout came from several directions.

"Yes," she said. "Miracles of my making!" she sneered. "You'd all be dead without me."

"And not dead with you, kinslayer?"

The assembly murmured darkly as Thyri's eyes fell on her questioner. The man's hand trembled, his fingers touching at the hilt of his sword. "Draw it or leave," she said coldly. The men around him pushed him forward, shouting at him to fight, their laughter and jeers growing louder with each passing moment.

"I suggest you leave," Thyri said. She stared him down, watching his eyes as he weighed his wounded pride against his life. He glanced nervously around, then turned away, departing silently amid a shower of flying mugs.

"Anyone else?" Thyri asked them.

Megan looked on distantly, breathing a slight sigh of relief that the gathering had not erupted suddenly into bloodshed. Thyri dominated their fears, at least, but the sorceress didn't care to guess where Thyri's address might lead them. To Megan, the night was rife with futility; though they bowed to her will, these men resisted Thyri. She would not forge an army this night, and even if she did, what use could it be, with *fimbulwinter* in Asgard and Ragnarok looming over the future like a fathomless, inevitable void? And these thoughts—Thyri could read them in Megan's eyes. Thyri fought them, the sorceress watching her with all the rest. Perhaps Megan thought of Ai'reth, his words and his visions. Perhaps she thought of darker things, sensing something of the strangeness of the night, and the events transpiring lands away, on the island of her birth.

Thyri calmed them with a wave of her hand. "I did not come tonight to command you," she said. "I do not ask a price for my part in saving you from death on the river. I ask for your homeland, and your gods. The lands of the north boil with the blood of our own kind. That is *wrong!* Don't you see it? You came south, many of you, in flight from that conflict! You should have come united! How else will the ways of our ancestors be preserved?"

"She speaks of Tangle-Hair!" a man near her whispered.

"Yes!" she shouted, seizing upon his utterance. "Harald of Vestfold has sapped the power of the north. I mean to bring him down, and all who wish to join me may do so!"

"You're mad!" someone shouted.

"Perhaps," she answered. "But perhaps not. Do you know the name of Rollo Anskarson? He who slew the overking of Jorvik? Well he commands the warriors of my ship, and he brings it here even now. It will arrive this night, and in the morning it will sail . . . north. You may choose: stay here and forget your past, raising children off the wombs of Frankish whores, or come with me. If you are not with me now, then depart! I do not need a host for this—only a core of brave, daring warriors."

Slowly, the assembly rose. When all had departed who would, only twenty men remained. In turn, they came before Thyri and knelt; she recognized several of them as veterans of the battle on the plain of Ethandune. One, a Sigurd Rolfson, had even been under her command. As he knelt before her, he lifted Thyri's scabbarded blade to his lips, then looked up into her eyes. "No finer Viking lives," he said, "than she who wields this sword."

She smiled at him, but it was a sad smile. She had but twenty men, off the crews of seven hundred ships. The rest—all weary of battle—had forsaken her.

Later, she and Megan lay awake in their tent, silent for long moments, awaiting the arrival of *Nightreaver*. What words they spoke were brief. "Is this wise?" Megan asked once, stroking Thyri's hair.

"No," Thyri answered, "but what use is wisdom? It is needed; I fear I will be mad without it."

"We could go alone," Megan suggested.

Thyri looked up at her. "We could. But then who will tell the tales of it? And after Harald's death, perhaps I shall have the fleet of Astrid's dreams. Perhaps the north can be united and made strong. . . . What else am I to do, Meg? I am cursed with a life with no direction, no great battles of any meaning. I can no longer simply fight and feel glory in the thought of sending my opponents to Valhalla. I have had no real purpose."

"And this is it—your purpose?"

Thyri didn't answer her; the words were causing her too much pain.

Rollo and *Nightreaver* arrived a few hours before dawn, and Thyri and Megan went to meet them. As she stepped upon the planks of the ship, Thyri finally felt the day's troubles slipping away, and she entered her cabin and slept.

Wind-Dreams

For the house of Kaerglen, it was likewise a long night, of no wind and little comfort. After Fand's haven, Tana retreated to her chamber where she laid the wishing stones before her and cast other spells that served up both excitement and ominous portents. For the first time, her sorceries found Seth—he *was* alive, and somewhere nearby. But she found also a dark cloud around Patrick, one that had not been there before. And as for Finaan, she could not find him; perhaps he had retreated behind his talismans and fled.

This was not true. Tana had become but a piece in a game, a game engineered by Patrick, a game that brought them all—just before dawn—to the roof of the east tower. Each felt suddenly compelled to go there, and each felt the thought came freely to his or her own mind.

Tana brooded, expecting Finaan's arrival either in fury or supplication, but it didn't happen. She wandered in her mind, wondering where it was taking her. After her vengeance in the grotto, she'd almost begun to yearn to see Finaan's face, how she might have changed it. And as her mind wandered, so did her feet. She found herself in the halls, climbing stairs, yearning to breathe the still air of the night. From the roof she might see more clearly, remove the confused emotions flooding her mind.

She reached the roof, but Patrick was there, his back to her, looking out over the battlements. She dashed quickly to the side and hid in the rubble of an old curtain wall of ancient construction. From there, she watched Patrick's back. He was there for a reason—looking for something. Seth? Some other answers in the night. . . . Tana fingered the wishing stones she held in her palm. What spell could she cast to kill him now, had she the need? By overpowering his talismans for but a brief moment, she could throw him over the edge of the wall, to a bone-crushing death below.

But new footsteps came and Patrick turned away from the wall, smiling; Tana had never seen such horrible depths in his gaze. His eyes shone almost red; she rubbed her own, fearing it was a trick of the night. When she looked at him again, if anything, the red in his eyes had grown brighter, more distinct.

The footsteps were Finaan's.

"How fares your father?" the one prince asked the other.

"You care?" Patrick returned.

"Of course."

"For him or for me?"

Finaan laughed. "For us, Patrick. Our plans of conquest."

Patrick smiled, the red beaming from his eyes. "Speaking of that, has my sister consented to marry you? Where is she anyway?"

"I—I don't know. Is something wrong, Patrick? You look strange."

"Nothing's wrong except you, Finaan. When did you promise Tana you would kill me? Here? Now?" As Patrick said this, his blade whispered free of its scabbard.

Finaan took two steps back and quickly drew his own weapon. "Must it be like this? I have not betrayed you, my friend."

"Not yet," Patrick laughed. "But should I wait for your betrayal? Who do you love more, me, or my sister?"

Finaan held his sword before him, then launched into an attack. Patrick parried easily, effortlessly, then, before Finaan could set himself up for a counterstroke, Patrick's eyes flashed blinding red, and the point of his sword cut across Finaan's stomach. Links of chain armor screamed out their agonies to the ill-forged night, and the prince from Erin fell to the roof, howling in agony.

Patrick stepped back and laughed. "Next!" he shouted, then he turned and resumed his post by the wall.

Tana watched, horror-stricken. This could not have been foreseen. She wanted to rush to Finaan's side, but the evil in Patrick's eyes had left her shaking and paralyzed. He had sorcerous power, and she had no idea of its source or nature. She had not been the only one who'd gained strength that day.

As she looked on, more footsteps came. This time, it was Seth.

How to defeat Patrick's new sorcerous alliance? Tana, frozen, watched Seth stealthily approach Patrick's back. She closed her eyes and warmed the stones in her hands with a slight charm; blue light bled from her fingers and she held her hand over her head, then sent a spear of the magic at Patrick's head.

Her brother easily dodged her attack and laughed as Seth challenged him with his new sword. Metal clanged loudly against metal as their blades met, and Tana sent forth another blue spear, forcing Patrick to dodge again, dealing the inevitable. "Run Seth!" she shouted. "Flee! He will kill you!" Her words were nearly buried under Patrick's laughter. Patrick's blade caught Seth's shoulder, and the younger brother fell to his knees. That was when Tana finally dashed into the fray.

She screamed as she charged, straight at Patrick. As she ran, she felt the wind and the sorcerous pulsing of the stones held in her fist. Patrick, smiling with his red eyes aflame, braced himself against her charge, but she stopped before she reached him, grabbing Seth's hand, at the same time letting the winds blow through her and calling upon all the power of the stones. In her fist, she felt them crumble, and for a moment all went blue, then Patrick's red magic roared forth, and she felt herself falling—an eternal descent—slowly to the stone of the roof. As she fell, she smiled. She no longer felt Seth's hand in her own; she no longer saw him, his blood or his cropped hair, his sea-weathered muscles, his gentle face.

She had saved him. With her last act before her defeat, she had given him, mind and body, to the wind. He would fly free where Patrick could not find him, and in the wind, he would learn and grow and perhaps one day return to seek vengeance for them all.

Tara

It was well into the morning when *Nightreaver* departed the camps of the Norse with its crew of twenty-five. Rollo herded the new recruits on board, then set sail without waking Thyri or Megan. The day was full of the sun, and the river burned blue now in Gerald's eyes— Gerald who spent most of the morning nursing his swollen head and recalling one after another of the puzzling incidents of the night before.

The wailing that filled the captain's cabin near noon was not heard outside its walls. In fact, Thyri herself could hear little more than a distant, warbling cry, like the sound of a faraway, dying bird, its agonies filtered through leaf and branch in the forest. She woke, however, with Megan's fingernails digging into her arm.

"Bean sidhe!" Megan spat. "I must leave, Thyri."

"Why?"

Megan laughed wryly. "A battle, one with meaning for me."

"How long will you be gone?"

The sorceress looked at her calmly. "I don't know. Come with me if you like."

"To where?"

"Kaerglen. Thyri—please—abandon this quest of yours! Send Rollo back with the others; I fear there will only be death for them if they stay with us."

"I can't, Meg!"

"Then I must go alone? Has our love weakened so?"

Thyri shook her head, her eyes suddenly brimming with tears. "I don't know what's happening, my love," she said softly. "If you want me, I will go with you, but let the

110

ship follow us. Cast a spell to speed its course. . . . Will you do that for me?''

Megan looked at her long, then nodded slowly. "It will be done. But hurry!'' She was already dressed, and the silver sorcery of her ring began to flow out into the cabin, tracing the outline of a gateway in the air.

Thyri threw on her sable cloak and left the cabin, glancing back briefly at Megan—now fully intent on her casting—and wiping a tear from the corner of her eye.

She took Rollo aside and quickly whispered her plans to him, then she ascended to the ship's prow and spoke briefly to the crew. "Something has happened,'' she told them. "We go first now west of Erin, and I must travel ahead. This craft will travel swiftly—more swiftly than any ship you've known, but do not fear. Stay aboard—Rollo Anskarson commands fully in my absence, and you must do whatever he says.'' As she stepped down, she added a battlecry, "Death to Harald!'' she shouted. It had a hollow ring to it in her own ears.

After she'd returned to her cabin, Rollo was left to handle the grumbling crew. "She goes ahead?'' they asked.

Rollo smiled at them. "Of course!''

"But how?''

"Have you noticed Eiriksdattir's companion? She of the dark hair and pale skin?''

"The servant girl?''

"No,'' he laughed. "The witch. Forget all you may have heard of Eiriksdattir, and sit and listen!''

So they did as *Nightreaver* suddenly lurched forward, speeding along the river at an incredible pace. Rollo, Gerald, and Rui sat across from Sigurd Rolfson and the other additions to the crew and began to speak, to weave the tale of the ship's origin in Jorvik, and the tale of the battle with Morgana in Jotunheim. They spoke long, and told all they knew except of their knowledge of the beast within Thyri, the beast that surfaced under the light of the full moon.

Rollo let Gerald tell them of their lives in the city of the Franks and how Thyri and Megan had set to saving the lives of them—the Norse invaders. So at least that tale

became known in full among Thyri's people, if only for a
short time.

When the tales were done, Rollo rose and, as if to prove
all they'd said, showed them the empty interior of Thyri's
cabin.

Thyri and Megan stepped out onto the crest of a hill.
Below them, in all directions, a great, verdant expanse of
grassland stretched to the horizon, bathing in the mellow
warmth of the late autumn sun. Puffy white clouds hung
above in the blue sky.

Thyri felt a sudden place within her breast, cleansing her
of the heartaches of the morning. This place was power;
she felt almost close enough to touch the clouds—their
illusory solidity, the banks of mist as she knew them as
Astrid had shown her. The eye deceived. . . . The swan
must seem a demon to the fly, and a mountain but an
anthill to Surt, to be passed *through* as easily as she and
Astrid had passed through the clouds.

She looked to Megan, wondering where they were; this
place certainly wasn't Kaerglen, but the sorceress had said
nothing since Thyri had left her to speak with Rollo and
Nightreaver's crew; upon Thyri's return, she had found
Megan's castings completed, and the sorceress set on packing provisions.

Megan broke her silence in this new world. "Coryn is
dead," she said softly. She looked fatigued; "We are
almost in-between," she said. "The one place in Midgard
closest to all the other worlds. One foot in the world of
men and, Mag Mor—Alfheim—just beyond our sight. Can
you feel it?" Her voice grew strained; she sat even as she
spoke, back against a great, undressed stone that stood
rooted at the hill's summit.

Thyri nodded. The sorcery here was palpable; she
stretched out her senses, finding in virtually every direction some hint of the pathways between the worlds. From
here, she might be able to get to anywhere, perhaps even
to Asgard itself.

Megan lifted a hand over her head and touched it
against the stone. "This is the Lia Fail, Thyri, the crown-
ing stone of all of Erin. In earlier times, it wailed, sancti-

fying a king's coronation. The powers of all the worlds would meet here, hosted by a Tuathan council.

"Yes, this place was much stronger then. I have only been here once before, but it has grown weaker even in these few years. It fades; the One God's cult has diluted much of its power."

Thyri looked off into the distance. She saw no signs of movement anywhere; were they still in Midgard? "How far from Kaerglen now?"

"Far, yet near. We could reach Castle Kaerglen in an instant, but I should rest. . . . No sense showing up exhausted for a battle." She tore two chunks off the haunch of pork. Thyri sat next to her, unstopped a flask of mead, and set it down between them. So they began to eat. After a time, the sorceress spoke again:

"Long, long ago," she said, her voice soft and distant, as if recalling something heard long before, "Midhir, lord of the Tuatha de Danann of Bri Lieth won Edain Echraidne for his wife. Scarcely had she shared his bed before Fuamhnach, Midhir's lover before Edain, grew so jealous that she struck Edain with her magic rod and changed her into a pool of water, and then Edain caused herself to change into a worm, and from there into a purple fly, a form from which she could escape no farther. The fly, at least, reflected her earthly form; it possessed a radiant beauty, while the beating of its wings produced a music unimaginable by human ears and filled the air with the scents of the spring rain and the passions of lovers.

"When Midhir beheld the fly, he knew without a doubt that it was his Edain. The fly stayed at Bri Lieth, and while it was there, he could not bring himself to bed Fuamhnach, for he loved Edain as the fly as deeply as he had Edain in her true form. So Fuamhnach consorted with her druids and created a magic wind which carried Edain away and buffeted her about over the Great Sea for seven long years. At last Edain managed to return, and she was found by Oengus, the son of Dagda and Boann, and the lord of the Tuatha at Brug na Boine. Oengus loved Edain as Midhir had, though Midhir had won her first; Oengus took her in, and created for her an elegant crystal sunbower in which she could hide from the wind of Fuamhnach.

At night she was able to attain her womanly form, and she and Oengus loved, deep in secret chambers of his sidhe.

"When Fuamhnach learned of the return of Edain, she stole away from Midhir and traveled to the sidhe of Oengus. The two spoke long, and in the end she convinced Oengus of Midhir's fervent love for her, and the wisdom of meeting with Midhir to smooth relations between them, as the one had long been distrustful of the other since the days when they had both sought the hand of Edain. Oengus left, and Fuamhnach snuck back and shattered the sun-bower, sending Edain away again at the mercy of her relentless magic wind. Oengus returned and learned of Fuamhnach's treachery; in his anger he chased her down and cleaved her head from her neck with his sword. The blow, however, did not dispel the wind, and Edain was forever lost to Oengus.

"Years passed, with Edain ever at the mercy of Fuamhnach's wind. Then one day the wind carried her into the home of Edar, a champion of the kingdom of Ulster, which lies north of here in the realm of men. She landed in the drinking cup of Edar's wife, and the woman swallowed her before she could escape. Thereafter, she was born as Edain, daughter of Edar, and grew up to be the most beautiful maiden in Erin.

Midhir learned of this and knew indeed that she must be the Edain he had lost long before. He came to her while she bathed with her maidens, and he sang songs of her beauty. But Edain did not recognize her husband; he only frightened her, and in sorrow, Midhir went back to Bri Lieth and the loneliness of his empty bed.

"The King of Erin at this time was named Eocaidhe Airemh. His druids decreed that he should marry none but the most beautiful maiden in all Erin. He sent out his men for the search, and they brought back Edain. Eocaidhe Airemh and Edain were wed right here, Thyri, in this very spot where we sit."

Thyri watched Megan curiously. She started to speak, to ask about the story, but the sorceress placed a finger to her lips, signing silence while she paused to tear again into the haunch of pork. After tipping the flask of mead, she continued: "Edain and Eocaidhe Airemh, as I said, were wed here. We sit on the Hill of Tara, the seat of power for all of Erin, all of Midgard. From here, the king may look out over all the lesser kingdoms.'' Megan waved her hand out over the view of the plain.

"As Odin may view the worlds from his seat in Yggdrasil,'' Thyri murmured.

Megan smiled, wiping the juices from her lips with the back of her hand. ''Just as. For years, during the Feast of Tara, the joining of Eocaidhe Airemh and Edain was reenacted for her by men and women assuming the roles of the king and his faerie queen, though the coming of the cult of the One God has banished this practice to memory. But Edain ruled as the queen of Erin at Eocaidhe Airemh's side; they loved, and from their love, Edain bore a daughter named Ess. They lived well and were happy, then one day Midhir returned, appearing to Edain in the guise of Ailill Anglonach, Eocaidhe Airemh's brother whom she had taken as a lover. Midhir came so to Edain and finally told her of her past and how he was her first husband and that she'd been lost to him. She remembered, but could not agree to leave with Midhir unless Eocaidhe Airemh consented.

"So Midhir went away and thought. When he returned, he challenged the king to a contest, and the king found himself unable to refuse such a challenge from one he saw as a god, especially since the terms gave the victor the right to ask whatever was in the loser's power to grant. They played at chess, and Midhir carefully lost at first. On his first victory, Eocaidhe Airemh ordered Midhir to clear these plains around Tara of rushes. On his second victory, Eocaidhe Airemh ordered Midhir to cut down the forest of Breag, and on his third, Midhir was ordered to erect a causeway over the moor of Lamraide, so that men might live more easily.

"But Midhir won the fourth game and told Eocaidhe Airemh that he wished but his arms about Edain, and a kiss from her lips. He left, promising to return in a year to claim his prize.

"When the appointed day arrived, Eocaidhe Airemh welcomed Midhir into his house, but he ringed it with warriors and locked all the doors. The precautions availed him naught; as soon as Midhir clasped Edain, he lifted her up and carried her through the sky window of Eocaidhe

Airemh's home. He cast the *feth fiada*, and they flew back to Bri Leith in the forms of swans.

"Eocaidhe Airemh was furious. He gathered his druids and commanded of them the location of Bri Leith and the secrets that would grant him entrance. He took his armies there and began to dig into the sidhe in search of Edain. Midhir came out and watched the destruction of his home with infinite sorrow and anger, and Eocaidhe Airemh agreed to stop on condition that Edain be returned to him. Midhir—the Tuathan lord—agreed grudgingly, but when he came again to Eocaidhe Airemh, he brought out a procession of sixty women, all of like form and raiment, and all appearing to be Edain. Eocaidhe Airemh had to choose, and his choice was as close to Edain as could be. He chose his daughter Ess and returned here to rule with a false queen. Midhir and Edain were reunited at last."

Megan stopped speaking, drinking deeply from the flask.

"Beautiful," Thyri whispered, her eyes now closed, her head back against the Lia Fail. "But I don't understand, Meg."

"Why I told you this story?" Megan smiled and stood. Swirls of magic began to flow from the ring. "I feel stronger now," she said. "Come." She began tracing the glittering edges of a gate in the air.

"Meg!"

The sorceress looked down, suddenly solemn. "I told you because it is a tale of my people. But mainly I told you what you've ached to ask, but never have. Edain was my mother." She paused, gazing out over Erin's four ancient kingdoms, lands that men could no longer find. "She was my mother," the sorceress repeated softly, her hand reaching down for Thyri's, "by Coryn Kaerglen."

Tana and Finaan

Awareness came slowly, filtered through a sea of malevolent, burning red, a red that haunted her vision even as she opened her eyes and painfully looked around. She was in a room, a circular chamber high in the west tower of the keep, she suspected. The only light came through two thin slats—perhaps as wide as her hand—in the wall near the ceiling.

Outside, it was day; here it was only dark and red; she was awake several minutes before realizing she wasn't alone. She crawled blindly across the floor, and her hand slipped in a slick pool of blood, cracking her elbow against the stone. She fell, then rolled against Finaan's still body. Patrick had imprisoned them together! She placed her ear against Finaan's chest; his heart yet beat, but only just. Struggling, she pulled his shirt and his rent mail over his head, then she gingerly traced his wounded stomach with her finger; the gash was deep and caked with clumps of dried blood. His breathing was shallow; she was surprised he still lived at all.

Slowly, she gained her feet, trying to shake the red shadows from her mind. What power did Patrick have with which to defeat her so completely? She could imagine only one source, but of it she scarcely dared to think. If the prince of Kaerglen had summoned the Prince of Darkness, then all hope was surely lost. The island, steeped in sorcery already, might very well sink under such an evil weight. She found the chamber's door and tested it, finding it locked. She whispered a charm and placed her hand over the keyhole, when the door suddenly burst open.

She had not caused this; Patrick's bulk filled the open

frame. His red eyes blazed into the room, turning Finaan's flesh the color of blood and his blood the color of coal. Tana backed away.

"Do you think your sorceries will work now, sister?" Patrick asked. Something had changed in his voice. It was deep and coarse, like the voice of an animal. She didn't answer; she just let him laugh. "Yesterday, I allowed you power. Today I have taken it away. Your spells will not work, I'm afraid."

"We need food and water, Patrick," she said at last.

He grinned at her. "If you are hungry, Tana, then certainly you should eat. Raw flesh should provide you a great deal of strength." He laughed, and slammed the door shut.

Tana stumbled back to Finaan's side and fell to the floor, retching at the thought of Patrick's suggestion. Finaan was nearly dead. . . . She too would die, but he couldn't expect her to—no. She took Finaan under his arms and pulled him away from the pool of his own blood, then she leaned back against the wall under the window and placed his head on her lap. There, in the dim light, she looked down into his face. It was pale and peaceful, free of all the demonic qualities she'd found in it in the past. She looked at it closely, running her fingers gently over his eyelids. She almost cried; she saw now what she'd desired to see the night before. As she gazed at him, she found within herself love, but not the love that she'd feared in his absence, that she might somehow have come to love *him*. Instead, she loved his life and knew at the same time that she'd won their battle, but if he lived, he could only be a friend, nothing more. Too much pain had passed between them for him to win her heart.

"Brigid," she prayed softly. "Let him live. Let us live in this dark place, let us defy my brother. We have no food and no water, so must I draw strength for us from the rock?" The hand on Finaan's brow—the hand with which she had held the wishing stones the night before—began to glow a soft blue as she spoke. So, Patrick had not stolen all of her power! She brushed this hand over Finaan's body, over the wound in his stomach. He stirred slightly under the sorcerous caress.

When she was done, she touched the hand to her lips and felt a wetness like water in her mouth. She touched her eyes, and the last traces of red fled from her vision, then, with Finaan cradled in her lap, she drifted off to the borders of dream, keeping one eye slightly open lest Patrick should ever again open the door.

Wildfire

Between the worlds, Thyri and Megan suddenly found themselves fighting for their lives.

Always before, time had seemed scarcely to pass in the moment between entering the gates of Megan's sorcery and emerging on the other side, whether that be an inn on Kaerglen Isle, or the crest of the hill of Tara. Now, something had gone terribly wrong. Before them blazed an inferno, an immense tower of fire within which figures writhed and faces moaned and twisted into horrifying masks of pain. The fire burned Thyri's flesh (though she really had no flesh in this place) and her eyes (though she could not truly see). She felt Megan near her, but she knew not where, and the fire drew her in, like a magnet drew iron, like water drew rain. She tried to swim away, but she had no arms. She screamed, but heard no sound, and she even prayed—against all the wishes of her heart—for the beast to take her and free her from this prison that drew her relentlessly, moment by moment, nearer to its fiery heart, so great was the pain she felt in every part of her being.

Such agony—she would rather walk again the rivers of blood of her early nightmares. She would rather taste again the blood of a man, than endure this another moment. She screamed out to Megan, fearing the sorceress had abandoned her. Was this the price she must pay for doubting their love? Was this where her torments would end, in a caldron set on devouring her whole? The faces in the fire—she felt she knew them; she feared she was becoming a part *of* them. Perhaps it was her own face there, twisting before her.

* * *

After an eternity, silver erupted into her world, and she suddenly felt grass under her feet. Megan's body lay collapsed on the ground, and Thyri fell next to her, her blood pounding in her ears, her hand reaching out to Megan's, pulling her closer to her lover to make sure she was alive. Megan's head lolled slowly toward her. "Must sleep," she whispered. "Was . . . mistake, I think, to gate for the castle. . . ."

Thyri watched Megan's eyes fall shut before letting her own close. She quickly entered dream—dream that for a while remained haunted by the horrible fire that had almost consumed them both.

Patrick summoned his dark master to cast thunderclouds into the bright afternoon, then he summoned his armies—his men of Kaerglen and Finaan's men of Erin—for his self-styled coronation. He was to have been crowned by the Priest Brenden, but he'd locked away the clergyman and assumed the burden of the ceremonies himself.

Under blackened skies, they erected a pyre, and onto the pyre, Coryn's body was laid, its pale flesh almost translucent in the dark light. The red burned freely in Patrick's eyes as he lorded over the assembly covering the entire hill below the castle.

Queen Moira, looking old and gray, stood crying at Patrick's side. She fretted about Brenden—whom she couldn't find—and looked nervously from time to time at her son. As the torchbearers approached the pyre, Patrick turned to her. "Join him," he said, pointing at her. "In days past, queens ever died at the king's side!" She cried out in protest, but his red eyes locked on hers and her feet began to move of their own accord. Grumbles were heard throughout the ranks of the armies, but they stifled when Patrick's gaze fell down on the men. Slowly, Moira mounted the pyre and stretched out on the wood, next to her dead husband.

Patrick grinned and ordered the pyre set alight. Coryn yet wore his crown; as the flames shot high into the sky and the queen's screams grew piercing, Patrick walked through the fire and, unscathed on the other side, he placed the crown of Kaerglen on his own head. "I am

King!'' he shouted, so loudly that all in the city and port heard his words.

Behind him, his mother's screams reached an ear-shattering pitch for a moment, then only the flames could be heard as Patrick stood there, gazing out over his kingdom.

Thyri woke near dusk, a wretched taste in her mouth and an ache in her heart, as if, in the ordeal of the gating, she'd been physically burned. She rolled over and looked up; the branches of bare trees hung overhead, and leaves blanketed much of the ground around her. Beyond the trees, the sky looked dark and stale, as if a storm threatened to brew, but a storm without the strength to bring rain. Megan lay still in the grass and leaves next to her. Not far away, Thyri heard the music of a running stream, and she began to crawl toward it.

As she drank the water—handful after handful—she wondered what had happened. What could have thwarted Megan's sorcery so? The last time she'd been here, the land had known but one threat, that of Pye, the wizard of the Blue Moon. But she had killed him—ten years before as time passed on Midgard. Ten years. . . . That would put Seth and Tana in their teens; Moira would be old and frail, and Patrick would be in the prime of his manhood. And with Coryn's death he would be king.

Still, Thyri could make little sense of it. Why had Megan so desired to return? She cursed herself for not having questioned the hasty action; as it was, she'd hardly thought of it, hardly thought at all, so absorbed she'd been in her own plans. She'd followed Megan recklessly, like a child. She'd forgotten the dangers of such unthinking haste, and they'd nearly died because of it. Thyri shuddered, thinking back on that fire. Of all she'd suffered, that had by far been the worst. Who had the power to inflict such agony?

She emptied her flask of mead, filled it with water from the stream, and returned to Megan's side. There, she wet her hand and brushed it over the sorceress's face until Megan moaned, then she tilted Megan's head and let water from the flask trickle between her open lips. After a moment, Megan coughed and sputtered, opening her eyes.

She took the flask from Thyri and drank deeply from it, and Thyri went to refill it and let Megan drink again before they spoke.

"Patrick," Megan said, her thirst finally sated. "Somehow—some way—that was Patrick's doing."

Thyri listened; it was strange hearing the name of Kaerglen's prince on Megan's lips. Thyri had mentioned it in the past—talked of the time when the young whelp had tried to take her in the baths of the castle—and Megan had scarcely acknowledged knowing of the name. Yet Patrick was brother to her, if not in blood then by name. "Megan Kaerglen," Thyri whispered, testing the sound of it. If the tale she'd heard on the hill of Tara were true—and she had every reason to suspect that it might be—then much of her own past had suddenly and unexpectedly changed. All these years, she'd thought Megan a former mistress of Coryn Kaerglen, but never his daughter.

"The power of this land has been changed," Megan said, sitting up. "I can feel it." She breathed in deeply, whispering words of enchantment under her breath and pointing at the leaves around her. Nothing happened until the silver of her ring flickered forth; only then did the leaves flutter and rise from the ground. "I'm all but powerless," Megan sighed. "They've cursed all the land with the One God's blessing; only my ring has the power to overcome it, and I've spent most of its power over the past few days—much just in bringing us here."

Thyri frowned; they'd faced this before—Morgana had sapped all of Megan's strength and left her near death for weeks on end. Yet Morgana had not had the power of that inferno. What had earlier seemed but a diversion from her quest northward now threatened to prove fatal if they didn't quickly change their tactics.

"Patrick," she said thoughtfully. "How much strength have you left?"

"For battle? I fear he's allied with the One God's enemy, Thyri. Against such darkness, I can do nothing."

"Then don't try," Thyri said. "Can you learn for me the truth? Who is where? Who fights for whom, and for what? Where the powers reside?"

"Perhaps, but not here. The One God's blessing clings

well to soil, but not so well to stone. Find me a circle or a cave, and I will try.''

Thyri nodded and left, letting the senses of the beast rise within her as she scouted cautiously over the land.

As the night grew dark, she carried Megan to a cavern she'd found in a hill several hundred paces away to the south. To the north, she'd found Megan's old home, the little hut near the cliff's edge that looked out over the northern sea. She was glad Megan had not returned them inside the place, for surely their enemy knew of it no matter what the sorceress had done to grant them safe arrival. And she must have done something, else they'd have been slain in their sleep.

The clouds hung heavily above them as Thyri entered the cave and laid Megan down on her sable cloak. From there, the sorceress smiled. "I could have walked," she said.

Thyri smiled and kissed her. "You need all your strength now.''

"You as well, white-hair.'' Megan pulled her down, tears rising to her eyes. "Don't forsake my love, Thyri. Whatever has come between us, it cannot be stronger than my heart.''

"Nor mine,'' Thyri whispered. But so much had happened. "It's just me, Meg. I feel so lost.''

"So you need battles? I think you've found one here. . . . After my castings, you must leave me. I will be too weak to be of any use.''

While Megan prepared herself, Thyri hunted in the night, returning with two rabbits, which she butchered and wrapped tightly in cloth so that Megan would have food even if her legs failed her. She brought water also, and went to Megan's old hut, retrieving baskets which she filled with berries. All this, along with a neat stack of wood for fires, she laid near Megan's side.

Then the sorceress cast her magics, her ring blazing silver that danced in the air above her. Thyri held her hand and sat alert, her sword ready, awaiting any threat from without. When Megan finally opened her eyes and spoke, she told her this: Patrick was indeed king, and his brother Seth had disappeared, though Megan would not name him dead. Tana, the princess, waned, imprisoned in the west tower of the keep, and with her was a prince of Connaught who had betrayed the king. The armies under Patrick's command comprised over ten thousand men, though many feared their king's unearthly powers gained in a recent alliance with the One God's enemy. What resistance remained—what group of men still faithful to the old powers—had its greatest strength among the bandits in the forest, a half day's journey southward.

Nightreaver would arrive within three days. That was it; then Megan slept.

Changes

Thyri left after covering the mouth of the cave with a tangled mass of leaves and fallen branches. She assumed the sorceress had retained some defense against attack—her ring had kept a slight glow at least—but Thyri saw no point in allowing anything, man or beast, to happen upon Megan by chance. After constructing the barricade, Thyri went north to Megan's old hut where she rummaged through a trunk of clothes, emerging with a long, green, hooded cloak that hid her features well and would aid her in blending into the foliage of the forest. At her waist, she strapped her weapons belt with her sword on one side and a long, thin dirk—almost a half-sword—on the other. Thus armed and disguised, she started south.

She knew the lay of the land well; she'd wintered on Kaerglen that first year of her curse, and the trees around her reminded her of the internal battles she'd waged under the eye of the full moon. To a degree, she felt the pain again, but she'd since defeated much of the horror, and learned to accept something of the dark side of her fate. And the forest seemed to greet her with its memories, of paths she'd followed, of glades where she'd rested. She knew of the farmers and shepherds of these parts, and of the occasional stable where she might find a mount. She went first to the nearest of these, taking her pick of three horses while the owner—a wealthy merchant escaped from the city, by the look of his house—slept, unaware of the pale, snowy-haired thief from the north.

Yes—snowy-haired. Time had passed, and each year had colored Thyri more pale and less the blond of her youth. Each year had colored her more in the shade of the white beast within her.

On horseback, she sped southward, slowing only when she reached the dark forests where Megan claimed there were bandits. The quickest, surest way to find them, she knew, was to let them find her. So she kept her steed reined in to a steady, even pace.

As she rode, she again recalled Astrid. She'd spent little time on horseback since their days together; she'd either been at sea or on foot, in battle, in some wilderness, or in a city full of men. Sometimes, with Astrid, she would just ride, the miles dissolving effortlessly beneath pounding hooves, or afternoons melting away at lingering gaits with words seldom spoken—but a glance could betray her heart to Astrid. But it was while passing through a forest much like this that Astrid had come to her end. They'd left the road to slay a man-killing wolf, but instead Astrid had fallen, and Thyri had come by her curse. So the dark shadows began to leer at her anew with their memories, spectral wolves among the trees stalking her on either side, calling to her with deep, mournful howls—howls forged in her own mind, howls shaped like those of the beasts who'd loved her in the new land across the waters. Howls of her own making—there were no wolves on Kaerglen Isle.

No wolves but one.

The arrows came first, as she'd expected; she depended on the sorcery of her sword, which she held limply by its hilt, to send them astray of their mark. The fifth rune of Odin gifted her by Scacath had saved her before, as it did now. The arrows rained; Thyri didn't flinch though they came straight for her. Four of the missiles, though, thudded in near-unison into the flanks of her stolen mount. It bolted, and she leaped gracefully from its back, wishing it a safe journey under her breath as she stood to face her attackers alone.

For a few moments, the shower of arrows continued. She stood patiently, her face hidden in the shadows of her hood, her sword held calmly in front of her. After a while, about ten men stepped out onto the road before her; she sensed an equal number did so behind her as well. One man stepped forward, drawing his sword, brashly approaching until he stood but three paces away. Under her cloak, she smiled, but he couldn't see it.

"This is our forest, stranger," he said. "Do you have sorcery to turn aside my blade as you have my bow?"

She chuckled. "Only my own blade, if you consider that sorcery. Some have in the past."

"It's but a boy!" someone behind the leader exclaimed.

Thyri heard footsteps behind her. "Please have them stop," she said. "I don't wish to fight all of you."

"Then you will surrender your arms to us."

"I'd rather be a guest."

He laughed. "You're a brave lad to ride this wood. If not for the obvious value of your sword, I'd ask you to join us. Are you for the king, or against?"

"Which king? Coryn is dead." Her remark drew the expected response; they had not yet heard, so how could she (he) know? She heard other words as well—the name of Seth placed on her from behind. This she hadn't expected; she weighed it a moment and considered it useful, at least a mystery she shouldn't discourage. And if they thought her the prince, then they couldn't know him for several reasons, the main being his age of fifteen. He would be almost a man, his voice deepened by now, not at all like hers.

"So Patrick rules—"

"Unfortunately," she said, ending his absent reflection. "I hope you don't think it good news, else I'll have to kill you."

"Lad," he laughed, "you *are* a brave one. Lower your hood; show the face of one so brave as to threaten thirty men."

"No," she said. "Not yet."

He eyed her carefully. "What brings you here? You rode from the north, where there is nothing—how is it that you know of Coryn's death, and we do not? How does a boy learn such things where they cannot be learned?" Behind him now, whispers that included Seth's name grew more frequent. Thyri smiled; again he couldn't see it. He only saw her shrug.

"Perhaps I'll answer you, if you'll tell me you oppose the new king."

"It is Patrick, lad, that we've opposed all along. So you'll answer my questions?"

"In time," she returned. "I wish to speak to he who leads all of you. I need to know your strengths. What is his name?"

"Lugh," the man answered sarcastically.

"Very well," she said, chuckling. "Keep it a secret—that's your right. But take me to him. You may call me a prisoner if you wish, but I will not give up my sword."

He eyed her for a while, then sighed, almost smiling. She could see in his starlit eyes the same questions his men asked. Was this Seth before them? Had their true leader surfaced at long last?

"Come," he said. "Dawn approaches." He turned to his men. "It is well nigh time we returned to camp, is it not?" As they gave their assent, he turned back to Thyri and nodded. "Let's go then."

Ai'reth turned briefly away from Midgard and whispered charms against the realm of fire that tried, immediately, to suck him in. Such a realm he would not enter, no matter how strong its call. He was Light, and it was not, though its seductions spoke sweetly and offered him power. He *knew* where the powers were. This place had changed, so suddenly that he could not have foreseen it, but he smiled nevertheless. He had done well so far, hiding Thyri and Megan from the darkness while they'd rested, while the sorceress had cast her own spells. Simple charms indeed could deflect the evil eye. True, the enemy of the One God was powerful, but his ways were more like the old ways, stolen from the darkest priests of the ages. Ai'reth knew many defenses.

Yes, he had done well. He had saved the true prince with the gift of the sword of power, though the princess deserved credit as well. Yet without the sword, the prince would have fallen quickly, but moments after the false prince's alliance.

So what now? The powers were safe, the helpless hidden, and the white-haired joined to an army. She would have to face the false prince; indeed, only she was equal to the task. And Loki would not threaten yet, not even should he escape his prison, not on this island claimed now by a darkness more dark than he.

Ai'reth sat, half in Alfheim, half on the border of Midgard. The princess—she suffered now. And she was a power as well—how had Midgard come to harbor so many powers in such dark days? She had not the mettle of the two he knew, though. She was too young, and could greatly use his help.

So he reflected, rising at last, skirting southward along the Midgard border, crossing through half-worlds when they would shorten his path. He would not risk any quicker means of movement, not this close to the fires; the sorceress had made that mistake and paid dearly for it. Ai'reth took the lesson to heart.

He approached the old fortress, passing through its walls, then fully into Midgard. All the worlds touching here grew hot from the nearby fires. He hid in shadows awhile, waiting to learn whether the false prince knew of his entrance. After a time, he turned his talent out, seeking the princess's light.

It was a strange quest, this one for Ai'reth. Castle Kaerglen reeked of hidden sorcery, the footfalls of ancient powers and the decaying glow of the Tuatha de Danaan, all of it subdued and shriveled up, however, by another light, the light of the One God's magic, the crosses of the sacrificed son he discovered at every turn, feeling more and more the weight of Klorista's words that day before S'kiri had died. Such simple spells they were, these that bound up the ancient mysteries and caused them to shrivel. He dared to touch one—just a small wooden talisman nailed to an oaken door—and it burned and numbed his fingers at the slightest of contacts. After that, he kept his hands close to himself, understanding all of Klorista's fears and praying ever more fervently that he had chosen the proper path, that Thyri and Megan might be the ones to save them all. Should they fail and their worlds suffer Surt's fire, what if the One God's enemy then directed his inferno there? And after that—if these simple talismans had such power—what if the One God himself came?

Such thoughts so darkened his mood that he scarcely noticed Tana's light at first. He followed it, reaching a door, guarded and warded by sorceries he understood, yet sorceries directed against she who was inside, not he, who wished to enter from without! So confident was this false prince. Ai'reth grinned—baring his sharp teeth—and pushed open the door. Her blue-white magic struck him in a soothing wave, and he revealed himself to her half-open eye.

"Hurry," he whispered. "Escape you can, but be quick!"

She looked at him oddly, started to speak, then looked down at the man she held in her arms. "Did Brigid send you?" she asked.

"Ai'reth sends himself. Hurry!" He moved forward, examining the man's wounds. The princess had sealed them with her blue magic, but the life blood was weak within him. . . . Ai'reth cursed softly, and took S'kiri's Queenstone from its pouch; he pressed it against the man's wound, digging in his claws around it, and incanting words of healing and life. After a moment, the man's eyes fluttered open. Would that the Queenstone could have revived S'kiri so easily. Too much life force in a felnin. The man's *yangi* began to shine with its normal, weak strength, and Ai'reth quickly returned the Queenstone to its pouch of safekeeping and glanced back, involuntarily at the open doorway, for fear the false prince might have found them and shut it again. But no—it remained open. Perhaps they were more safe than he knew; perhaps the false prince was out, displaying his powers to others, forgetting his home and his prisoners there.

Ai'reth wondered on this; surely the One God's enemy could see them, so close to the fire as they were. Or could the fire's eyes be blinded, able to see only where it was invited to look? Whatever the reason for their safety, he was thankful for it.

Finaan stood with Tana's help. His eyes were a while adjusting to the light; by the time he could see, they were already moving—behind some creature that looked like a clothed, walking cat. As the image registered, he shook his head, but Tana held tightly to his arm. "He is a friend," she whispered. "One of the elder races. Please trust him, Finaan. Our lives are in great danger."

Danger, he thought. From Patrick? What on earth had happened to him? In the grotto, Tana had bewitched him, pitching him back into her past, making him feel all her pain, all Seth's pain, and then he'd returned to the present and found her gone. He'd sat on the rock and cried, understanding how he'd lost her forever on that day of youthful lust long ago. He'd fled to the shore below and spent hours in mourning, unable to decide anything, scarcely able to think. And when he'd regained the courage to climb back to the castle, to risk seeing her again face to face, he'd instead been drawn somehow to the roof of the east tower. There he'd found Patrick—a strange, changed Patrick—and they'd fought. He remembered a blinding red light, pain after that, then nothing.

Now Tana aided him. The pain—he'd felt it in his stomach. As they hurried along behind the cat-creature, Finaan explored his flesh. He had a long, deep scar across his abdomen, but it felt healed, ages past. The cross he wore around his neck was gone; his sword was gone, as was his shirt, but he wore the same pants he'd worn that last day of his memory.

He felt as if he'd been dead and brought back to life. In his dreams-near-death, he vaguely remembered Tana in them, but not the Tana at his side. In his dreams, she had tortured him, again and again, with the memories of her pain, taking pleasure in her revenge. When he glanced at her now, he found only concern in her eyes. Much had changed, and he had so many questions, but he asked nothing, for fear that the sound of his voice might spoil something, ruining their escape, or revealing it to be but another dream and thus end it. If this was a dream, he didn't want it to end.

After descending the tower stairs, they each took a hand of the felnin and passed through the stone wall of the castle. Outside, the morning sky was dark and brooding with only a paler tint in the eastern sky betraying the passing of a recent dawn. Then, their fingers still caught in Ai'reth's hands, they came into another world, an indistinct world of purple lights and uncertain winds, a border-world at the edge of Midgard. Ai'reth led them north, quickly, through half-worlds, in and out of the border as he had come there.

Tana marveled at the journey, while Finaan grew ever more fearful that he did, in truth, but dream.

They came into a northern forest before they finally stopped. Tana heard the voices of men nearby and pulled Finaan down into a crouch behind bushes.

"If she asks," Ai'reth whispered behind her, "was Brigid who saved you, not myself."

"If who asks?" Tana turned around, but the felnin was already gone.

Warriors

The man who escorted Thyri to the main encampment of the bandits was named Ailill, a name which, once Thyri heard it, sent her thoughts back to the tale Megan had told her on the hill of Tara; such a misty, elusive tale it had been, with gods changing other gods to water, and gods changing themselves into flies. The way of the world when the Aesir and Tuatha de Danaan had both been strong. Thyri felt a sadness that she'd never asked Megan more of the gods of her people, and a sorrow that Megan had seldom volunteered a tale in her desire for Thyri not to know the full truth of her past. Perhaps such tales were painful for the sorceress; she was apart from her mother's people, and yet not really a part of the world of men. In a way, this had unrooted Megan's life in much the same way Thyri's curse had unrooted her own.

Yet Thyri could do with more of such tales. As Megan had told it, Thyri had felt young again for a time, the way she had felt when as a little girl she'd heard the tales of her own gods from her father.

The leader of the bandits was absent upon Thyri's arrival, forcing her to endure the early morning in a tent alone with Ailill. The man was pleasant enough, but Thyri grew tired of talk and impatient of waiting. In time, when they were finally hailed outside, her spirits lifted when she saw the face of he she sought, a face she knew—not the one she'd most hoped for, though she knew Cuilly would be too old for this. It was Dearen, the man who had come to lead her charges after her departure from the Kaerglen Guard so long ago. She smiled under her hood as she

134

approached him, then without warning, she threw the hood back. For a moment, he looked at her as if stunned, his mouth falling slightly agape, then he grinned broadly and let our a whoop that attracted the attention of all in the camp. "Thyri!" he shouted then. "The legend yet lives!" He came to her as if to embrace her, then caught himself, smiling uncertainly. "You choose your moments, don't you?" he asked in disbelief. "I have just learned from the south that Coryn is dead."

"I know," she said.

He shook his head, smiling at her, then turned to address his men. "All against the new king!" he shouted out. "Let Patrick tremble when he hears that she who slew the Blue Moon stands against him! All you too young to know the tales—this is no wench come among us, but the finest warrior by far these eyes have seen. And to all you who whispered Prince Seth as I entered the camp, hear this! I'd rather this one among us, than ten rightful kings of Kaerglen! Speak ill of her, and I'll have your head!" With that, he turned back to her and invited her to council, in the open air where they could keep an eye on the darkened sky.

With Dearen and his lieutenants, Thyri discussed Patrick and his dark alliance. It came as news to most, though Dearen had heard something of it along with the news of the king's death. He told Thyri something she didn't know: Patrick had ordered Moira onto the pyre with Coryn. This disturbed Thyri deeply, driving home a new understanding of the dangers they faced. Before, Patrick had been Moira's pet, seemingly the only true object of her love. If he'd turned on her so easily . . . The darkness within him had to be strong indeed. Yet he was new to it from all accounts; they could use this to their advantage.

There would of course be a war. Though Dearen was pleased with Thyri's arrival in the camp, they yet sorely needed Seth, if he could be found. They needed the rightful heir to show to the people, else they'd be defeated quickly and all hope would be lost. With Seth, they might cause confusion and desertions among Patrick's ranks in the heat of battle. Otherwise, they were outnumbered better than ten to one; Dearen had less than a thousand men.

So they discussed the prince. Thyri could offer nothing but that he should still be alive. As the discussion prolonged itself, Tana chose her entrance. As if from the air itself—her sorcery fed by the faith in the old ways among all in the camp—she and Finaan stepped among them. "My brother lives," she said, "and he is safe."

As the shock of her entrance passed, cries erupted among those who looked on. "It is Connaught! We are betrayed!" came the shouts, tens of fingers pointing at Tana's companion, as many arrows notching into suddenly battle ready bows.

Tana turned on them. "No!" she declared. "He owes his life to me, so that makes it mine to take or leave intact, not yours!"

Dearen, still seated, glanced at Thyri. "If not a prince," he said, "it seems we have a princess."

Thyri remembered Tana, the little girl who'd escorted her to Megan's bedchamber in the castle. She looked up at Tana now, the young woman whose fear of the situation was betrayed only by a slight trembling of her hand. Thyri smiled, doubting anyone else had noticed.

The council continued on through the day, Tana at Thyri's side. The princess spoke vaguely of the whereabouts of her brother, for how could she explain to them how he rode free on the wind? She herself was unsure in ways of what she'd done. With assistance, he might return to Midgard, anywhere at any time. But could he now if she called him?

Before they'd joined Thyri, she and Finaan had hidden while she'd attempted sorcery to call Seth back from the wind. Either her spells had failed, or he had not heard her. So what, in fact, could she tell them but that Seth was alive and safe for the moment from his brother?

In an act of humility and of his own accord, Finaan stood behind Tana, baring his naked torso for all to see until someone finally asked of the scar, and he replied the wound was Patrick's doing, and he would have his revenge or die in the process. Beyond that, the prince of Erin said little until the talks turned to discussions of Patrick's armies and his strengths. Only then did Finaan sit and become an equal among them; of the captains under the king's command, Finaan knew a great deal, perhaps even more than Patrick himself. And in the course of his contribution, Finaan pointed out that over half of Patrick's forces owed their primary allegiance to Connaught, not Kaerglen. Was he not, then, more valuable even than Seth? Might he not, in battle, turn over half the king's armies against the crown?

As Finaan said these words, Thyri laughed. He was right, and even she hadn't thought of it, though her lack of foresight had been rooted in ignorance of this aspect of the conflict. Dearen, however, cursed himself affably; he should have known, and he'd had ample time to beat Finaan to the observation. As the idea developed, Finaan stood, his self-assurance finally reemerging after all the trials of the morning. "If any here still see treachery in my heart, he may kill me now." He looked around, at the ragged crowd of men gathered around the central council. No one challenged him, and he spoke again, "We may not have Seth, but if we attack quickly, before Patrick can fully turn my men against me—and he will surely attempt this when he learns of my escape—then we can defeat him. I have heard talk here that we should wait, redouble our efforts to find Seth, but such a wait could cost us dear. I regret that in past years I've sought the rightful prince's death, but were he to join us now I would rejoice with the rest of you. If the prince remains hidden, we yet have among us a rightful heir to the throne. Who here says Princess Tana could not be queen of Kaerglen?"

All eyes then turned to the young sorceress, and she felt the weight of their stares. She smiled for them, but inside she prayed fervently for Seth's return. Not once in her past had such a suggestion occurred to her, and the thought of the responsibility—the safekeeping of all on the island—made, moment by moment, each stare more heavy than the last. Under this weight, she couldn't flinch; she had suddenly entered an alien world—the world of battle and armies—but she knew enough of it to understand that showing her fear could cost them all the gains and hope of the day. Only yesterday, she had asked her father for hope, but she'd never considered that the hope might lie with *her*. She'd gained in strength, but had she the strength to challenge Patrick for the throne itself?

Shouts had arisen around her—distant shouts, as if the

turmoil in her own mind pushed the external world ever away from her, forcing her to flee against the weak resolve of her reason. They were cheering her, these distant shouts, calling her queen, assuming the royal blood in her veins equal to the task. Even Finaan, for he led them in their shouts; and beneath his stare, he smiled at her. She wished she'd had the thought to speak of this to him before he could thrust her so in front of all, unprepared as she was. But she had failed to consider the eventuality, and she'd forgotten the nature of Finaan's essence. He was a man of power, used to wielding it, used to seeking it. Patrick's sword had only subdued his nature for a time; she'd failed to foresee its rebirth.

Something began to draw her back—Thyri's hand on her own. As she returned to them, she noticed the ache in her cheeks; her smile hadn't faltered. Her reason had forced the acquiescence of her body even while her mind had fled. But Thyri had sensed her failure in that moment.

"Do not despair," the swordsmistress said softly, so that only she could hear. "All things may be righted in the end."

As Tana looked into Thyri's smile, she recalled the comfort it had given her long ago. It renewed her strength, returning her fully to the present. If necessary, she could bear the burden. This was the war, the conflict with Patrick she had to face in any event. Had she to assume the mantle of usurper, she would have to do so while Seth rode free on the wind. Thyri's smile revealed a hidden confidence, and Tana took it to heart. This was the woman who had once saved her father, delaying his death. And as her mind calmed, she remembered for the first time that day that Thyri meant something else: She was a friend to her sister. Surely the swordsmistress would have news of Megan. . . . Tana ached to ask it, but held back the question before it could pass her lips. This was not the place; few on the island knew the name of Megan Kaerglen, and fewer still held it dear. Should she mention it, they might realize that yet another heir lived, an heir with an older claim to the throne than she. Should she mention it, they might take her words as a rejection of their allegiance, see in them her weakness and reluctance toward her heritage.

Thyri's hand remained on hers; the swordsmistress yet smiled, as if seeing into her thoughts. She spoke again, softly again: "She lives," she said, "though she has aided already all that she might. We shall win this battle, Tana, and then you will meet her. Many things will change."

Tana thought on that. Yes, things would change; things had already changed. There would be a battle, a war. She had seen but one in the past, and that only in her winddream on the hill below the castle. How had that one fared? For all she knew, the Tuatha de Danaan had all perished in their world away from her own. How much might their defeat change? Where would it lead? If the gods warred, what meant the petty wars of men?

The council went until dusk. As Dearen's men erected tents for those who had newly come among them, Tana found herself nervously facing Finaan. There were wounds she could see in his eyes, and the dark evil she'd grown so accustomed to finding there had fled. But would he renew to her now his pledges of love? Would he fall to his knees and plead with her to bed with him? Would he force upon her such questions? She couldn't read the answers in his face; the wounds of his eyes were too deep to allow any other feeling an escape.

So he gazed upon her and time passed in silence. He reached out to her and took her hand lightly in his own. "Thank you," was all he said, then he turned away, leaving her to watch him depart. At that moment, Thyri called to her, bidding her to come and sleep.

So Thyri and Tana came to share a tent over these days. It must be written that Thyri never once felt the lust for the young princess that she might once have felt in earlier years. Tana had many of the qualities Thyri desired in her lovers: strength of resolve, physical beauty, and the vulnerability of inexperience. Tana might have had the tranquil side of Pohati, the shy hesitancy of Akan, or the untapped tender passion of Megan reborn. But this speculation falls flat before the winds of reality. What happened at night in the tent they shared compared most to the nights Thyri had shared with Astrid upon first arriving in the world of Scacath, only then Thyri had had the questions and the other had had the answers. With Thyri and Tana, this was reversed. As they lay down to sleep, they would talk, slowly and quietly, Tana generally asking and Thyri answering, reassuring, complimenting, inspiring confidence or mystery as the questions required.

From time to time, however, the roles would reverse. As they rested, letting their talk grow softer and gentler with the approach of sleep, Thyri said to Tana, ''So Brigid did find you. . . .''

The words puzzled the princess; she took them as some unexplained mystery concerning the appearance of the felnin in her locked room that morning. In fact, Thyri was remembering a night in the land of the Saxons, the night Gerald had led her to a place of power to summon Megan to her side. The place had been Brigid's, and Thyri had spoken long with the goddess. In this discourse, Thyri had told Brigid of Tana, and how the magic of the old ways was strong within her. The goddess had replied that the finding had already been done.

Tana answered a simple yes, ending, so far as she was concerned, all questions of her escape from her brother. Nothing more was said on that matter in any case.

Fire

The alliance led by Dearen, Thyri, Finaan, and Tana began its march southward the next morning. They moved as quickly as they dared without risking complete exhaustion on the dawn of the battle; it took them nearly a week to gain the southern reaches of the island.

They were a motley army, these bandits: ill-equipped, some carrying no more than a bow and a quiver of ten arrows. One day, Thyri took it upon herself to count the longswords among them, and they numbered less than two hundred. That explained, at least, Ailill's words concerning "the obvious value of her sword" that night on the road in the forest. By confidence they were driven. Thyri would have held them back were there not so many unknown factors unsolved without the battle begun. She deeply desired to confront Patrick herself and see this new power of his through her own eyes. And if Finaan *could* bring half his army to their side, then this might become possible.

Patrick, in his arrogance, let them come, not bothering even to interfere with their swift passage, instead preparing his men to greet them; over these days of his waiting for the final defeat of his last enemies on the island, he moved his forces to the plain named Dagda, an ancient battlefield some two miles north of the city.

Before this, Rollo and *Nightreaver* arrived.

The voyage over the seas passed uneventfully, except for its speed, which often caused alarming creaks through *Nightreaver*'s hull and the unexpected illness of many of the veteran seafarers aboard. Gerald spent it deep in thought, his memories of The Emporium yet fresh in his mind. As for the sea—he recalled the name given it by the poets of his people. Whale's road, they called it. Yes, he realized, but *Nightreaver* traveled far more quickly now than any whale ever could. No leviathan of the deep stood a chance of hindering their journey.

As for Rollo, he had no problems with his new crew, the sorcery of the vessel bespoke all the power of its owners, such a power disallowed any thoughts of mutiny or any lesser disobedience.

The time, as well as the leagues, passed swiftly.

Megan's sorcery propelled them through the island's mists, then let the ship idle. Rollo would at least have the decision of where to land. It was late afternoon; in the distance those in the rigging could just sight the port. Rollo directed them north of it, putting *Nightreaver* to anchor in a cover five miles upcoast of Port Kaerglen itself. From there, he, Gerald, and Rui manned a landing craft with eight other men, and they put this smaller boat to water and headed south to learn the state of things on the island in a less conspicuous manner than docking *Nightreaver* at port, letting all witness its wolfshead prow and the uniform black of its wood.

The port they found seemed abandoned. Beyond it, the light of a huge bonfire blazed into the sky, at first seeming as if the city itself burned. Rollo led them cautiously onto the docks, then—having little inspiration concerning future courses that might reunite them with Thyri—he started them toward the distant, billowing clouds of black smoke.

As they passed the hovels and houses of the seamen and their wives the streets remained abandoned. Upon occasion, Rollo noticed faces disappearing quickly from open windows when he turned his head toward them. Something, surely, was amiss in the city. They came to the port wall and passed through its unguarded gate, then kept in a line toward the fire. From time to time, Rollo thought he saw a castle on the hill far beyond; the smoke was too thick to tell. As they grew ever more near, they saw the crowd.

*   *   *

The bonfire burned at the edge of the city, a sea of people surrounding it on all sides. Someone stood on stacked rock at the foot of the flames, clearly the figure of man cut into silhouette by the glow beyond. Rollo thought, even at this distance, that he could almost hear the man's words above the roar of the flames and the shouts of the mass of men. For the most part, they were armed men. Nearing them, he discerned a fanatacism in their eyes, another thing adding to his disturbing impression of the scene. He was unsure of the nature of the wrongness until they drew up and into the fringe of the crowd, and he saw a man he knew: Rorvald Arngrimson, a veteran of Guthrom's campaign against Alfred, a man who Rollo had once heard express a desire to abandon the Saxons and seek out the turmoils of Erin. Well, Rollo decided, he had obviously found them.

So Rollo approached Rorvald, placing a hand on his shoulder. The other Viking turned to him; in his eyes was the absence of sight, the vacancy of the blind, of the seer or invalid. Rollo cocked an eyebrow and greeted the man. "Hail Rorvald!" he declared with a wink. There came no response. Every muscle in the Viking's body seemed to bid him to turn, to face himself toward the bonfire and the figure lording over it. Rollo could hear his words now; they were vile, repulsive words, but there was a sorcery within them, a sorcery that bid him listen, to look, to match their evil with whatever evil he might find within. He began to mumble to himself to shut out the sound.

A short distance away, the others waited. Several of the Vikings stared now at the bonfire; Rollo grabbed each and pulled him to the ground, bellowing into his ear until he was certain that he'd returned him fully to the present—his present, and, he hoped, Thyri's present. He gathered them all and spoke to them: "For now, let us stay here. Stand and face the fire lest we become discovered, but don't stare. Keep your eyes moving. Trade tales with the man next to you. Talk of anything, but keep talking; there is a powerful sorcery here to which we must not succumb."

"Then let's leave," Gerald suggested.

"In time perhaps. I'm not yet certain what to do; what if Thyri is among them?" he asked, waving his arm at the crowd. "I agree we should not stay long, but allow me leave to think. As we stand here, should the man next to you move forward, grab him and throw him to the ground. We cannot lose a single man to this sorcery, else we all may be lost.'' With that, Rollo spread them out, and he thought: It was true that they shouldn't stay. He could feel the call grow stronger the more he tarried. They could hide in the city, as some obviously still did, but perhaps those were only women, children, and old ones. This crowd before him was an army, mostly soldiers, but looking around he saw blacksmiths and weavers, tailors and fishermen. Those men of the city and port with the strength to do battle had been called. That could mean only that battle brewed.

Battle against Thyri? Or another? The swordsmistress had told him precious little before her sorcerous departure from their ship. All she'd said had hinted at an innocent, short diversion, not a conflict, certainly nothing like this. He wished he could approach the fire, if only to see for himself what sort of man controlled this. And then he was guessing it was indeed only one man; he didn't really know enough to be sure. But if all the folk of the city and port were already here—all the able bodied men—then there had been a sorcerous summoning, followed by a binding into this crowd. Perhaps it *would* be safe to hide now in the city; they had seen no riders there, no evidence of an ongoing search for more blood.

If this were true, what should be his decision? He needed the rest of his men in any case, and that meant sending the boat back to *Nightreaver* to bring them ashore. If Thyri was not in this crowd, then he saw no reason to stay. If she was, failing to find her soon would result in his own loss of himself to the dark power of the fire. So he thought.

At the bonfire, events moved on. Onto the stone platform, more stones were raised, cut stones, as of an altar. A bound man, robed in white, joined the master of it all, standing there as an object of the crowd's jeers. He was laid onto the altar, and the lord of the bonfire approached, touched him, then held up a bloodied hand for all to see. Though Rollo's mind was far away, Gerald's wasn't, and he couldn't resist peering intently at this new development. In the one man's hand, was the other's still-beating heart.

Though none of *Nightreaver*'s crew knew this, the robed man was named Brenden, the priest of the One God Moira had brought with her to Kaerglen's shores. All his life, he'd striven to bring the island under the One God's care, and in addition, he'd acted as tutor to the children of the king. Patrick dispensed with him as easily and more cruelly than he'd dispensed with his mother.

When Rollo at last pulled back his men, shaking each to chase the absence from his eyes, he formed them for a stealthy departure. He made them crawl to the nearest building so that a watcher might not witness their escape, then he led them back through the city, through the port wall, and to an abandoned hostel near the docks. By this time it was dusk. He gave them rooms, and sent two men to return with the others from the ship.

As time passed, the weird assembly below the castle went on, its participants never seeming to falter, sustained by the same sorcery that held them in place. After another day and night of it, they began to move; Rollo had scouts follow their passage from a distance. He who ruled the fire led his army north to a plain and kept them there. Rollo began to see the battle looming ever nearer in the future. All this time, no one reported Thyri or Megan among the strange army's ranks.

The crew of *Nightreaver* followed, keeping a mile or more to the west; from the occasional absent-eyed scout that came plundering through the woods, they hid. It wouldn't do to kill and alarm the army of enemies to the west. Rollo camped them in the hills over the army's plain, and there they spent two nights awaiting the clash, enjoyable nights on the whole except for the frosts, which they could not risk countering with small fires. Rollo was certain that discovery now would mean their end. They'd been lucky enough to get this far. Instead, they drank. On leaving the city, they'd plundered the abandoned shops, departing with provisions enough to last them two weeks or more.

From time to time, Rollo worried about *Nightreaver*'s safety. He'd left no one to guard it, and while it usually went to anchor protected by the sorceress's charms of invisibility and more, this time no such protection had been granted it. After their first night in the hills, Rui Taichimi announced that he would travel to the ship to verify its continued well-being. Rollo spent much of that day in worry, worry only relieved when Rui returned near dusk to assure him that all was well.

During these days, Rollo sent out his own scouts. On their second day, one from the north returned to report sighting a small army moving toward them. Eiriksdattir strode at this army's head, but the servant girl (the sorceress) was nowhere to be seen. Even so, elation grew among Rollo's men, despite the scout's estimation of Thyri's meager forces. Rollo thought on the news awhile, then sent the scout back with a message for Thyri: He had arrived, and awaited her orders. If need be, he could join her that night.

Her message came back thus:

Wait. Watch the battle—we are sorely outmatched. Cut arrows for Rui, and choose a tree on the battlefield in which to place him, then plan to get him there and command the Norse swords to guard him and advance before him if possible. Cut him arrows, Rollo—as many as you can; you have seen the forces we face.

There may be tricks in the heat of battle, but let's not depend on them. Their leader must be slain, though this may not be an easy task. But, be strong, and don't join me. Stay hidden. Choose carefully the moment of your attack.

Rollo heard the message and sent other scouts. From them, he learned of a low hill topped by three trees about a hundred paces ahead of the western flank of Kaerglen's horde. Their description of it puzzled Rollo; it sounded too round and flat to be natural. It was probably the cairn of some ancient, fallen king. Rollo hoped the dead would be in good spirits when battle came to disturb the peace. Assuming Kaerglen's army would charge, the little hill cairn would find itself in the midst of the conflict on the western flank.

They passed the rest of that day and early evening fashioning arrows for Rui. Before they slept, word came that Thyri had reached the south and camped on the northern edge of the plain. She expected battle at dawn.

The night left them huddled in their furs within hastily constructed shelters, each lost in his own thoughts. Just before sunrise, Rui stole away from the camp to take his position in the appointed tree. When Rollo wakened, a nervous Viking confronted him with this news and gave him the archer's message. Rui had seen the lay of the battlefield and wished to ensure his usefulness. During the charge now, he would be able to add his arrows to the rain of the others without being noticed.

Rubbing his eyes, Rollo stared at the man, saying nothing.

"He says he can kill fifty or more before sword ever meets sword," the Viking continued. "After that, he can keep the hill clear long enough for Thyri's forces to gain it and guard his position. Now we'll be free to join in whenever and wherever you choose, regardless of the archer. He also said you could kill him afterward if you wish, assuming you both survive."

Rollo grunted. It was a good idea—good if Rui had indeed gained his post undetected. But the archer could at least have cleared it with him, if only because Thyri needed to know of it. After a moment, he told the man to get word to the northern camp.

"It's already done," the Viking returned. "Erling Hallfredson has gone and returned. Thyri knows."

Rollo gave him a brief, twisted smile, then went to rouse those of his men still asleep for their short trek eastward.

And so the stage was set for the battle of Dagda's Plain.

Blood

They came in one massive, unthinking wave, with a furry that surprised even Thyri, though she'd considered over and over again the possibilities of the battle in recent days. Patrick had retained no commanders in the merciless process of indoctrinating his army, and they were more than the ten thousand reported by Dearen; they were well over fifteen thousand with the men of the city and port included.

They charged blindly, out of blind loyalty. Only one mind operated to capacity among the entire horde, and that was the mind of Patrick himself. Thyri found herself wondering whether he was so drunk with his power that he'd abandoned all his past knowledge of tactics to depend on sheer might alone. Perhaps the evil within him simply desired death, and the more the better, it mattering not whether the death came from his pawns or his enemies. In a way, this made sense; he'd had ample time and opportunity to undermine their rebellion in far more subtle ways. And it yet surprised her that Rollo had managed what he already had.

Patrick's charge began from his encampment in the southern half of the plain. Without this further description, the picture of the battle is incomplete: Though covered with heather, Dagda's Plain was scarcely featureless, and the hill from which Rui would launch his attacks was but one of many. In addition, in recent past the south had boasted a small village, at the center of which was a small chapel, built by Brenden and Moira in their crusade to take the One God's cult to the people. In his arrogance, Patrick

148

had let the chapel stand so that it grew from the center of his assembled army like the last bastion of Light, a thing to be mocked and leered at by all nearby. It was a small building, able to hold but seventy worshippers at most, but it had sufficed for the villagers, and they'd built it on the site of an ancient temple to Manannan. It was of plain oak, and decorated all around with the crucifix talismans of the god to which it had been dedicated. Patrick had ordered those that could be moved be turned upside down; other than that, the upright crosses seemed to cause him no trouble in any case. Such were the mysteries of the One God's cult, and the cult of his enemy.

With this—the One God's edifice—as a backdrop, began Patrick's charge. The king himself kept to the rear, greedily anticipating the death to follow, urging his forces on with shouts and curses.

Thyri had formed her army in a great wedge, weighted to the west. As the charge unfolded, she sent a messenger to Rollo with new instructions, then she too ordered her forces forward.

She'd spent long hours on recent nights discussing Patrick with Finaan, hearing tales of her enemy's prowess, trying to piece them together with her memories of the impertinent adolescent she'd known ten years before. Through Finaan's words (and Tana's, to a lesser extent), she'd followed Patrick's growth, spending endless hours attempting to dissect his personality, to forecast his tactics, what he would do. This was how she'd been taught, by Scacath, to understand her enemies. Now, the entire effort seemed pointless, so changed had the king become. Patrick's only tactic now seemed to be control, a tactic that spelled trouble for their plans to rally the forces of Connaught against their former leader. Patrick's army would be lessened in its overall strength because of it, but it still outnumbered hers by fifteen to one, and when she considered the ill-equipped state of her men, matters became even worse.

As they moved forward, Thyri glanced at Finaan and saw his eyes. There, she saw thoughts identical to her own, though the consolation in this was questionable.

In her tactics, however, remained some small hope. For

Finaan and Tana, she had chosen another, smaller hill—
this one obviously a cairn—about forty paces north of
Rui's position. Her wedge rushed forward, passing it,
those skilled in the bow dropping to their knees as soon as
the two armies came within range. She'd ordered them to
stagger and time their shots, spacing them two seconds
apart—Rui Taichimi's most comfortable, effective speed.
They did this, notching arrows and firing by the beat of a
drummer. Rui quickly caught the rhythm of it, and the
front ranks of Patrick's charge began to fall, slowing the
advance of his western flank.

Under cover of the archers, the point of the wedge and
nearly all the forces behind it made straight for Rui's hill.
Finaan, leading Tana by the hand, gained the other hill
Thyri had chosen for him. As Thyri passed, she had
another reflective thought, unusual in that she generally
left evaluation of conflicts until after they'd transpired: By
rights, Patrick was the defender and she the challenger. By
rights, the hills were his to claim and defend. By rights . . .
In terms of the warrior, the new king of Kaerglen had lost
all reason. It was a good thing, and she wondered how
Rui had foreseen it. Had he not—had Patrick decided to
man that particular hill in the night with his own forces, he
would already be dead. Such, however, was not the case.
Rui's bow rained death into the enemy ranks; given the
time and arrows, he could slay them all.

When Finaan took Tana by the hand and split to the
west with about fifty men, Thyri herself broke ranks with
another fifty and headed east, leaving the bulk of her
forces to form a thin wall that would stretch from about
thirty paces south of Rui's hill to link with Finaan's. Her
best fighters—led by Dearen—were at the point, to defend
against a flanking maneuver that might break through to
the west and surround Rui's hill. Her biggest worry was
that such would happen, allowing Patrick to cut her forces
in two, centered around each point of her defense. In such
an eventuality, the sheer weight of his numbers would
ensure his victory. She worried also for Tana; she'd wondered long on whether she should bring the princess into
the fray at all, but the advantages—assuming the possibility that Patrick's unrelenting control on his forces might
diminish—outweighed all other considerations. In one sense,

if it didn't come to that, and events forced them to attempt a normal, military victory, they would fail and all end the day dead.

As Thyri split from the main wedge, she glanced westward to see Rollo's entrance upon the field of battle. The Norse—all brave, hardened veterans—raced for Finaan and Tana, to form a shield-wall of defense if they could make it in time. She smiled at Rollo's quick reaction to her last order. With him defending Tana, she could lay some part of her worry aside. And she knew that no matter the odds, the Viking would glory in the battle, instilling his bloodlust in all those around him. She wished him well and many more battles before his ascension to Valhalla, then turned her mind fully to the task at hand.

She went east, becoming the wildfire, the wild card, the unexpected thorn in Patrick's side. With her small wedge, she would meet Patrick's frontal assault, hold back his forces, deny him the advantage of flanking her army and coming back around to assault the western slopes of the hills from the north. The arrows of the archers slowed progress to the west, placing dead bodies in the paths of the attackers, obstacles to hinder Patrick's advance. And as the dead were overstepped, more fell on top of them, creating small mounds, further hindering the king's momentum. And much to Thyri's surprise, the missile fire was never returned. Patrick had armed his men with sword and mace, the weapons of eye-to-eye death, and little more. If they survived long enough, victory itself might become conceivable.

As it was, with Patrick's eastern flank unhindered by missile fire, Thyri was the first to meet the enemy with sword. Her attackers fell, left and right, their mindless assaults offering not even the slightest challenge to her blade, a weapon trained to defeat the most skilled in combat, a weapon that had tasted more blood perhaps than any other in all of Midgard. She plowed through them, never losing her stride, killing anything around her that moved. Unfortunately, her men did not fare as well. When Patrick's followers fell, no sound at all issued from their lips; it was as if they were already so close to death that all she did in killing them was to complete the transition. Her own dying, however, made their agonies known; the screams filled the air around her. She faced a truly relentless tide with fifty men. Before the battle had been joined, she'd wondered whether she should take a hundred; now she was glad she hadn't. Within minutes, she stood alone against the rabid horde. Even surrounding her, they posed no real threat. As she had when fighting Alfred and the Saxons, she became a machine of death, scarcely thinking, merely reacting, Bloodfang lashing out with death in all directions.

Just before this—in hearing the deaths of the last of her men—she hoped the west fared better.

Rollo shaped the shield-wall just after the battle was joined before the hill of Finaan. In the process, Egill Hakison fell, as did Hrethel of Vestfold, a Viking who had joined with Thyri because he knew Harald Tangle-Hair and had battled for him and been wronged by him in an uncertain affair involving a contest that by his telling he should have won. So Rollo formed the shield-wall with less than twenty men. Though he knew Gerald to be an able swordsman, he knew also that the Saxon was unversed in the Norse ways of battle, and he ordered Gerald up the hill, to be the last defense of the royal blood which they all fought to protect.

And the enemy came. Over the fray, Rollo could see the southern forces fared slightly better due to Rui's skill with his bow. The far southern line, though, looked to have fallen, and Rui's hill would soon be beseiged. Yet Rollo shortly had no time to consider the south. The weight of the enemy pressed against him, urged on by a tall, dark-haired whelp on horseback whose eyes glowed red and whose mouth had twisted into a permanent, grotesque, grinning leer—the lord of the bonfire. Rollo knew him with certainty though he'd never before seen him so close. With the presence of this leader, the fury of the attackers reached frenzied heights. One by one, the Vikings of the shield-wall began to fall. When a mace cracked suddenly against the head of Thormard Rurikson, the sound so loud that it rose above the din, Finaan of Connaught took Rurikson's fallen weapon and broke through the shield-wall from behind, entering the fray with a blade of blinding speed.

Rollo shouted at Finaan for a few moments—after all, what had they to protect if their charges abandoned their haven?—but then, seeing the prince's blade flashing red with fresh blood, seeing the enemy fall before him like wheat in a ripened field, he understood. As Rollo had heard Thyri's plans, the prince of Connaught—merely by his presence—should have turned some of the enemy to their side. That hadn't happened, and now the prince saw their defeat looming, all the while knowing of the prowess of his own swordarm. He could have been Rollo himself, as well as he fought, and for this the Viking could fault him not at all.

But Finaan could not remain content to face the enemy and take down ten times his own number each minute. He carved himself a path toward Patrick, and the king did not flee—if anything he came closer, and when Finaan reached him he dismounted. All this time, but one image burned in Finaan's mind, one image of the many Tana had granted him, the image of Patrick's face, his cruel smile as he sat hunched on the rock of Tana's grotto, listening distantly to words coming from the mouth of the monster whose weight bore down on top of him and whose loins pounded into him with a frantic fury he could no longer stand. This image he had—it was the image of a sister looking pleadingly at her brother, her brother who sat by idly while she, only ten years old, was raped.

Amid this fury, Finaan's sword met that of her former friend. In the first moment of his attack, he caused his enemy to retreat, but then the red flashed once again in the eyes of evil and Finaan again felt the sudden, unexpected pain of iron piercing his flesh. This time, Patrick's blade found not his stomach, but his heart, and Finaan fell dead to the ground, unable to hear Tana's cry of depair behind him.

Changes

Thyri killed, Bloodfang biting into flesh and bone in all directions, sending streams of blood into the air as if she were the center of a bright, red fountain. Only when she'd cut her way through Patrick's ranks did she call to him.

Behind her, the flood had passed through the breach allowed by her fallen men. It had grown distant, begun to skirt around the north to come up on the far side of the hills as she'd feared. And from what she could see, the line between her two hills had broken, the defenders forced to guard the entire circumference of Rui's hill, though luckily the breach had been at the south end and Tana still had a good number of men to protect her. But as time passed, they wouldn't be enough.

Thyri let her voice erupt over the battlefield, a crackling, strangled voice, full of fury and hatred. "You are nothing, little boy!" she screamed out. "My sword is stronger than yours!" Her words were meant only for him, meant to recall for him the memories of his defeat long ago at her hands, the time in the castle when he'd tried to take her, and she'd instead mocked him. She laughed now, a demonic sound that managed to turn even some of the heads of Patrick's men. She berated him, cursed him, repeating over and over again the same words, the same laugh, until she spied him among those gathered around Tana. So deep was her fury that she scarcely noticed Finaan's absence from the hill. And now she called to him more strongly, "Dog!" she cried. "Face me now! Come and try to take my body! Have you no lust inside you! Has a king no loins? Where is your fire? Burn me, you son of Loki, if you can! If you dare!" So she went on, until at

154

last he turned and stepped away from the battle so that naught but dead bodies lay between them.

Thyri moved like a cat, like a hawk against her prey. She gave him no time to think or consider; she hit him full force, her blade whirling, propelling him ever backward toward the south—if she could do anything, she wanted him well away from his men; if Tana's presence could mean anything, they needed Patrick well away from the fray. So Thyri fought him; he parried her attacks well, but after the first minute of their battle she had learned his every move, his every attack, his every counterstroke. All the while, the evil red sorcery burned in his eyes; she could sense its power without feeling it. She fought him, insulted him, and cursed him, the invectives rolling off her tongue to push his ire to furious heights. She insulted his swordsmanship, his manhood, and his cruel, twisted face. She knew him now, and she knew that she could kill him if only she could be sure she could slay the man within him without unleashing the evil source of his power.

That red evil became her true enemy, the man hosting it merely its tool. She didn't dare tempt it; with her curses and insults she fought to bring the man to the surface, to bolster the man's anger, to make him a crazed slave to his own pride. She fought, smashing him to his knees with one mighty overhand blow. In that moment she could have darted in with the dirk in her left hand; against a normal man she could have buried it in his heart, but she feared what the evil might do to stop her. Instead, she took a step back and ripped open the front of her shift, baring her breasts, running the blade of her dirk over her own flesh and digging it in slightly so that she drew a thin line of blood over her own skin. She laughed then, and skipped past him to the south, toward the small chapel at the center of what once had been a town. As she passed him, she spoke softly. "Come, Patrick," she said. "Come show me your manhood. Take me on the floor of the house of the One God, he you've rejected. Show me your power!"

She glanced back only briefly to make sure he followed her.

Rollo watched Thyri's handling of their enemy with something akin to awe. With the king growing smaller and more distant, Rollo began to hope that the mindless assault against his shield-wall would lessen. But it did not; whatever distraction Thyri had provided, it was not enough. If anything, the fury of the assault increased. He was down to twelve men, and even with the others fighting on his side, there were places where only one man stood between the blood-thirsty mass and the princess behind him. He began to call out to Thor, to Odin, to whatever god would listen. He battled, his every muscle straining with the ache of it, and he did not intend to die this day. He had long since lost count of the number that had fallen before his blade.

Tana looked on, terrified, her heart still screaming after the death of Finaan. Next to her stood Gerald—to her but a strange Saxon whose eyes never left the fray below, whose body and sword shifted from side to side, dancing around her as he moved to cover one possible breach in their defenses after another. And then Patrick's men did begin to break through.

The Saxon leaped to her defense, cutting down one assailant only to find two more taking his place. The sides of the hill became slick with blood. When three men rushed at Tana at once, she grimaced as Gerald threw himself before them, gutting one, cleaving deeply into the next's neck, and feeling the bite of the third's sword in his side before running his Norse blade through the man's heart and pushing him down the hill, there to impede the progress of two others attempting to climb up. And as Tana looked away from this, her eyes found only the endless sea of their enemies. To the south, only a few she knew to be friendly remained. Among them was a strange, olive-skinned warrior, a man with a face like a cat's—Rui Taichimi he was, the archer, though the princess could not know this. Still, his sudden appearance in the battle with a sword in his hand was enough to turn her thoughts from disaster. By his looks, he reminded her of the Tuathans and of the felnin who had rescued her from Patrick's prison. She thought, and knew she had to revive her hope, else would it end like this? Would the red sea overwhelm them, slay them all? This Saxon who fought bravely now, one hand clutching at his side, the other guiding his sword to the heads and hearts of those who wished them death—would he die in vain?

At first, she shouted to them, calling out her name, calling herself queen, but they wouldn't listen, their mindless assault persisting. She began to despair, then caught herself. Holding up her hand, she whispered prayers to Brigid and called out the name of her twin. The blue sorcery of the wishing stones began to light the air above her. She called out to her twin and tried to feel the wind, to make it blow through her, to find Seth within its substance. All around her, the dam that held back the flood of death began to break. An attacker's blade cut through the Saxon's leg, and her defender fell to one knee.

Below, those Tana knew were far more dead than alive. Then, without warning, she felt the wind's answer. It came into her body through her breast and blew down her legs and up again, through her belly, back through her breast and into her shoulders and up her raised arm until it circled in her hand full of the sorcery of the wishing stones. She spoke other charms and ancient words until the wind emerged suddenly from her palm, and she felt like the earth, the wind a river and a waterfall cascading from the cliff of her hand. She dared to look to her side, and she found substance coalescing there, the wind gaining form; she turned back to the sea of madness below and shouted into it. "Behold!" she cried. "It is the true king come to cleanse Kaerglen. Behold him and know he is the true heir of Coryn."

Before her, the Saxon painfully gained his legs to slay two others who had nearly reached her. He staggered a few more steps before falling and rolling slowly down the hill.

As she watched Gerald's descent, Tana suddenly heard a new voice—one she had lost to the distant past. It had grown deep and resonant, and it sounded out, a single word that rang out over the entire battlefield. "Stop!" Seth cried, and all below fell suddenly silent.

Tana glanced at her brother, then turned suddenly away when a boot thudded heavily onto the earth on her opposite side. She turned to look into the gaze of a blacksmith, a man armed with a mace held high in the air, the weapon ready to fall and crush her skull. She flinched away; at the same time, the man shook his head, looked at her with suddenly focused eyes, and fell to his knees.

In the chapel, Patrick knew none of this. He had followed Thyri inside, leaving sorceries behind to bolster his army's resistance to Tana's call. But he had failed to think of Seth, his brother who had not died but had disappeared on the breath of the wind. So it was that, though the battle without had come to a sudden end, he and Thyri remained locked in their private duel.

For him, she had ripped open her shift. He intended to take her.

Thyri goaded Patrick to the altar, then again thrust her sword between them. The red yet burned in his eyes, but here she felt more safe to face it. Here was the house of the enemy of Patrick's ally, and here was the privacy to protect her from what she feared most deeply; here she could risk Patrick's death without fear that the wrath of his power might engulf the entire battlefield in flames, the terrible inferno she and Megan had just barely escaped. So she pressed him, displaying the true worth of her skill for the first time. Her attack bit deeply into his chest. To his credit, he moved quickly enough to avoid it landing on his neck. Her second thrust left him no such escape; her blade sheared through his shoulder armor and pierced his skin, and in that moment he realized his error and understood her ploy. In that moment, the red power of his eyes lashed out to consume her blade and toss it aside, parrying her stroke in the way that no normal weapon could. She had defeated him in the ways of battle, but he would yet have her. He had power she couldn't possibly resist.

Now *he* pressed *her*, wrapping his sorcery around her like a great, blood-red talon, lifting her from the floor, squeezing her so that her lungs could not inhale and her blood could scarcely force its passage through her veins. Thyri felt a sudden twinge in the back of her neck, and the lust of beast surged forth.

Could she *remember* it, the death of Patrick would have played much like the death of Erik. The wolf emerged, shaking off its red fetters in a matter of moments, brimming with the forces of Chaos and nightmare to meet the sorcerous attack with fangs and claw. When it was done, Patrick's body lay torn on the chapel floor, his blood flowing in slow streams to form a pool at the foot of the altar.

Idylls

Over those short, fateful days following the death of Coryn Kaerglen, the island endured its painful rebirth, a time that quickly became legend, haunting the songs of the people for years to come and immortalized in poems and sagas (as well as here). The queen few had known or loved was dead with the king. The priest of the One God named Brenden—who had come to Kaerglen to extinguish the ancient fires—was dead as well. Patrick had spilled Finaan's blood, Thyri had spilled Patrick's, and the island had a youthful, rightful king to help in forgetting all the death. Those pawns of Patrick who had survived until the end went back to the city and port, there to begin peaceful lives anew; even the warriors went to take up the trades left vacant by fallen craftsmen, merchants, and artisans.

Of the warriors: Dearen was dead, his skull crushed in the onslaught fueled by Patrick's lust. Rui suffered a long, shallow wound on his left shoulder, but otherwise survived. Rollo ended the battle drenched in blood, though none of it was his own. He had left, however, only five of the Norse come from the riverbank of the Franks.

Gerald lay near death, with wounds too many to count.

At battle's end, silence reigned—a silence split abruptly moments later by sudden screams from the south. Only when Thyri emerged from the distant chapel, raising her sword high for all to see, did the survivors of Dagda's Plain burst into cheers. They went to Seth and lifted him up, chanting songs of elation as they carried him southward, on toward his castle. They attempted the same with Tana, but the princess shrugged them away, ordering them

160

back to clear her path. Then, unaided, she slid and stumbled down the blood-soaked hill to kneel next to the Saxon who had so bravely defended her life. His body was bent and torn; she began to cry and leaned close to him, praying that he yet breathed. When she heard the faint, labored efforts of his lungs, she summoned the blue power to her fingertips and touched each of his most mortal wounds, stemming the flow of blood from where it still came freely. After a time, she looked up and ordered a flat construction of wood, a construction on which to lay the Saxon to keep him still for a journey back to the castle.

When this was done, she went to Finaan, her tears finding a new life. She ordered him lifted from among the dead, to be buried that same day among the graves beside the chapel wherein Thyri had made final their day's victory. As for the rest of the dead, that very moment Rollo led a crew of fifty in digging graves around Rui's hill. Still, the work would take them days. The hill itself became known as Archer's Tower, the glory of the ancient king encrypted beneath long forgotten. Legend would quickly have it that, during the battle of Dagda's Plain, a foreign god had come to the aid of Kaerglen and, from Archer's Tower, slew tenfold more men than any mortal warrior that day save perhaps Eiriksdattir, the bane of the Blue Moon, the wildfire that would ever break loose and come to the aid of Kaerglen in its darkest moments. Or so it is said in the city and port.

Megan, wakened though yet weak, was brought south and welcomed back into the royal house by Seth and Tana. Only these three remained to carry on the legacy of Coryn mac Fain, the mortal of Erin gifted the island by Fand, wife of Manannan, nearly a century before. Under Seth, Tana, and Megan, the old ways were reborn, and those of the people in which the old flames still burned soon went to the wood and built new altars, havens of worship for the gods abandoned by their former king. During the ensuing weeks, Seth ordered a new circle of stones erected in the center of Dagda's Plain so that all in the future would know what forces had emerged victorious. And yet he refused a purging of the One God from the island. While in the port, he had come to know some who had

made the One God their own and found a peaceful comfort
with him. On the chapels built by Moira and Brenden,
Seth decreed thus: Should those living near wish them
burned, then they should be burned; should they not, then
the buildings should survive. Too much blood had been
spilled already, and the people, he said, had a right to their
gods, whatever gods they might be. In any case, he decreed the chapel at Dagda's Plain should survive and be
preserved as a monument to their victory.

But Megan returned. Thyri greeted her sadly, the
swordsmistress's days haunted darkly by all that had transpired. She saw no room for love in this aftermath; she
walked the halls of Castle Kaerglen a silent, grim ghost.

Tana, though, was too young to let war fully extinguish
the fires of youth within her. These fires she tamed, and
she guided them all into the wounded body of Gerald. He
should have died by virtue of his countless wounds, wounds
so dire that no sorcery could quickly heal them all. Instead, Tana tended to him over the days, parceling out her
magic (even refusing Megan's offers of help, though Gerald could not know this at the time), and spending long
hours at his bedside, speaking to him tales and the hopes
and dreams of one just entered womanhood. Over these
days, Gerald came to know Tana more fully than any
other, even Seth who had been her companion in childhood; often, the adult emerging from the child bears little
resemblance to its past life, just as the butterfly emerging
from its cocoon reveals no kinship to the leaf-eating worm
in which it was begun.

And slowly Gerald recovered under the care of the
princess sorceress. He became used to her smile, her soft
voice, and her simple, flawless face framed by her flowing
brown locks. He knew pain—terrible pain that would waken
and cause him to scream out in the night. Even at such late
hours, his calls would ever bring the princess, and he later
learned that she slept alone in the room next to his so that
she could always answer his calls. And when she'd come,
his pains would lessen, her voice a soothing balm, her face
like that of a goddess in the candlelight.

*   *   *

For Thyri, the days brought no such respite. Megan spent long hours with Seth, holding his hand through one royal decision after another in order to teach him to be just, to respect the thoughts of those both like him and unlike him so that he would never err and act as his father had. It came to pass that for the time being, he would have no other counselor. The decision on the One God's chapels, in fact, had been Megan's, and it must be written that the sorceress found great pleasure in these acts, for she had at long last regained her littlest brother who had been little more than an infant when she'd been banished to the north years past. And she'd regained as well the respect of the crown under which she'd been born.

To the slayer of Patrick, the sorceress yet swore her love, but the days left Thyri alone as she had no desire to use herself in the making of a new king. Had she interest in such things, she would have long before taken a kingdom of her own to rule, and if she was to involve herself in it, she would do so only in the north—in the north after she'd freed it from the shackles of Harald of Vestfold. She found some consolation in the presence of Rollo and Rui, but even that grew painful. On idle days, near Rollo, she could not shake the memories of their one afternoon of love from her mind. She would look at him and feel him inside her again, or rather feel the ache to have him inside her again, and these thoughts of lust she rejected, so strong remained the taste of Patrick's hot blood in her mouth. But with her, Rollo wished desperately to leave, to take to sea and continue Thyri's quest against Harald with their crew of five. Rollo's taste for battle had not been sated at Dagda, not because he hadn't exacted his share of death, but because he could not think it a real battle, it having been no more to him than a mindless slaughter of enemies driven not by noble purposes but by the absence of their thinking minds.

Once again, as events would have it, Thyri had found herself on Kaerglen with winter approaching, confined to land while ice descended to lord over the seas. Even had they departed directly from the land of the Franks, they would have risked some ice in northern waters. Now after their delay, the northern approach would be impossible. So once again she was forced to winter there, though this time she hadn't a willing, undistracted lover to warm her nights. And amid all this, she had the full moon with which to contend.

Rollo brought *Nightreaver* to the port, and Thyri spent the first night of the next full moon in her captain's cabin where Megan had once conjured a mystical landscape on the wall, a gateway into distant, otherworld forests where she was free to roam and hunt far away from the realm of men. When the change came over her there, she entered the painting, only to find its forest burned, its life fled. Consumed by her hunger, she ranged far, and only luck allowed her to find and kill an old buck near midnight. The next night, and all nights of the full moon after that, she spent trapped on the island—not even daring to attempt the pathways between the worlds—preying in the north on wild boar and deer and the sheep of farmers when necessary. She grew detached, noticing but scarcely caring about the blade Seth now boasted at his side; to Thyri's mind, that Megan had never bothered to explain this only proved how far distanced they'd become. Beyond this, her mood grew so dark that she would sometimes make herself long absent from the castle, spending weeks and sometimes months of the winter alone in the northern woods, alone with her thoughts and the burdens of her curse. And there, she began once again to dream.

She had dark dreams, dreams in which she slew all she loved, her fangs tearing out the throat of Megan, then moving on to Gerald, Rollo, Rui, Sokki, even princess Tana. Since Astrid's death, Thyri had never weathered well the idle days free of conflict; in the past, she'd survived only by taking a lover, but a lover now she refused to accept.

One dream, above all others, came to her again and again. She would find herself on a plain of ice, where the wind itself pounded her, forcing her to fight merely to keep her feet. Against this wind, she would walk, painful step by painful step, until the wind abated and she realized now that she walked as the wolf; the lust then in her heart would be great. She would walk, her claws digging into the ice until she came upon a frozen lake, and in the lake she would see faces, the faces of all those she'd ever

known: Her mother, her father, Erik, Akan, and Megan . . .
on and on until the faces became strange, became the
faces of gods. And all these faces gazed at her with lifeless
eyes, and the wolf within her would claw at the ice above
them, at each in turn in this endless dream. The part that
was herself would mourn the dead eyes, while the part that
was the wolf would hunger for them, its fury growing ever
wilder since, when her claws had cut deep enough to
uncover flesh, the face would disappear, revealing itself as
but a reflection or a trick of the ice.

In this dream, the last two faces were ever the same.
First would come the sad face of Astrid, a face that even in
death tried to smile at her. The wolf would dig, and Astrid
would disappear. She'd move on, and the last face was her
own. By now, the wolf's lust would allow no control, and
it would dig quickly ever deeper, and at last reveal flesh
frozen under the ice. In that moment—her own cheek
bared to the hunger of the beast within her—she would
always waken, her sweat like ice on her skin in the winter's cold, and she would lie sleepless then, until dawn.

When spring came, she departed on *Nightreaver* with
Rui, Rollo, and the five surviving Vikings. Gerald did not
go with them; he might have, had Tana not begged him to
stay. He had become her sole confidant, and with her he
felt more alive, more meaningful, for she ever asked his
council and took it for wisdom. Among Thyri, Rollo, and
Rui, Gerald lacked that gift.

On the docks of Port Kaerglen, Thyri bid Megan
Kaerglen, sister to the king, a silent farewell. All the
sorrow of their impending separation lived in their eyes.
Thyri did not even ask Megan to join her; she knew the
workings of Megan's heart and could not forget the tale
she'd heard on the Hill of Tara. The sorceress had found
again her family, her banished past, and Thyri could not
bring herself to ask her lover to abandon it. But even so,
she could not abandon the demands of her own history. As
Thyri looked into Megan's eyes, she realized that their
love was far from dead; it was merely wounded, and given
time the wounds would heal. Given time, they would
reunite, just as they had after Thyri had left before to
travel west to where the sun spent its nights and had found

instead the new land of the Habnakys and the Arakoy. On the docks then, she reached out and touched Megan's cheek with her silver gauntlet, then *Nightreaver* was set, once again, upon the seas and guided to its northerly course.

Book IX:
EIRIKSDATTIR

As I write, this tale seems to race away from me, becoming its own creature as the tapestry of the Norns wraps more tightly about it, as surely as the entrails of Narvi, Loki's son, hardened and bound his father in the darkness of a cave where Loki's wife, Sigyn, held a bowl above his face to catch the dripping venom of the serpent bound above her husband.

All I have seen. . . . All that I know. All these gods with their own fates bound to Midgard—the One God's inexplicable rise, the fading of all the rest. I still do not profess to understand, at least no better than I have learned through Megan's words, or from Klorista through Ai'reth. But in the nine worlds lorded over by Odin, all the prophecies of the Sibyl save the last have now transpired behind what I have written. So long ago, it seems, I wrote of Thyri's return from the new land astride Astrid's winged steed. During that flight, Astrid told Thyri of the death of Balder, the signing of the coming of the end. So it happened, and Fandis and others prophesied the coming of *fimbulwinter*, the prelude to Ragnarok. But more transpired.

I still do not fully understand Loki's purpose in his meddling with Thyri—his games. For him—by the Sibyl's reckoning—the events that followed Balder's death were tumultuous. And he never caused true harm to Thyri; not when he forsaw the demise of the Black Rabbit and caused the girl Elaine to be in its midst; not when, disguised as Al'kani, he tormented her; not even when he wakened Morgana. And the raft that turned into snakes before my eyes—that must have been some weak manifestation of his power, even though he was bound that very moment.

What else might explain it, yet not explain it, if not the Trickster? Perhaps the raftsman had manifested the One God's enemy, though I find no sense in that thought. He never assailed us or hindered us, and without us, Patrick would surely have prevailed at Dagda. Perhaps, once again, I simply fail to understand; the One God's enemy does not seem to glory in worship, only in death. The lack of sense I see here comes from the means. The snakes and the laughter bore all the marks of Loki's nature, and it must have been him unless I'm further mistaken and the truth will have it the One God's enemy and Loki boast more similarities than I perceive.

But that set aside, by my reason, Loki has either sought Thyri's undoing, or he has sought in her an ally. The latter possibility puzzles: In past acts, he hardly wooed her; he only complicated her life, tormented her. Were his manipulations so subtle? Did he seek to torment her to draw her to his side solely by nurturing the darkness of the Chaos within her? As for Thyri's undoing—he hardly came close to success. But *were* that his goal, only another mystery could explain his failures: Odin, who seemingly remained ever distant, and yet might have watched over Thyri all the while, diluting Loki's influence while allowing her torment for reasons of his own. The keys to these riddles escape me. But I do know things. Even Odin was bound, in essence, to his foretold fate.

By the prophecies sung by the skalds of the north, a darkness hung over Asgard after Balder's death as all who lived there knew what it portended. Time passed, the gods mourning and Loki growing ever more confident and brash of his victory. He had his own prophecies, the Trickster did. He was part evil, part closed—part Chaos. He had his own prophecies that said that no prophecy could bind him, bind Chaos. So he battled on in his own inexplicable way.

It came to pass that all the gods went to Aegir's hall in the sea next to the isle of Hlesey for a feast. They went in friendship, wounded as they were by the passing of Balder. When Loki entered and saw that Thor had not yet arrived, he leered at them and began to insult each of them in turn, sparing none—not even Odin, whom he accused of being a witch. This went on and on, the gods growing enraged, and Loki's insults growing ever more sharp in their twists of spite. At last, Thor arrived, and Loki insulted him as well, though when Thor's anger grew and all the worlds began to tremble with his anger, Loki made a hasty retreat, fleeing to a remote haven on Midgard.

This must all have occurred while Thyri, Megan, and the crew of *Nightreaver* were trapped on the seas of Jotunheim. Deciding Loki's transgressions had exceeded the rights of his divinity, the gods pursued him, led by Thor and guided by Odin, who could see all from his seat of Valaskjalf in Asgard. They caught him, even though he nearly escaped in the shape of a salmon. In their vengeance, they took his two sons, Vali and Narvi, and put them together, working sorceries upon Vali to turn him into a monstrous wolf. The wolf Vali leaped at Narvi and tore him apart. The gods then took the dead Narvi's entrails with which to bind Loki in a dark cave, and they bound a serpent above him, there to drip poison down upon him until all fetters would break before the end of all things.

Already, Loki's other offspring—begat by the giantess Angrboda—awaited that same day, and powerful they were. Fenrir the wolf lay fettered like his father on the island of Lyngvi. Jormungard the serpent lurked under the sea. Hel waited in Niflheim, where Garm lay chained, guarding the entrance to her world.

The other enemies of Odin and Asgard ranged free throughout Jotunheim and Svatalfheim, and even Alfheim and Nidavellir. Megan's people, the Tuatha de Danann of Alfheim, fought in vain all this while to stem the tide of warring giants marauding from one world to the next (as Tana saw well in her wind-dream). Meanwhile, the Norns relentlessly wove the inevitability of Ragnarok into their tapestry of life. Of these giants, the sons of Muspell, the legions of fire commanded by Surt, wreaked by far the most destruction. So it went on, intensifying on all worlds save Midgard as the *fimbulwinter* fell on Asgard and the Aesir saw the coming of the end.

What to write here of Ragnarok? This is how the skalds tell it:

The three winters with no summer between them—

fimbulwinter—will fall upon Midgard, and mothers will seduce their sons, and sisters their brothers. Skoll will devour the sun, and Hati will devour the moon. All the stars will go out.

Great shudders will wreck the body of the earth, and no stone will survive without damage. Three great cocks will crow, alerting and awaking all the giants, all the warriors in Valhalla, and all the dead in Niflheim. All fetters will break: Fenrir will run free, Garm will stretch his horrible limbs and howl out in ecstatic, demonic freedom, and Loki will emerge from his cave and set sail for Vigrid, followed by all the legions of the dead.

Fenrir and Jormungard, Surt with his giants and his sword of fire, Loki and the dead, and army upon army of giants—all these will cross Bifrost, the rainbow bridge, and enter Asgard, the land of the Aesir. Bifrost will collapse behind them, wrecked by their immense weight.

Heimdall the watchman will sound his great horn, Gjall, and it will be heard throughout all worlds. All the gods, the Aesir, the survivors of the wars in Alfheim and Nidavellir, and all the warriors ascended to Valhalla—the Einharjir—will arise and go to Vigrid behind Odin to meet the invasion. As they clash, Midgard will shudder, and destruction will lord over it. Two humans—Lif and Lifthrasir—will see what happens and escape, and they will hide in Yggdrasil, clutching in terror as the great ash trembles and the battle goes on.

Odin and Thor will lead the charge of the forces of Light. The All-Father, wielding his great spear, Gungnir, will meet Fenrir, and Thor, Jormungard. Then, immortals will begin to die. Heimdall will kill Loki, and Loki will kill Heimdall. Garm and the one-handed Tyr will kill each other. And Surt, with his flaming sword, will kill Freyr of the Vanir.

The greatest matches go on. Thor, the mightiest of all the gods, will kill Jormungard the serpent, but Thor will be poisoned, take nine steps back from his victory, and fall down dead. And when Odin witnesses the fall of his son, he will be overcome with grief and forget, only for a moment, the danger of Fenrir before him. In that moment, Fenrir will swallow the father of the gods.

*   *   *

The skalds tell this tale well. Over the centuries, all the world's shoesmiths have tossed aside scraps of leather for one purpose: For the shoe of Vidar. For as soon as Odin disappears into Fenrir's gaping maw, Vidar will rush forward and use this shoe to prop open Fenrir's jaws while he tears apart the wolf and avenges the All-Father's death.

Then Surt will burn all, setting all the worlds alight with his flaming sword. Everything will die, save Vidar and Thor's sons, Modi and Magni, and Vali and Vili and Ve and Honir. And Lif and Lifthrasir, the humans who had fled in time into Yggdrasil to hide.

So it will all end, leaving the seeds for a new beginning. Balder and Hod will come back from the dead, and the world will be a better place, for much evil will perish at Ragnarok on the plain of Vigrid.

Yes, that is how the skalds tell it. How it is told, as if it has yet to come.

Ice

The harsh, northerly wind whipped back Thyri's hair, pummeling into her face, which grew red as if burned by the sun. But it was the cold that dug into her, the newly cracked winter greeting her with its biting breath. Ice still floated in chunks on the water.

Had she cared, she could have avoided this by tarrying another fortnight on Kaerglen, but she'd refused to consider the thought. And the ear-blistering cold—she reveled in it, summoning it against her skin, seeking its frigid bite. She left it to Rollo to navigate the ship around the worst hazards. She didn't care; some madness inside her almost wanted her to jump in and embrace it all. She finally felt free from the shackles of winter. She had but seven men under her command, and she felt as if she commanded an army, as she'd not felt since she'd led the Habnakys against Aralak's hordes in that war across the great ocean.

Winter's end, traveling north—free of the dreams that had haunted Thyri's nights these past months. No nightmares could now intrude upon her will. She would go north. She would have Gyda's head before she returned to Kaerglen. Megan could no longer understand her. . . . The objections in the sorceress's eyes, as they'd stood there on the docks, only proved how far apart they'd drifted. The thought left a bitter lump in Thyri's throat. She swallowed it and turned her thoughts outward, into the cold. Perhaps this was *fimbulwinter* bearing down on her from her homelands. Perhaps Megan's ravings of Ragnarok on Asgard alone were wrong. All these affairs of gods— what were they to her? *Nothing. Embrace the cold, Chaos. Take it inside of you. Make it your bones and your blood*

*and your heartbeat. Your breath with which to burn all
who stand against you.*

Behind her eyes, a great serpent rose up from the water.
Jormungard, poison dripping from his fetid, gaping maw.
He fanged the clouds, then swooped down over her, his
sibilant voice oozing into her, through her eyes, not her
ears. *You and I,* he said, *we ssshall dessstroy them all.
With you at my sside, I might devour even the One God
himssself. With our brother Fenrir, we sshall tear Midgard
assunder, and people itsss fieldsss, my ssseed in your
womb.* . . .

The earth cracked, a horde of wolf-headed vipers rising
from the depths. Behind them, fountains of blood spouted
from the rock. The vipers grew wings and flew, dragons
to lord the air above their father in the great sea that
strangled Yggdrasil. Clouds of black poison washing through
Alfheim, engulfing all in their path. The fall of the thirteen
elven kings: the king over the mount, the lord of the
golden briar and thistle, the standard bearer of the treedrytes,
the king of oaks, the lord of the swallows . . .

Mad, Thyri thought distantly, *I'm going mad.* The shadow
play of the apocalypse yet faded, in and out of her vision.
Gods, she thought. Damn them all. The power surging
within her was *hers.* She was a warrior, and she would
have her battle. These visions tugged her this way and
that, but never away from her sword. Odin had abandoned
her long before. She may not serve him now, but neither
did she serve another. Not Loki, not the serpent. Not the
wolf with eyes like prisms and the fur of frost.

She still remembered the faces in the ice—they'd burned
themselves into her waking mind. She could feel her claws
digging in toward them; always before she'd fought the
feeling, now she almost welcomed it.

By the stars, they came within a day of the northern
reaches when all changed. It was just night, and the lights
of the gods danced mysteriously in the sky above. Yet
Rollo guided *Nightreaver* on, standing on the prow next to
Thyri and peering ahead, his eyes picking out the great
chunks of ice just in time to call out his orders to port or
starboard.

Under the play of the heavenly lights, figures began to

take shape in the air before them. At first, Thyri thought it another vision, but when gasps came from behind her and she felt Rollo stiffen, she knew suddenly the vision to be truth. The figures—wispy and ghostlike—coalesced, glowing like new stars in the heavens, their white armor and golden blades shining as brightly as the moon itself. They were the Valkyrie: Host Fetter and Shrieking, Spear Bearer, Might, and Shield Bearer . . . *Shield Bearer*, Thyri grunted, *Astrid*. Since leaving the new land, she had seen her cousin only in dreams. Now on the northern seas, the Valkyrie had returned.

"Hail!" Thyri greeted her. *Astrid, my love* . . . The Valkyrie were armed; on their faces she did not see welcome.

It was Astrid who spoke to her: *"You cannot pass, little one."* Thyri glared at her, and tears came to her eyes. *"It is Odin's wish. You must turn back."*

Thyri drew her sword and held it up in the air before them. "I will not!" she shouted, full of madness. "I am the wolf, and I will have my blood!"

"You are not the wolf, little one," Astrid replied. *"Did Scacath not teach you well? Why do you lust to be named The Usurper? Wars rage among the gods, yet you wax insane, questing to bring new battles when the battles are nearly done."*

"But it is Gyda, my love!" Thyri cried. "Gyda who has caused the lands of the north to be soaked in blood. Once I abandoned them, but they are the lands of my birth, and they cry out for justice."

Astrid looked at her long. *"Gyda is nothing,"* she said at last. *"Harald is nothing but that he has made small kingdoms, small jarldoms, into nations. And nations they need to be; Midgard changes, Thyri. One thing ends, and another begins."*

"No! You speak like the dead king of Kaerglen who gave up his land to the One God because he feared the battle needed to stop him!"

"Then perhaps your dead king was right."

Thyri waved her sword again in the air, then spun, pointing it at her crew. With the appearance of the Valkyrie, Rollo had ordered the sail slackened. Now she ordered it filled. "Forward!" she commanded. "Else I will have all your heads!" Yet despite the menace in her eyes, none moved. Next to her, Rollo gripped her shoulder, then moved on. He took the guide rope of the sail and made it taut, pulling until the sail filled and *Nightreaver* again moved forward. With the motion, Thyri turned again to Astrid and glared. "We will reach Vestfold or die!" she shouted.

With that, the Valkyrie said not another word. Astrid broke from their ranks, her steed—named after Loki himself—carried her forward, and she raised her great golden sword into the air and brought it smashing down against the wolfshead prow, splitting through the wood, then shearing down through the hull itself, the ship screaming as the Valkyrie's sword tore the prow asunder.

Nightreaver lurched, then it pitched Thyri and her crew unceremoniously into the sea.

Magic

Rollo spat the brine from his mouth and clung to the side of the floating, icy island that held him above water. Rui had already climbed up onto its flat surface; the archer lay there, heaving softly, his bow gone, as was Rollo's sword.

Nightreaver sank behind them; as Rollo looked back, the last foot of the ship's stern slipped silently beneath the waters, leaving hardly a ripple behind. What moved on the surface of the sea was the work of the wind. Two other Vikings clung to a similar island—he could see them now on the other side of the ship—even so, as he watched, one slipped under and did not reappear. The other tried to grab him, failed, then saw Rollo and attempted to swim the distance through the freezing water. Halfway there, he too floundered and sank, and Rollo and Rui were alone. Their three other men had never surfaced—they, along with Thyri—had been swallowed by the sea. And all this the fault of the Valkyrie. Rollo cursed them, damning them if they hadn't stayed in their spirit forms to escort his five fallen warriors to their rightful seats in Valhalla. This was not the way. Could Thyri have truly perished and he survived? He'd always imagined their last battles, his sword next to hers, his flesh always succumbing while her body churned on, one sword laying waste an army of thousands, man by man.

Now he froze. His legs went stiff with the cold. He tried to pull himself onto the ice as Rui had, but the cold had worked into his arms and they failed him. He cried—barked—out his pain, and after a moment the archer crawled to him and took his hand, pulling him up to safety—a freezing safety, though one much less quick and sure than the waters beneath. On the ice then, he and Rui collapsed against each other, and Rollo let the cold surround his head and steal away his thoughts at last.

He dreamed. He dreamed of lush, sweltering southern forests, places he'd never seen with his own eyes but had only heard whispers of in late-night taverns. In the forests were trees the size of giants, and insects the size of birds. The birds themselves spoke—real words in a language he could not understand. And in all the trees—quiet kings of earth, greenery, and sky—were cats.

Ai'reth watched the moments pass with a deep frown cutting furrows into his forehead. The Valkyrie had had no right! Did they seek the downfall of their last wild champion? Had they sided now with Loki, even as he lay chained? From his haven next to Midgard, Ai'reth looked on; the white-haired power sank, then suddenly twisted away from Midgard toward him. So great was the fury in her eyes that he fled for cover, emerging only when he was sure she'd passed. By then, the mortals he could have saved had all perished. Except these two still on the ice, the two he knew better than the rest for their ties to Thyri were strong. He let them lie there, let them alone until sleep came to take their minds away. Then he cautiously stepped out into Midgard.

Even Ai'reth felt the bite of the north wind's breath. This was weather for ice giants, he thought, not felnins. He went quickly to them and dug his claws into their shoulders, then said spells to take them all away from the cold.

Once on the Midgard border, he carried them one by one to the safety of a half-world (where it indeed sweltered, and there were insects the size of birds), then watched over them awhile before taking up his finger drum and tapping a simple charm that would revive his low-born charges.

In his dream, Rollo suddenly wakened. But for Rui sitting next to him, shaking the clouds of sleep from his mind, Rollo would never have thought this place to be true.

Before them, tending a fire on which a haunch of wild boar roasted, was a creature, half cat, half man. The creature looked at him and grinned, fangs bared in the light of the fire. "I am Ai'reth," the creature said. "I am a felnin."

Rollo cleared his throat. "The ice?" he asked after a moment.

"It was cold, yes. No place for life to be left to perish. Your clothes have dried now—they are there, on that limb." The felnin pointed to a nearby branch from which hung Rollo's furs and Rui's silken dress and cloak. Before seeing this, the Viking had not yet grown aware that they were naked. He rose unsteadily, then began to dress, glancing back at the felnin. "Where—" he began.

"It doesn't matter," the creature interrupted him. "Where you should not be. We must leave soon, else we'll attract powers you will be too slow to escape." Ai'reth grinned again. "And to the other question I see floating behind your eyes—the question you don't dare to ask—I tell you she still lives. She you call Eiriksdattir. She lives."

"Where?"

"Everywhere."

The answer caused Rollo's ire to flare, his hand moving to his side where there should have been a sword but there was none now. "I don't play games," he said abruptly. "With cats or anybody. Where is she?"

"On her own path," the felnin answered. "You cannot follow her now. She has moved beyond this, beyond her agonies of recent years. She walks a path only she can follow." With that, the felnin took the pork from the fire, hacked away a chunk with a small knife and offered it to the Viking. Having nothing else to do, Rollo sat down to eat it.

Later, the felnin let them sleep again. On awakening, they were led on a curious journey, through wooded land, then charred forest. Over beaches that turned suddenly to gold-paved city streets and then back to forest. Time passed, and the felnin finally stopped them in a small stand of wood from which Rollo could hear distant laughter. "Midgard again," Ai'reth said with a smile, then he disappeared.

*   *   *

Following the laughter, Rollo and Rui came to a tavern. The night was late, and there were few guests within. Those there spoke the Frankish tongue, and Rollo cursed under his breath when he heard this. After all their travels, they'd but returned to the place they'd departed.

The guests—three drunken swordsmen who taunted each other continuously while pawing at the sole, homely serving wench—failed to notice the newcomers until they'd sat and ordered mead. Then they turned their insults in Rollo's and Rui's direction. Demon, they called Rui, and spawn of the devil and more. Rollo allowed such words to be said for only a few moments before he rose abruptly, went to the nearest man, and punched him heavily in the mouth before moving on to the next two. As the servant girl brought their mead, Rollo tossed Rui one of the fallen Franks' swords, took another for himself, detached three pouches of coins from three belts, and signaled his companion that the time had come to leave.

Back in the night, armed and moneyed again, Rollo held a finger to the wind to test it, trying to grant moment to a decision that he knew no longer mattered. As they set off on foot, the two warriors each fell back to their own dark thoughts. As for Rollo, he could think of no future course, no direction that might be better than any other. His thoughts were filled with Thyri, and he was certain—so certain he could not entertain even the slightest hope or doubt—that he would never see her again.

Chaos and Rune

Along the pathways, Thyri raced. *I am the white beast,* she thought, *the mistress of this world.* She became the wildfire, the wolf, the heartbeat of Chaos. Through her mind tumbled the promises of Jormungard, those words he'd spoken to her before the death of her ship. She held them close, for if Odin had sent his Valkyrie against her—Odin who had allowed her torture and curse all these years—then who might she call a friend? She took Jormungard's words to heart and held them there. Behind her, she sensed the Valkyries' pursuit. She would not think of them, only of her quest.

Thus she locked up her thoughts, fearing any digression, knowing the pain she would feel if she set her mind free. Astrid had been her first love, a love pure and never tainted by doubt or sorrow until the end. A love of youth, without the sorrows she'd come to find with Megan. She could not face such thoughts. She could not let the Astrid in her heart transform into the Astrid standing against her. She might have tried to think the Valkyrie's attack on her ship an illusion, a trick of some enemy, but she knew Astrid too well. No sorcerer in the world could show her an image of Astrid and trick her into believing the illusion. Their pasts had bound them too tightly together.

On the pathways then, she ran. The Midgard gate she sought came quickly, and she surged through it, Chaos bursting into the realm of Harald. The fires of his great hall burned in the distance, but she reached it in moments and barreled through the door, pushing servants aside, feeling every bit the wolf though indeed she had not changed form. Only her eyes held the beast's red hunger,

180

like the eyes of Erik, the eyes of Patrick, eyes she had always despised.

In the depths of the hall, she did find Gyda, she who had once been princess of Hordaland, daughter to the king who had ruled Thyri's people. But the discovery was not made in Harald's private chambers; it was made in his hall of women. Thyri burst into it, sword in hand, and held herself back, so unexpectedly did the colors, the occupants, and the lay of the room strike her.

The place was large, almost a cavern, with a huge fire in its center around which girls draped in silks lounged, rubbing oils and perfumes over bare limbs, their own limbs and those of others. After a moment's pause, Thyri strode among them. The women, terrified, cleared out of her path, and when she whispered the name of her whom she sought, several terrified fingers lifted into the air to point nervously in the same direction, the direction Thyri then went. When she found the princess of her homeland, she found something quite different than what she'd expected. Sitting at a stool, the woman rubbed powders furiously into the wrinkled skin of her neck, cursing under her breath. Thyri saw her eyes first in the mirror she held before her. Gyda's eyes, even, had lost their life, and beneath them were dark purple patches, the heavy marks of the years.

As Thyri looked into the eyes, so did the princess turn to see Thyri. In that moment, Thyri knew she could not be mistaken. This was, in truth, Gyda before her, but not the power-hungry vipress she'd hated all these years and resolved at last to hunt. Once, this woman might have been beautiful; now she'd fallen victim to the ravages of time. Her wrinkles did not stop at her neck; they spread out over her face, and her bare breasts hung limply on her chest, empty sacks with little power to stir the loins of a man, much less a king with all these women from which to choose. So Thyri stared at her, unable to speak, her sword dropping limply to her side.

Behind her then came a voice, one full of laughter. "So princess!" a harlot said. "Here is another taking your place in the king's bed! How long has it been? How many years?'' The voice did not wait for an answer; it melted quickly into laughter that echoed, never quite fading into silence.

Thyri turned and glared at the source, catching another glimpse of the female paradise in which she'd suddenly found herself. She'd heard long past that Harald had taken over seventy wives, and collected more each day, but she'd never imagined that Gyda would have been just one of them and not the highest of them all. In all these years, Thyri had misjudged this king—this ravager of all the north. And as for the wrinkled creature before her—what satisfaction might her death now bring?

Asking this question of herself, Thyri turned away. As she passed through the doorway, she again met Astrid, the Valkyrie's sword now sheathed. *"So now you have seen,"* Astrid said.

Thyri lowered her eyes, then Astrid reached forward, lifting her chin. *"You cannot usurp Harald to unite the north, little one. It is too late."*

Thyri felt tears welling up in her eyes at the sight of the beauty of her cousin.

"Look," Astrid continued, and she waved her hand; the air beneath it shimmered, and Thyri saw Harald, a king that she knew had to be Harald Tangle-Hair, though he was neat, and walking with another man who named him Fair-Hair. She could hear their words. *"So you will join me?"* the king asked. *"By Odin's beard,"* the other answered, *"I swear."* Flanking each of the two men were Vikings—strong elite guards of their royal charges. The second man who spoke with Harald had a voice stained by the twist on Norse of the Danes. She witnessed an alliance formed by Harald himself. There was no belligerence; the guards of the two kings did not carry themselves warily. They joked with each other in fact, and several of them carried flagons of mead in their hands instead of swords.

"You see?" Astrid asked after the scene had played out. *"The union of the north has been Harald's from the start. Before my death, I was a fool to think otherwise. It is not your destiny to take his place, to renew the bloodshed."*

"Then what is my destiny, Astrid?" Thyri asked, finding her voice at last. "Where must I go from here?"

Now the Valkyrie smiled but did not answer. Slowly, she began to fade.

"Astrid!" Thyri cried. "Take me with you. I cannot abide by this world another day!"

"*You can,*" the Valkyrie answered distantly. "*And I cannot.*"

From the hall of Harald Fair-Hair, Thyri wandered, she as directionless as Rollo, full of mourning, of a lost possibility, of lost glory. She cared not where she went, yet her feet propelled her to the sea, and there onto a merchant ship whose captain gave her passage without question.

She did not speak words; she simply boarded the ship and sat, heedless of the crew's prodding, a prodding that ended abruptly when one among them suggested she could be the kinslayer of Hordaland, Thyri Eiriksdattir. Bloodfang—her name and deeds were legend. And so the ship set sail, Thyri ever distant. If she had a clear thought at all, it came when she saw, around the neck of one of the crewmen, a small talisman shaped after the crosses of the One God. At the sight, she spoke, asking the man why he would wear such a thing. Grinning, he told her how it was a token of his past, a part of his plunder on his one raid to the south. She asked him if he would so quickly display any of the symbols of Loki, and he gave her a curious look, but he did not cast the cross into the sea. Thyri said nothing after that.

They docked, and she wandered ashore, through a bustling port in which she heard no words of war, only talk of merchants' goods and travel. She wandered on, and once away from the docks, the land began to call her back. This was the land of her youth to which she'd come. This was Hordaland, where she'd grown as a girl, where she'd lived and learned from her father, where she'd played with Astrid and Skoll and then mourned Astrid's departure when she was but seven and left only with her wonder at the affairs of the gods.

On these roads, Thyri moved again, her feet finally finding direction. They carried her home.

*   *   *

Yrsa—her cousin, Astrid's younger sister—worked on tanning hides in the unkempt field before the hall of her youth. Thyri approached slowly, then stopped ten paces away, waiting for the woman's eyes to rise. Memories surfaced slowly—memories of rumor heard long past from Anlaf Olafson in the land of the Saxons. These fields had been burned, he'd said. Yes, she thought, noting a distant, charred tree, but they were alive again, and her elders' hall had survived. Was it a trick, or had Anlaf also told her that Erik had once sought Gyda's hand for himself? Could that have been true, before he'd sought her death? She would never know.

"Begone phantom," were Yrsa's words when she first sensed Thyri's presence.

"I am no phantom, cousin," Thyri replied. "But I am weary, and home at last."

Yrsa stepped away from her work, squinting in the afternoon sunlight. "If you be my uncle's daughter," she said, "then you are not welcome here."

Thyri smiled sadly. "Are they all gone?" she asked.

"All you knew? Those you did not kill? Yes—they are gone, all but me. And if you wish to kill me, do so quickly and be done with it. I have no defense. My husband, Leif Hallson, is away to the south on campaign."

So the marauding yet continued, at least in part. "I will not kill you," Thyri told her. "You are the last of my kin."

"What of Erik?"

"Dead," Thyri whispered, adding no more.

"Then leave. They call you kinslayer here; I will not have you in my house!"

Thyri looked at the trembling woman now brandishing a tanning knife in the air. Yrsa was brave, as brave as she'd ever been. She knew the ways of the runes and had once attempted Thyri's death through them. But she had no real power—in their family, all that had been given to Astrid and herself. All others had been forced to live in their shadows.

She thought these thoughts, and she began to turn away. Yet as she did so, the afternoon seemed to fade into the distance, and on the road leading up to the hall, another approached. It was a stranger, a man draped in brown cloaks and sporting a wide, floppy hat on his head. Thyri abruptly stopped; the rider's steed walked on eight legs.

As the stranger approached and Yrsa saw what Thyri had already seen, she gasped, letting her tanning knife fall to the grass. She knew the lore well; only one rider in all the worlds boasted such a mount, and that rider was Odin, the father of all the gods, and the father, in the distant past, of them all.

The All-Father stopped time; the birds and insects of the fields ceased their chatter, and the sun grew more distant, though a warmth seemed to rise from the ground. He stopped before Thyri, paused a moment, then raised the brim of his hat. One eye was patched over, ruined ages past during his self-sacrifice as he hung from the branches of Yggdrasil. Thyri looked into the other eye, finding a gaze infinitely more fathomless than any she'd ever known.

"I end your pain," the All-Father said. From his cloaks, he brought forth a golden ring and held it out to her. "Wearing this, the moon cannot harm you."

Thyri reached out hesitantly, taking the small band of gold. She realized in that moment that she had forgotten the passing of the days. Quickly, she counted them back; were she not mistaken, this very night the moon would again be full? "Why not before?" she asked him, the question freeing itself before she could test its weight.

"We all must suffer," he answered. In his presence, she could find no argument. By his patched eye, he proved wrong all she might say; as she knew the lore, from his sacrifice he had gained his runes of power, and she herself had lived through many a battle with the aid of but one of them—his fifth rune—the rune placed by Scacath on her sword that gave it power to deflect all missiles.

"It tests our mettle," Odin added enigmatically. "You are much more than you think, Eiriksdattir."

"But what? What am I?"

"You will learn," he said, then he winked at her with his one eye and tugged at Sleipnir's reins, to head back down the road away from them.

*   *   *

Thyri knew not how much time passed before her thoughts turned outward. By the sky, dusk neared, and on her hand she felt the warmth of Odin's gift of gold.

In her other hand was Yrsa's. When her cousin saw the focus return to Thyri's gaze, she began to lead her, slowly, toward the hall.

Idylls

That night of the full moon, Thyri went out, laid her sable cloak down on the ground, and gazed up at the sky and the stars. The moon yet seemed to glare at her, but the ring on her finger—Odin's ring—felt warm and it sheltered her. Let the moon glare. . . . The longer she gazed up, the more the warmth spread through her even as the chill winds of night began to whisper through the trees. The stars—she wanted to reach up, pluck them from the heavens, and draw them inside her. She almost felt that she could. As Valkyrie, Astrid had flown among those stars; perhaps she, as well, would gain that privilege in time. All this became possible once Odin had come to her. But he had taken so long. . . . Her wondering was idle; she'd nearly hated him over the years he'd shunned her, but she couldn't hate now, not after seeing him with her own eyes. And he had not spoken so darkly of the future. All of Megan's dark forebodings of Ragnarok fell before the power of the All-Father's visitation.

Thyri spent the entire night there, under the stars on her sables. Never had she known such peace. Though she thought of it—realizing the source of her past pains had been vanquished—not even her separation from Megan bothered her. She was happy to be alone here, to confront herself and her past, and Megan had no real place in it. Megan's presence would confuse her memories, distract her mind, fill her senses with something other than this quiet peace, a peace for which she had so desperately ached over the years, what she had needed all along: solitude in silence, and a mind free of guilt, anguish, and doubt. The anguish was gone; the moon, above her yet powerless, was proof. And Odin had taken from her the guilt, even the deaths she had inflicted on her family. He had not accused her; *he* had not named her kinslayer and demoness.

So the night passed. . . .

Thyri thought back on that time in Alfheim, the night from which Megan's sorcery had shielded her memory. As she thought on it, it came back to her, a whole memory: her unease in the felnina, the arrival of Ai'reth, her confrontation with Erik, and his death. She could remember it all. Had Odin changed her so completely inside? Could she remember, and remember without pain? Even understanding? Megan had been right; with Erik, she'd done everything she could do.

But that was the guilt and anguish. Since that day in Alfheim, she'd tortured herself over her love for Megan, even doubted her lover's sincerity. And why? Lifted now of her curse, Thyri's doubts melted away into meaninglessness; something weak inside her had given birth to them, and she was stronger now. She'd imagined her love supported only by Megan's ability to give her pleasure in spite of the tragedies of her life, the curse in her blood, and thought Megan's love nothing but pity or some perverse attraction to Thyri's nature. No, love was much more than that. It had to be. She felt free now of everything on which she'd imagined their love was based, yet she could feel her love all the more for it. She had hurt her lover gravely. That would have to be repaired.

In time . . . right now she had this peace, and Megan still had the affairs of Kaerglen to manage. There was no need to hurry back. She decided, at least, to stay through the spring. Their reunion then would be that much sweeter. And Megan, no doubt, could find her if necessary.

And so Thyri came to stay in the hall of her youth. What it had been in the past was gone. To the little girl, the hall had seemed huge, almost a castle. When she'd returned from time to time after her training under Scacath— when she and Astrid had warred together under their king, Ragnar—the hall had grown smaller, though still spacious and always alive with activity and the heady smells of cooking and mead. After Astrid's death, it had all become like a foul, festering wound on her soul. Still later, when she'd returned after her first ordeal with the moon, when she'd killed her mother, her brother Halfdan, and her uncle Egill and found her father dead as well, the hall had hardly touched her, so consumed had she been with grief and hatred of her own very life. Yes, then it had been like a stark, bare dream—an empty shell, a house of weak, impotent ghosts, a thing with walls, a meaningless place defining only by chance the distinction between the warmth inside and the cold without.

Since then, when she'd happened to dream of the hall, she'd dreamed it as either pain or nothingness. Her dreams had never carried her back to the warmth of her youth. So now, returned home, her heart embarked on something of a rediscovery. Within the walls, she found comfort, like the contented afterglow of love. She didn't feel herself a child again; rather, she felt the child she had once been there with her, guiding her, showing her happy memories and simple thoughts.

The weight of her curse had been lifted.

As for Yrsa, who had borne over the years a hatred for Thyri akin to Thyri's long hatred of Gyda—the All-Father had torn down and rebuilt her world in a matter of moments. She cared for Thyri as she would care for any high-born guest of her husband. In Leif's absence, Thyri was all she had, and she insisted on playing the servant though Thyri refused to assume the mantle of master. In time, Thyri's calm eased her cousin's demeanor, and Yrsa began to allow Thyri to help in the kitchen when she prepared their meals, and they took to spending the evenings together, sometimes in silence, but often talking at length of their youths and their lives, Yrsa at once working diligently on her leather, and pressing Thyri for every detail of her past and Astrid's past, and Thyri asking Yrsa, with equal enthusiasm, of her own life, of her knowledge of the runes, of her husband, and even of the arts of shoemaking and of the kitchen.

Through Yrsa, Thyri began to regain something of the normal, rustic life that might have been hers had Scacath not chosen to take her from her family and set her on a course far different from that she'd expected as a young girl.

*   *   *

Such was Thyri's last idyll, the meeting of her present with her past. Odin had gifted her with an eventless sort of serenity, all traces of the wolf whisked away, or, rather, hidden from her heart and mind by the power of his gift to her. But one event of note did happen there, an event of transcendence, of another kind:

One day, with Yrsa absent, gone into the village to sell the fruits of her labors, a young, would-be Viking came onto their land and bellowed out the name of Eiriksdattir.

Thyri was in the barn. "Hail, stranger!" she called out. She waited for him to come to her.

He showed himself in the doorway. He was young, still a boy with but a wispy, downy growth for a beard. In his eyes, she discerned both determination and fear. He spoke abruptly. "Eiriksdattir," he said, "I would battle with you!"

"I am Olga," Thyri countered, looking puzzled. "Eiriksdattir does not live here—she hasn't for many years."

The boy, irritated, tossed a sword at her feet. "You lie!" he insisted. "I have heard whispers, that Eiriksdattir is returned to Hordaland. You must be she."

"Why?"

"No more words! Take up that sword and fight me!"

Thyri bent, glancing up at him. "Why would you battle Eiriksdattir?" she asked. "She would kill you."

He laughed. "Then I would find Valhalla, wouldn't I? But perhaps I would kill you, no? Then my name would be known throughout the north as the slayer of Thyri Bloodfang."

"I am not she."

"Pick up the sword, or I will kill you without it!"

She grasped the weapon's hilt and stood. Years before, Thyri had been accused of being a wench impersonating a swordsman. Such an accusation had always pushed her ever more close to fury and battle; now she played the part willingly, becoming in her mind a milkmaid, a simple farmgirl. When she tried to heft the blade, her wrist collapsed under its weight. She dropped it, its point digging into the ground perilously close to her foot.

She jumped back and almost fell. She looked fearfully at the boy, then smiled. Instead of battle, she offered him her hand and seduced him.

That nameless young warrior had Thyri in a way that no man ever did, in the way that Gerald and Sokki—even Rollo—had dreamed. She fell back on the fresh hay, her hands, shaky and excited, running up her legs, hiking her shift up to where the boy could see the mound of her womanhood emerging slightly from the shadows. In her mind, all thoughts of swords and death and battle had vanished. She felt both innocent and wanton, as if she were still discovering the sensations of her flesh, as if she had had but a rare taste of love and wanted it again but knew only how to ask and not demand. When the boy knelt before her, the fear of innocence came into her eyes, and the nervous ecstasy of a virgin on her wedding bed washed over her loins as he kissed her thigh.

As his excitement mounted and he crawled on top of her body, she let him rip open her shift, savoring every infinite moment of anticipation before his lips touched her breasts. As he entered her, she clung to him, and only then did the past intrude dreamily on her thoughts. It flowed in almost magically, merging with the cascades of sensation that flowed from each caress: The boy became Akan, Rollo, Hugin, Munin, Gerald, Sokki—every man she had ever had, and every man who had ever wanted her. She gave herself to them, a sacrifice on this primitive rustic altar; she held them, together and separate, and she kissed them and wept, out of sad pleasure, out of joy and sorrow for the lot of men in this world, for their beauties and their lusts. She felt pure again, as pure as the blue of the sky, as the black of the night. Gyda, Yrsa, Odin—and now this boy—had made her clean. Stripped free of the stains on her soul, she could at last truly love.

All the while, Bloodfang hung in its scabbard on a peg inside the room of Thyri's childhood. She hadn't seen it in weeks, and she'd almost forgotten it was there. While the boy labored above her, she nearly *believed* that she was Olga, and not Eiriksdattir at all.

When the moments of passion ended, the boy fell asleep in her arms and she held him until he wakened. Near dusk, he left, promising to return after the spring's campaign. He never did. Under Harald's banner, he was the first to fall in an assault on a renegade Danish reaver. As he died, he thought of his lover, the tender white-haired woman of the

house of Eiriksdattir. Her name—Olga—was on his lips as
the last of his blood spilled onto the deck of his ship.

Nothing else of much import transpired for Thyri until
the end.

On Kaerglen, the making of Seth the king went on.
Megan lectured her brother constantly on the arts of lead-
ership, arts she herself knew mainly from Thyri. Though
the sorceress busied herself all the more as time went by
and still no word came of Thyri, her thoughts did begin to
turn relentlessly back to her lover. She began to worry;
through her sorcery, she lifted for a time the mists that
shielded the island from outsiders, from foreign ships.
Seth questioned her, and she knew not what to tell him,
except the truth. She wanted contact—news from the outside, of the world, and possibly of Thyri. Her powers had
not returned to her fully since their battle with Patrick, and
she knew no other way. And even if she could, she told
him, more powerful sorceries could draw to them, in these
dark times, evil they were not prepared to face.

But she had to know, so she lifted the mist, though she
did in her own way ask and receive the king's consent.

After but two days, a small ship came into Port Kaerglen.
On board were Rollo Anskarson and Rui Taichimi. They
went to Megan and told her what had transpired on the
seas south of Vestfold. Astrid had crushed *Nightreaver* and
they—and Thyri—had been pitched into the sea. They
described their savior and Megan immediately knew him,
but what had finally become of Thyri, she could not know.

The news did little to improve Megan's mood. But she did
know from Ai'reth through Rollo that Thyri had survived
the Valkyries' attack. Her thoughts turned ever more to her
sorceries, even in these dark times. She'd regained some
part of her strength, only it remained true that its use
would not, and could not, be wise.

But if Megan knew her lover, she would have continued
on; the loss of a ship deterring her not in the least. She
waited impatiently for news, word from afar that Eiriksdattir,
the berserk, had stolen Harald's kingdom for herself and
now brought the northern fleets south to make all of
Midgard tremble.

Meanwhile, came other news: There would be a wedding. More must be told: The love of man and woman grew finally between Gerald of Jorvik and Tana Kaerglen.

If indeed there was a day of transition, it came in mid-spring, when all the castle was alive with activity. The folk of the city and port roamed the halls freely as Seth had ordered the fortress painted white, inside and out. And with the common folk among them, gossip had quickly spread of the princess and the Saxon who was ever to be found at her side. On this day, the gossip was worst, as it was the day to paint the halls.

Before the decree, Tana had persuaded Seth to leave the depths of Kaerglen untouched, and on this mid-spring day, to escape the stares and the knowing smiles, she took Gerald by the hand and led him down to the grotto. There she showed him Fand's haven.

Of what transpired there, the writer will say little but that it was beauty reborn and that the love was untainted, a joyful love never marred, even by what was to come.

One month later, Gerald and Tana were wed.

Ragnarok

In late spring, Thyri awoke one morning with thoughts of deep reflection. At her bedside, she set to combing her hair, and when she was done, when her white locks shone with a tender glow, she began slowly to braid—a ritual she had long since abandoned. In her fingers, she held her rune-bead, and she did each braid carefully, recalling all of her victories of note and the lessons hidden within them. She braided knots she had never braided before, victories far in the past that had eluded her at the time, revealing themselves only now. When she'd finished this endless process, her braids were two hundred and thirteen. Finished, she affixed her rune-bead, and rose to retrieve her sword.

Yrsa saw her as she passed through the halls, moving like a serene goddess. She did not question her; the last woman of the house of Egill sensed a strange presence in the air, and she knew somehow that this, above all things, had been foreshadowed by the All-Father's gift to her cousin.

Yrsa did not know this—nor did Thyri—but Loki had burst free of his fetters a week past, and that night, just before the break of dawn, Heimdall's horn had sounded to alert all the worlds. Yet it had not been heard on Midgard.

This morning had been sent to Thyri by Odin himself, and it needed no explanation. The white wolf had to prepare. And Odin sent to her as well his last messenger— the last messenger he could trust as the warrior himself scarcely understood his purpose. But the messenger nevertheless was dispatched.

* * *

As Thyri donned her sword, Ai'reth stepped into Midgard before her. The felnin looked up at her with enraptured eyes, and it was long before he spoke. "There is one who loves you, white-hair," he said. "One who needs you now, and you must come."

"I am ready," she said. Her gaze remained distant. He had the thought that he might have asked of her anything and had the same reply. Yet he didn't question her; he took her hand and led her onto the Midgard border. Once there, he started onto the pathways he'd planned—the careful ways that would hide from all eyes—when suddenly a sorcery erupted from the Queenstone in its pouch, throwing a gate before them which they had no time to avoid. They stepped through, into the grassy courtyard of Castle Kaerglen.

The sudden force of the sorcery rippled through the worlds to shake the trunk of Yggdrasil itself. On Bifrost, Loki's head turned, and he smiled. One power had been hidden from him these past months, but now, just before the battle could be joined, he sensed it anew. Ordering his forces on, he disappeared briefly from their midst.

Megan stood among the orchids, reflecting also on the past, when Thyri's presence struck her in an unexpected shower of magic. She turned to find her lover in full battle gear before her, the morning sun glinting off her unsheathed sword. Next to Thyri, the figure of Ai'reth shimmered, then faded into the next world and they were alone.

From a window above, Gerald witnessed Thyri's arrival, and he raced for the stairs, calling out the news to his wife.

Thyri came into the present, Megan before her. If anything, the beauty of the sorceress had grown, overwhelming all the wonders of Kaerglen's garden. In that moment, she would have taken Megan and sealed anew their love on the grass— just as they had on reuniting long ago in that place of Brigid near Jorvik—had another not suddenly appeared in their midst.

He was tall, draped in black, an evil, two-bladed sword jutting from his gauntleted hand. Megan reacted immediately, a giant spear of her silver magic flying in a burst toward the intruder's face. He laughed at it once, then turned back the silver, striking it into Megan's chest without giving her a moment to scream. Ever slowly, to Thyri's heightened senses, the sorceress collapsed to the earth.

Eiriksdattir turned on the man, launching swiftly into the attack. "I will fight you," the man said, laughing, "and best you as well."

"I cannot be bested," Thyri growled. "Not since my youth has another blade found my flesh."

"Mine will," he replied, and she felt a searing pain in her arm. She fought harder; entering the mind-of-the-tyger, sequencing her attack to end in a crushing blow that could not be blocked by the best sword in Midgard. But block her the man did. They went round and round the garden, skipping over Megan's fallen body. Thyri thought of nothing but her opponent; against him she focused the very essence of her skill, the full force of her battle fury and her strength. She felt her mind fall away, the point in battle when only blood began to matter, when she would kill and kill again like a machine. Yet the man before her would not fall. She had not even scratched him, while she herself bore now countless wounds off his blade.

From the entrance to the courtyard, Gerald and Tana looked on in horror.

There was a way, Thyri knew. A way she could best this man, best any man, or any god— she had now guessed him a god, though his power would not let her see him as Loki. Still, even a god might fall before the hunger grown within her but leashed only by the ring she wore on her hand. She could not die this day, not with Megan already fallen, not after all the blood spilled to rid Kaerglen of Patrick's evil. If she fell, this evil would simply take his place.

Megan would die.

Seth would die.

All would be lost and meaningless.

Thyri launched a final assault with all her mortal fury, then backed quickly away and threw off Odin's golden ring. The beast surged already within her, and it took her more quickly than ever in the past. To Gerald and Tana, she became the beast the moment the ring left her finger.

So it was. The white wolf leaped at Loki only to be engulfed by a terrible red fire. In the distance, she heard laughter, laughter that rang and echoed off the walls of Castle Kaerglen. But when she landed, Midgard fell away from her.

From the portal Gerald crept hesitantly toward Megan. He lifted her under her arms and carried her back to the safety of the castle, all the while looking nervously askance at the monstrous white beast that lay motionless on the grass.

Chaos

She walked on Bifrost, her weight as great as Jormungard's and Fenrir's, they who came behind her. Her lover strode at her side; his tall dark body a part of hers. For him she would do anything. For him, she would now slay gods.

They descended to the Plain of Vigrid below, there to meet the assembled Aesir. So pitiful looked these gods, Odin with his dead men, the Valkyrie on their puny winged steeds, the pathetic little gods of Alfheim, most already dead, consumed by the hunger of the giants behind her, the Jotun who loved her and held her name on high, Surt with his flames and all those behind him. It would be an easy day. Her lover whispered to her the name of Thor, and her mouth watered at the thought of swallowing the thunder. She would devour him, and then feast on the legions of Odin.

With Loki she touched upon the ground of Asgard. The ranks of the gods awaited them in the distance, all but Heimdall who stood with drawn sword, barring their way. Beside her, her lover cursed and launched himself at the watchman of the gods, their blades crashed together while she led the others forward. On the Plain of Vigrid, the Aesir and their forces began their charge. Her lust for blood grew. Thor—her first enemy, her first meal—came in the forefront; she ran toward him, Fenrir who would destroy the All-Father running at her side. She watched Thor's eyes lock on Jormungard's, he who came behind her, more slowly. She would beat the serpent to victory. So consumed with her hunger did she become that she raced ahead, outdistancing even Fenrir himself. But together, at the forefront of their host, they made for Odin and his son, the leaders of the enemy. Together, they would dine.

They grew ever near, close enough to see the faces of those they would devour. Her gaze bore down on Thor, but she turned it once toward Odin, and the All-Father winked, and she suddenly remembered that wink from her past. *What am I? You will learn.* . . . The wink released her; her body, without warning, came to a halt.

Where was she? This all felt like a dream, yet never had a dream felt so real. She heard words in her head. Loki's voice: *Thor! Kill Thor!* Odin's voice: *Turn, white-hair! Behind you!*

Such a dream. . . . She glanced back to see the Midgard Serpent, Jormungard, poison dripping from his great scaly jaws. In her mind then she heard Loki's scream as he fell before Heimdall, the saddest of all the gods.

In the distance, Thyri saw Scacath, the swordsmistress of all the Tuathans; she had survived all the battles before this. Thyri watched her use her sorcery to propel herself through the air, into the very midst of the ranks of the Jotun. The Valkyrie, too, flew ahead, diving down around the fiery head of Surt, using their steeds to dodge his deadly sword. Even as she watched, they began to fall, one by one, from the sky.

And so Jormungard approached behind her and Thor came closer. Fenrir, now far ahead of her, met Odin with force enough to shake the plain beneath her. She looked from them to Thor, then back to Jormungard, and snarled, turning suddenly on the serpent. Thor would have to find another fight. . . . In one great leap, she landed before the serpent, he who had whispered seductions to her on the Midgard seas. She leaped again, onto his back, her fangs digging deeply into the place behind his head, where all his struggles couldn't turn his deadly head to attack her and free himself from her locks of her jaws.

And so did Chaos ride the monster whose thrashing tail swept over Vigrid, crushing whole legions of giants under its weight. Chaos dug in her fangs and held on, raking her claws forward, over his eyes, blinding him. She rode him until Vidar, fresh from avenging his father's death by the fangs of Fenrir, came to cleave the head of the serpent in two.

Thyri released her jaws, feeling exhaustion wash through her every limb. She felt herself growing smaller, until she lay on the bloodied plain, scarcely able to move. But she was a woman now, and what was left of the war of the gods continued in scattered pockets. Before exhaustion finally overtook her, she saw Thor emerge from the fray, the smouldering head of Surt held high in his hand. This was a day of victory for the Aesir, and she had done her gods the highest honor of all.

Thor, proudly showing the head of the fire-giant king to all—by the prophecies of the Sibyl— should have been a ghost. By the prophecies of the Sibyl, the Thunderer had died by the poison of Jormungard, and then at Ragnarok's end, Surt would have set all the worlds alight.

All the worlds, she heard whispered in her ear, *save Midgard*. She turned her head to see Megan stooping over her. The sorceress smiled and helped her to her feet, then she led Thyri over the battlefield, through the legions of the dead, even past Astrid's fallen body; before his death, Surt had exacted his toll.

As Megan led her away, Thyri could find no further mourning in her heart. To her, Astrid had perished long before. And if she'd died now, it had been in the only battle that mattered. Thinking this, in the distance she heard the elated battle cries of the Tuathans as the last of the giants fell before them. As with Astrid, Thyri could find no mourning if Scacath had fallen. This had been a day of victory; the battle had gone past dusk, and now the waxing moon shone brightly overhead. Odin had died, Heimdall had died, and so had Freyr and Tyr, yet the Aesir remained powerful under Thor and the end of all things had not come to pass.

Behind them, they heard a great crack as worlds split apart, no longer bound together by Odin's power. Megan put her lips to Thyri's ear. "Midgard has fallen away now," she whispered. "Into the hands of the One God."

So split finally from her past, Thyri walked, supported by the one she most loved, under the moon that had been her enemy. Her last thought, just before Megan cast a sorcery to carry them far away where they might at last share solitude, concerned that moon:

If Skoll had swallowed it before Ragnarok, how then did it yet shine?

Thus was the truth of Ragnarok.

On Kaerglen, time passed, Rollo and Rui joining the watch over the fallen wolf in the garden, and Tana watching over the sorceress stricken by the force of her own magic. Near dusk of that day, Tana came to tell them that Megan had disappeared—not a mystery, but a fading she had witnessed with her very own eyes. The sorceress had gone, the reasons behind such a thing to remain obscured for a long while.

With this news, Gerald moved hesitantly for the wolf. He reached it, stooping down to touch its fur. In days past, he had heard Rollo's pained laments countless times over, that his life had no meaning without the white-haired swordsmistress of the north. With the body of the wolf at his feet, Gerald felt much the same.

I, GERALD

I

Here ends the tale of Thyri Eiriksdattir on Midgard, with Gerald of Jorvik stooped beside the body of a white wolf, and Thyri herself nowhere in sight, for she has departed, forever, from this world.

The tale, however, has not yet ended in full, for Gerald is there, next to the wolf, and he wonders and mourns. In his heart, he knows Thyri has departed, that this beast is no longer her but simply a part of her, the dark part, but dark no longer without her. He thinks the beast is dead, but on the contrary, as he reaches out to touch it, it rears its head and bites his hand, then races away, never to be seen again on Kaerglen Isle after Rollo and Rui step aside to allow it passage through the castle.

Gerald stays near the ground, holding his hand, a new terror filling his heart.

When writing of Gerald, I of course write of myself. I remember very well that day and the days that followed. The full moon was but a week away, and my hand bore the throbbing, painful mark of the beast's fangs.

The day before the first night of the next full moon, I traveled far from the castle, taking with me several large skins of wine, all of which I emptied into my stomach before dusk. As it was, I passed out before the sunset. Later, in the middle of the night, I woke to get sick and found myself in the arms of my wife. She had followed me; she admitted that she knew my fears and my intentions, but had stayed silent while I'd waited for the moon to go full because she knew I wouldn't believe her if she'd said I'd feared in vain. She'd known through her sorceries

202

that my blood was yet clean. The wolf that bit me was no longer *were*.

Nevertheless, that bite was Thyri's, and it's stayed with me, as surely as if it carried her curse. In that bite, and the pain it's left in my hand, reside all the memories of the years I spent with Eiriksdattir, and, moreover, there is the lust there, the lust to know more. I felt it then as I still do now, though the telling is done. I must soon leave it, unsated.

So I bore her wound, and as time passed I realized fully that she, and everything she'd brought with her, was gone. I grew obsessed, testing Tana's love for me to its limits. Thyri's absence made her hold on me all the more strong; I had to have her back. I felt I couldn't live until I regained her, if only in part, and so my lust for more bid me leave, and in the still of the night, with Tana fast asleep, I set out on a quest of my own.

I wandered that night, coming first to a circle of stones. I sat in the middle holding my arms up to the sky, invoking every name of every god I knew or imagined. None heard me; only the wind answered. It seemed that an eternity passed, but when I finally rose, the night remained young. I moved on, reaching next the abandoned temple of the One God where Thyri spilled Patrick's blood.

As I entered, I could almost feel the fury of that battle anew—the screams outside, Patrick's fear, and Thyri's wrath. The Christ on his cross gazed down upon me with his tragic eyes, and I kneeled before him, pleading that he lift my agony, that he give me Thyri again, that he tell me all the things I never dared ask—yes, even that he make her return and love me at least once before her death. Once again, I had no answer. The Christ's eyes did not move. The cross would not bend and let him step down. In another corner, the Virgin beckoned to me and I knelt before her, pleading the same things, receiving the same silence. Again, eternity passed, but when I left, it remained night.

It was a night, somehow, that lasted forever. I wonder now whether it wasn't some spell, some dark spell cast upon me in the wake of Thyri's passing. But as I count my enemies, those who might have had the power, I count them all dead. Who knows? Perhaps it *was* that bite. In any case, I lived all this, though how or why I'm uncertain.

Exiting the One God's temple, exhausted from my pleadings, I thought to return home to my wife, to try to forget it all, to live out what years I had left in happiness. Couldn't I see that? Couldn't I let Thyri die and live my own life in peace, without her chaos, her adventure? I was no longer young, but I had a beautiful wife and we might yet have children. Might that not be enough?

I thought and wandered, away from the chapel and its graveyard—all those souls lost on Dagda's Plain. I had almost reached the road back to the city when I met the dark priest.

He was cowled; I could not see his face. He stood before me, and as he did I felt cold, as cold as I had that day when Morgana died, in her sorcerous, fierce winter. And yet I couldn't move, couldn't flee. He stood before me, dark, scarcely more than a shadow, and he spoke to me. "Ask," was all he said. His was a sibilant voice, the voice of a snake.

Without warning, all my pleading issued forth anew. I wanted to know all; I wanted Thyri's love, her memories, everything. The dark priest listened until I'd poured it all forth, and then he spoke again in that hissing voice: "If you have all this, when it is done, will you give yourself to me?"

I stared into his shadows. "Yes," I said. "If you can give all this to me, I will be yours."

"Forever?"

"As long as I live."

"Your life is much longer than you know," he hissed.

I eyed him anew, but I heard my own voice, speaking as if it had a life of its own. "As long as I live," I repeated.

"Very well," he said, and he told me the formula for the pool of blood, the liquid talisman that has granted me all the knowledge I wished, the source of my own sorcery, the thing I came to name after the dark priest, after reflection and discovery of his nature. The thing I call Satan's Chalice.

*   *   *

On that night, I stepped upon the path that led me here to this writing. All the while Tana has stayed with me, comforting me in the night, even asking how my work has fared. Honestly, I do not understand. She must have felt, often, that Thyri stole me away through this work like a lover, that my mere act of writing, not to mention the experiences of Thyri I had in my research, proved my unfaithfulness. No, I do not understand love—Tana's love and how it has kept her bound to me. Not that I would lose it; were it possible, I would burn this manuscript, all this work, if it might give me a day longer with her than I might be allowed.

But I feel drained. The tale, in truth, is done, and Satan's Chalice, in my final researches of Ragnarok, runs dry with only a thin layer of red powder on its walls to betray what it once contained. After following the dark priest's formula, I first used it to learn that Thyri had not, in fact, died, but had passed, willingly, with Megan into . . . whatever world the sorceress had chosen. My feelings on that day were those of great elation. Last week, I exhausted the pool looking at the same moments of Thyri's life, the moments of her final passing from Midgard. Somehow, it seemed fitting that the last blood of the pool reveal to me the same scene that I saw in the beginning of my sorcery. With that willful act of voyeurism, I brought the end back to the beginning. And I have few questions left that I would ask the pool, the main concerning Ai'reth. I cannot claim to know what became of him, only that he did not take part in Ragnarok. I lost touch with him after he brought Thyri back to Kaerglen. He seemed to disappear then entirely —at least to my sorcerous eyes—and perhaps the speculation closest to the truth might be that he was in fact a minor aspect of the All-Father's mind, and having performed his last useful act, he'd returned promptly to join with his source.

In any case, now I rest. All promised to me by the dark priest has transpired but the act of love with Thyri herself. All this time, I have felt that one request of mine hanging over me, hanging over my bed while I loved my wife. All this time, of all that I asked, that is the one request I would have first taken back, but now, when I think of it, I feel a strange peace within it, perhaps the peace of my salvation.

If the dark priest cannot deliver it—and with Thyri departed, it hardly seems likely he can—then our contract remains unfulfilled.

II

At night, howls from distant forests somehow rise high above the city to reach the walls of this castle. I hear them, though distant they are. Some nights I have stayed awake, straining to detect this distant howling of wolves.

Yes, they have multiplied again on Kaerglen Isle. I wonder whether that wolf Thyri left behind in this world has mothered them. But whence came the father? Some escaped pet of some trader? Some stowaway on an anonymous ship? Or were the consequences of Ragnarok more deep than I've described? Might another have been freed of the curse? My imagination has taken flight on those sleepless nights—after all I've witnessed, this puzzle of wolves where before there were none smacks of mundanity, and yet . . . What if another were freed of the curse? What if that one were myself, created and freed in a moment when that which was once part of Thyri bit my hand? What if that part of Thyri has mated with a part of myself, and it is my children that I hear calling to me?

Such imagination . . . I cannot discuss such things with Tana. After all that has transpired, she says to me always, "Have hope." To speak this of the wolves—she would think me mad at last. Perhaps that is true; I have not discussed these howlings with anyone. Perhaps they howl only in my mind, a haunting from Thyri's past.

As I've reflected, I'm amazed to find my sanity relatively intact, so many pasts I've absorbed into my own. Occasionally, when some little thing—some noise or some smell—triggers a memory within me, I discover that the memory is not mine, but Thyri's or Rollo's. When this happens, it is fleeting the way that dreams are often fleeting in the morning. But it is a strange feeling while it lasts; should such memories come more strongly and more often, I fear I truly would become mad.

I feel a strange kinship with Thyri's brother Erik, more so him than Patrick, son of Coryn, though he as well cer-

tainly suffered the ultimate fate for which I am destined.
Erik, however, was twisted by much the same forces as I.
Erik's weakness was the history of his kin and the paleness
of his own shadow next to those of Thyri, his elder sister,
and Astrid, his elder cousin. Even his elder male kin—
warriors all.

Twisted—when he was younger, he revered Thyri, so
why did he become a tool of evil and seek to kill her? I
wish now that I had researched this deeply; in this I can
now see where my work has surely lacked, for my sorcerous omnipotence over it seems less omnipotent with each
day, now that it is done. Yet I can imagine Erik's sleepless
nights as if they had been my own (and I have had many!).
His thoughts would have boiled with visions of his par-
ents' deaths, the plague of his sister's curse that was
responsible, and his own aching ambition to equal her.
And this maelstrom of thoughts—might it not have attracted *temptation?* On a world defined increasingly by the
lore of the One God, temptation in the form of Lucifer
might have reached even one in the north, and then whispered promises into the chaos of Erik's mind. What might
have been promised? Many things: That he might have
vengeance on the curse that destroyed his family; that he
might himself, rival its power; even that he might, in
killing Thyri, assume the mantle of her power for himself.
All these whispers—and I stress that I only imagine them—
might have tricked Erik into a contract like my own.

However it happened, he came to serve the same master
as I, with his service rooted in the same essential reason:
Thyri Eiriksdattir. Erik and I—we must both have lusted to
possess, to change, even *to become.* Such lusts transform
into a sort of madness when we have not the power to
fulfill them. And our madnesses have led us to the same
end. How many others have walked this path?

How many others will walk it?

The mists have lifted. Kaerglen now lies fully in Midgard.
Tana says . . .

I'm sorry—something has happened and I am called
away.

III

He has come. Too soon! Even now, Tana entertains him in the dining hall, for all that I know she is terrified by his very presence. She walks like a ghost these days, her sorceries fading noticeably between each dawn and dusk.

Last week we returned to the grotto, and she told me of all Brigid had taught her there. I listened, though I already knew the tale. I couldn't tell her that I knew, that I had spied on her through Satan's Chalice as surely as I had violated the intimate privacy of all whom I have loved. So she told me again and I listened. Then she cast spells, to call to the goddess. We had no answer.

And Tana—my beloved wife—she has sought gate upon gate into other realms where we might follow Thyri and escape. The gates are all gone now, eight of the nine worlds released from their bindings to Midgard. And, as written, what sorceries that still work here fade by the day.

The mists that hide Kaerglen from the world have lifted.

But Tana has been brave and fought to persevere. For a short while after I began this, I kept secret the pool and its power. The secret could not last long; when at last I told Tana of the pool's power, how it seemed to grow and not weaken at all, she even tested it. The visions did not come to her, and to her sorceries, it would reveal itself as nothing but a pool of blood. She told me that its magic was beyond her, and its power only mine to wield.

While she fades.

While the worlds shook at Ragnarok, splitting apart, the Aesir and the Tuatha de Danaan abandoning Midgard to the One God and his opponent.

My master.

The darkness in him—he does not shield us from its power as he hid it from me that night we met—is a void so black that the night outside, which I see through my window now, seems the most transcendent of dawns. I must cherish this pale night, burn it into my memory, that I might remember it in that void.

Too soon he has come! Tomorrow, Tana and I would have set sail for Tara and the Lia Fail, where Thyri and Megan rested on their journey here after Coryn's death. If

a gate to other realms remains, it would be there, where all
sorcerous pathways intersect. We cannot leave now. . . .

But I am husband to the sister of the king!

Seth knows nothing of this—Tana forbids telling him.

The dark one—she speaks to him now.

I write in circles.

My mind burns; my hands shake.

He has come; even now his dark clouds fill my heart.

IV

I have slept. How long? I sit here, and find before me
the pages penned last night. What have I written? My
mind still burns, but I have dreamed a dream, a horrible
dream, but one so real I feel I've lived it.

I must tell it. I must find in it a way out.

On a moonlit beach, black water coming in with the
rising tide . . .

Do angels howl and leer? I saw them above me, a
grotesque procession, a parody of the One God's host.
They had faces like dogs and horns like goats. Their wings
were white, but they had no feathers. They had the wings
of huge, white bats. They howled a cacophonous dirge,
their serpentine tongues dripping green and orange spittle
down into the black water, where it burned and sputtered,
releasing a foul stench beyond description. This procession
turned, circling above me, coiling about itself like an
endless snake until the highest disappeared into the night
and I found myself at the bottom of this nightmarish,
writhing, leering whirlpool of monstrosities. And all of
them whispered my name.

Some force (Within myself? Without?) pushed me back
to the sand so that I stared up at the stars and moon
through this ghastly circle. Swirls of smoke, from where
the stench rose up from the water, danced over me, pene-
trating my nose as if alive. I felt bound to the earth,
unseen bonds strapping me to the sand. I could not lift
even my head.

I wanted to run, to race down the beach, up a cliff, up a
mountain, into the clouds, the heavens, the depths of the
sea. Anywhere. I forced my eyes shut, and found another

vision there, a vision of a burning cross, the cross of the
Christ. Nailed to the wood was Thyri, her flesh aflame,
and then the procession entered this vision as well! A
leering parody of beauty with orange eyes and green fangs
thrust unexpectedly before my eyes. I could smell its
breath—more terrible even than the stench rising from the
water. This face peeled away my eyelids as if they were
merely the curtains of a stage. The whirlpool nightmare
returned; the visions meshed and combined. Thyri hung
there in the center, burning on that cross.

The whirlpool descended until its bottom tier reached
the sand. Then it whirled tighter. I could feel them now,
mere inches from my body on all sides. Just then, the
cross began to spin, the flames giving way to spears of
light. Faster and faster. . . . It became a cloud, and the
cloud pelted me with rain and hail, snow and ice. I grew
cold and numb in an instant. The cloud became the sun,
and it burned me, the lurid angels howling and weeping
their delight. The closest began to lick the sweat from my
skin.

Slowly, as the bile rose to my throat, the sun became
the moon, and the moon became Thyri. Only now she was
naked, glowing, as beautiful as ever I'd seen her, nay,
more beautiful than ever. She walked down a silver ladder
from the sky until she stood at my feet. And there, she
began to run her hands over her body, over her breasts and
thighs. Some of the dark angels broke ranks and surrounded her, kissing her, biting her, and she answered
with caresses of her own and moans of ecstasy.

I still felt the bile in my throat. I still felt this horrible
revulsion, but, just as some power pinned me to the sand,
some darkness raised and hardened my manhood at this
sight above me.

"He likes you, my pets!" Thyri said, grinning and
falling before me to her knees.

I cannot write what came next, for never might I have
imagined such horror and beauty possible in the space of a
single moment. I endured, trapped in this nightmare. I
endured, and felt pain and pleasure, attraction and revulsion, and everything—every feeling known to man—in
between.

I yet shake as I think on it. I want to purge it from my mind, but it will not go away. And yet, though I know whence to seek relief, I cannot yet go. I know what power gave me this vision. That power is here in this castle, awaiting me, dark and patient, wielding its boundless, malicious evil. He toys with me, but he has tried to cheat me!

Yes! In this vision lies the seed of his defeat, for did he not promise me I would love Thyri? Is that not why he sent me this dream? Is that not why he made the dream so real and powerful? Yet it was but a dream; it wasn't real. He does not hold power over Eiriksdattir. Even should he argue that he transported me to that beach, that could not have been Thyri herself who came to me. That was not her, not her love I felt.

And that is what he promised me, her love. Her love as she shared with Astrid, with Munin, with Akan in her tent in the new land where they thought her akiya toyn, the wildfire, a goddess. With Pohati, gently, slowly, on furs as with Astrid. And with Megan, always with Megan—oh, Tana! Do not read this my love and hate me! It is you I want, but she is whom he promised me, and if he failed in this promise, then he cannot take me! Please understand!

V

I have played a game of words and lost.

"What is a dream?" he asked me, his voice a dark hiss under his cowl.

I was shaking, clinging to Tana's hand, staring into the darkness under that cowl. There was no face inside. Just black upon black. "An unreal thing," I answered resolutely.

"And what is a real thing?"

"Something that happened."

"So dreams don't happen?"

I stared into his darkness, trying to calm my body. "Yes, dreams happen," I said, "but the thing that is dreamed—that doesn't happen. It is an imagined experience, not a real one."

"So what makes a real experience?" he hissed out. "Something that you feel, taste, see?"

I nodded cautiously.

"But you feel, taste, and see in dreams, don't you? You

must explain to me more clearly the difference between dream experience and real experience. This is very important with regard to our business, is it not?''

"Yes," I said, clearing my throat. "But in a real experience, you are *there*. It is happening around you."

"But that's true also in dream. Come, you must tell me the *difference*, and it must make sense.''

I turned to look at Tana then, but her head did not move; she stared into his darkness, unflinching. I squeezed her hand more tightly, but she did not squeeze back.

From the darkness, came a soft laugh. "She will not help you," he said. "I will not allow it, for this agreement we must settle is between us, not her. What is the difference between dream and reality?''

My mind burned with a cold fire, for what could I answer? He toyed with me; he had taken Tana away for some reason. Could she answer better than I? Could she help me win? What *was* the answer? *Simple*, the thought came into my mind. *Dream experience happens when the body is asleep*. That is what I told him.

"I agree," he hissed at me.

"But will you agree that dream experience is not real?" I asked.

"For settling our agreement? Yes, I will give you that. Do you agree? This is very important, as you know.''

"Yes, I agree, and I have won!" I shouted, laughing.

"No," he said, and the darkness flowed from his cowl, filling the room, then filling me with visions, of my past, of memories and things I have felt and seen.

Yes, he showed me again how I sat like a parasite inside Akan as Thyri loved him. And he showed me other times when I did the same, with other lovers. I felt again Thyri's touch, her lips and her body, and the thrill of joining with her. At the end, the darkness and the visions lifted, and my mind raced to understand, to reach a new battleground in this game, this dark and deadly duel that had suddenly trapped me. "But I was not *there!*" I protested.

"I have given you all I promised," he said, ignoring my complaint. "Now you must settle our pact."

"But I wasn't there!"

"Were you asleep?"

"No."

"Then it was real experience, based upon the terms that we just now defined."

With that, he rose. "You may go," he said. "My gifts have served you well, have they not? Do not despair. I am generous. I will give you until tomorrow night at dusk when the moon will be full. I think that then will be a fitting time to consummate our contract."

No longer able to bear looking at him, I nodded, I had lost. He lingered a moment, then left.

As I write, I turn that word game over and again in my mind. Could I have won? Could I have answered that real experience requires physical presence? Would he have accepted that, or would he have argued artfully until he forced me in the end to admit that, perhaps, no difference between dream experience and real experience exists at all? I think so. I think I was trapped before it had begun. That dream last night—the one he sent me of Thyri—that closed the trap. Had we argued until no difference existed between dream and reality, I might still have said that *I* must experience as *myself*. The dream covered that escape.

So I am lost to him, condemned to the company of Erik and Patrick and how many others? Tomorrow night, I must leave this world, and I will shortly set down this pen for the final time and go, to spend what time I have left in the arms of my wife. When all is done, she will have little more than these writings left of me; I would that I could have given her more of myself these past years. But I accepted this fate; it is my burden alone to bear.

As I write these last words, I am filled with a distant sort of hope. I have learned that immortality is fleeting, and eternity meaningless, for I know that even immortal gods can perish. These new lords over Midgard, this One God and his opponent—how long might they last? A hundred years perhaps? Two hundred?

I will wait. This Satan must perish as have other gods before him. Then, at last, I might be free.

Author's Note

This story was translated from an untitled manuscript uncovered by Lord Basil Horning during excavations he made before World War II. His notes describe its origin as a dark drywell in what was once a shrine to the Celtic goddess Brigid. In addition to the manuscript, he uncovered several jewel-inlaid human skulls. The discovery was kept secret from the archeological world—it seems Lord Horning was involved in occult researches and cared little for the methods of the hard scientific community of his day. Recent attempts to find the site of his investigations have failed.

In 1982, I was in the air force and stationed in San Angelo, Texas. A friend called me and, knowing of my interest in the legends of the darker ages of Europe, told me of this manuscript and that he had come into possession of it. He refused to tell me how, but he invited me to his home in Florida to examine it, so I took a week of leave. I drove to Dallas and got lost in the crush of international jet-setters at the airport. When I finally reached Florida, I was cursing my friend. But he gave me that which I had come only to see. He asked me to take it, read it, study it. So long as I respected the necessity of secrecy— not of the story, but of specific occult formulations contained therein—I could sate my curiosity, then return the bundle to him.

My friend would not tell me why parts were secret. I knew that he also had embarked upon various occult researches, and I assume that he'd copied the specific passages down, else he would never have given up the thing to me. In any case, I've not heard from him since that weekend, and his family believe him dead.

I've respected his desire for secrecy; in fact, I superstitiously avoided even reading the parts he'd singled out. The story alone fascinated me. At one university, I had fragments of the fibery parchment carbon-dated to circa 900 A.D. This meshes roughly with the times of which Gerald writes: the battle of Ethandune, the seven hundred–ship assault of the Norse up the Seine, and the reign of Harald of Vestfold all occurred historically in the late ninth century. The script itself was in a free-style dialect of the more formalized Old English found in the Anglo-Saxon Chronicle penned under the direction of Alfred the Great, and a kind professor from another university that shall remain nameless assisted me in unscrambling some of the more hastily scribed passages.

The adaptation to modern English, however, is mine and mine alone. Some of the names and some entire passages are modernized, some are not. Where the prose turns to modern forms and phraseology, I take full responsibility. I feel I am justified—my task was to retell Gerald's story, not to provide a literal transcription.

After much wrestling with my conscience, I burned the original manuscript. For one thing, my friend's death was surely related to his possession of it. For another, I am a novelist. Who would believe this story is true?

MDW

Danville, Virginia

10/88

The son of an Air Force officer, MICHAEL D. WEAVER spent his early years in various parts of North America and the world. He is currently settled with his wife in Danville, Virginia, where he makes a living working with computers. With BLOODFANG, he completes his first fantasy trilogy, the first two books of which were *Wolf-Dreams* and *Nightreaver*, both available from Avon Books. He has also had his first science fiction novel, *Mercedes Nights*, published to much acclaim. His second, *My Immortal Father*, appeared earlier this year.